M
Mother's
Secret

To Val,

Hope you will enjoy

my latest book

love

Julia Roberts

x

BOOKS BY JULIA ROBERTS

THE LIBERTY SANDS TRILOGY
Life's a Beach and Then…
If He Really Loved Me…
It's Never Too Late to Say…

Christmas at Carol's
Carol's Singing

Alice in Theatreland
Time for a Short Story

One Hundred Lengths of the Pool

As J.G. Roberts
THE DETECTIVE RACHEL HART SERIES
1. Little Girl Missing
2. What He Did
3. Why She Died

My Mother's Secret

JULIA ROBERTS

Bookouture

Published by Bookouture in 2021

An imprint of Storyfire Ltd.
Carmelite House
50 Victoria Embankment
London EC4Y 0DZ

www.bookouture.com

ISBN: 978-1-80019-276-8
eBook ISBN: 978-1-80019-275-1

PROLOGUE
Sunday, 17 February 2019

Taking one last look up at my mum's bedroom window, I pull the garden gate closed and lock it behind me. It feels cruel leaving her on her own, particularly as it's the last night she will spend in the house where she has lived her entire life, but I'm bone-achingly tired and I need some rest if I'm to cope with what lies ahead. I know I would be unable to sleep with Mum in the next room and I'm desperate for the comforting arms of my husband, Ben, after what can only be described as the worst day of my life.

I pull my quilted coat closer around my body in an attempt to combat the icy chill permeating my bones as I unlock my car, climb in and turn the key in the ignition. Driving along the deserted street, I'm grateful that we only live a short drive from Mum's. What is it the motorway signs say? DON'T DRIVE TIRED. Tired doesn't come close to the way I'm feeling; exhausted and emotionally drained would be more accurate.

Never has the red block paving of our driveway been more welcoming than when I pull in ten minutes later. Unlike most of the other houses on the street, ours spills light from the hallway through the glazed panels in our front door and a soft glow emanates from behind our bedroom curtains. Ben will be waiting up for me. He'll hold me and tell me everything will be alright just as he has a thousand times before, but this time I'm not so sure. I kick off my shoes and leave my handbag on the bench beneath the

hooks where I've just hung my coat. Climbing the stairs quietly
so as not to disturb our daughters, Amber and Jade, I push our
bedroom door open. Ben is already out of bed, the book he had
been reading face down on the covers.

'How are you doing?' he asks, wrapping his arms around me.
'I wish I could have been there with you.'

'You couldn't leave the girls alone,' I say, allowing myself to
relax into his embrace. The familiar smell of his cologne fills my
nostrils as I bury my face into the soft cotton of his pyjama T-shirt.

'Have you eaten today?'

'Not since breakfast. I couldn't face anything.'

'Danni,' he reprimands gently, taking my face in his hands.
'You ought to have something. There is going to be a lot to deal
with tomorrow. Look, you get ready for bed and I'll bring you
up some tea and toast.'

I haven't got the energy to argue. He disappears downstairs
while I head to the bathroom. I barely recognise the reflection
staring back at me from the mirrored cabinet. The paleness of my
skin is accentuated by red-rimmed eyes, underlined with huge
dark circles. I look as though I've aged ten years in the past eleven
months, and it isn't over yet.

On the way back to our room, I push open the door to first
Jade's room and then Amber's. I have a sudden overwhelming desire
to hold my girls, to draw strength from the softness of their skin
and the clean smell of their hair, but both are sleeping peacefully
and it would be wrong to disturb them. When I break the news
to them, I'll need to choose my words carefully and tonight I'm
incapable of that. Reluctantly, I tear my eyes away from Amber,
something I was unable to do on the night she was born. I lay
awake all night in awe of the perfect tiny miracle who lay sleeping
in the clear hospital cot at my bedside. Until the moment Amber
took her first breath, I didn't understand what was meant when
people spoke about a mother's love, but from that instant my life

changed. My love for her, and for Jade when she arrived three and a half years later, has continued to grow. The way I felt, clutching my babies to my chest after the pain of bringing them into the world, is imprinted on my heart forever. I am so thankful for the precious gift I was given. Ben and the girls are the most important things in my world, and we'll face what lies ahead together.

I'm climbing into bed when Ben reappears with the tray that he uses to bring me the occasional Sunday morning breakfast in bed. The toast smells appetising but my throat feels too tight to attempt it, so I pick up my mug for a sip of tea instead. It has the words 'World's Best Mum' emblazoned on the side in gold lettering. My hand starts to shake violently and the tears I have been holding back cascade down my cheeks like a waterfall.

Ben removes the mug from my hand and sets the tray down so he can hold me while I sob uncontrollably into his chest.

'You could never describe Diana as the world's best mum,' he says, stroking my hair back off my face.

'I know,' I manage through my tears, 'but for all her faults, she's still my mum and I love her. She didn't deserve this; no one does.'

CHAPTER ONE
Easter Monday, 2 April 2018

It's been unseasonably warm for most of the school holidays, despite Easter falling early this year. The girls and I have taken full advantage of the sunny weather and my time off from Woldington Library, where I work as an assistant three days a week. Today is a bank holiday, so Ben also has the day off and we've brought a picnic lunch to the seaside. I wouldn't exactly describe it as bikini weather, but once we've positioned our two brightly coloured windbreaks in a semi-circle in the dunes at the top of the beach, it's sheltered enough to enjoy our sandwiches in relative comfort with a view of the sea in the distance.

After lunch, we laze around reading for a while, something we all enjoy, before joining forces with another family for an energetic game of cricket. Chasing the ball on the wide, flat, sandy beach, a feature of this part of the Lincolnshire coast when the tide is out, is pretty exhausting and I'm ready to head back to my towel for a few more pages of escapism. Ben, however, has other ideas.

'Last one to the sea buys the ice-cream,' he says, setting off at speed towards the distant shoreline. I hesitate for a moment. Gone are the days when I would have to hang back to give the girls a head start and slow down as I approached the brownish water of the North Sea to let them beat me. Both our girls can now show me a clean pair of heels and are giving Ben a run for his money. I set off after them at a jog knowing any attempt at racing is futile and accepting that, as per usual, the ice-creams will be on me.

We've been bringing Amber and Jade on day trips to Mablethorpe, our nearest seaside town, since they were both toddlers, in spite of the less than happy childhood memories the place holds for me. My grandparents retired to a bungalow by the sea when I was a newborn, allowing my mum and dad to buy their house in Woldington. I have vague memories of visiting them for a few hours at a time when I was very young, but it wasn't until my brother Adam was born that I was allowed to stay over. What should have been a fun time away from home was anything but. My grandparents weren't the most warm or loving people and didn't seem particularly keen on having me to stay, but Mum was struggling to cope on her own with a twelve-year-old and a needy baby after my dad walked out on us. They tolerated me, often leaving me to my own devices in my bedroom or out in the garden if the weather was fine. I don't remember them ever taking me to the beach, which is probably why I don't have any hang-ups about bringing the girls here. At least I had my books for company, losing myself within the pages for hours on end and allowing myself to imagine that I lived a very different life from the one I was actually enduring. In a way, I suppose I should be grateful to my grandparents. Those hours alone contributed to my lifelong love of reading which eventually led to my job at the library, despite my lack of formal qualifications.

I can hear Amber and Jade squealing about how cold the sea is as they splash around in the shallow water along with a few other brave souls and several dogs who appear to be enjoying the experience much more than their humans.

As soon as she's sure I'm within earshot, Jade calls out, 'Can we get a dog, Mum, please?'

It's not the first time one or other of our girls have asked this question. I've tried explaining that it wouldn't be fair to leave a dog on its own in the house all day on the days I'm working, but they can always cite at least half a dozen friends with dogs whose parents are both at work full-time. The truth is, money's a bit tight so we can't really afford a dog. We'd be able to feed it, but vets bills don't come cheap and it wouldn't be fair to take on an animal and then be unable to care for it properly. Ben and I have discussed it several times and he's all for telling them straight that we can't afford it. I have a different reaction: they already do without a lot of things that their friends have, so I'm usually non-committal.

'Don't just say "We'll see", Mum,' Jade persists. 'That's what you always say.'

'How about we discuss it with Dad in the car on the way home?' I say, looking over their heads towards Ben. He's shaking his head, a mildly exasperated expression on his face.

'Can we, Dad?' Jade asks hopefully.

'Discuss it, yes, although I think you know what conclusion we'll reach.'

Jade pouts. She's normally a very mild-mannered ten-year-old, but she stubbornly refuses to give up on us getting a dog.

Anxious to avoid spoiling what has been such a fun family day out, I say, 'We should probably be making a move soon. It's pretty nippy now that the sun's going down.' I catch Amber's eye and continue. 'Who fancies hot chocolate instead of ice-cream?'

'Good call, Mum,' Amber says.

I smile my gratitude to her. Although only three and a half years older than her sister, she is more aware of the struggle we face to make ends meet and has already volunteered to get a Saturday job when she's old enough. I slip my arm through hers and we head back in the direction of our stripey windbreaks. Ben and Jade continue to splash around in the water before finally conceding that it's too cold and go racing up the beach to arrive ahead of us.

They collapse in a heap laughing, the petulance of a few minutes earlier seemingly forgotten.

'We should go to the beach more often,' I say, reaching to turn off the lamp on my bedside table later that night.

'Yes,' Ben agrees, 'although I could have done without the dog interrogation all the way home. You're too soft with them, Danni.' He reaches his arms around me and pulls me closer. 'Amber and Jade need to learn that people have to live within their means, or they'll get into all sorts of financial trouble when they leave home.'

I'm about to say we won't need to worry about that for years when the realisation dawns on me that Amber could be leaving in as little as four years if she decides to go to university. It's hard to visualise our home without our two girls and it brings an unexpected lump to my throat. There's a lot more to parenting than I'd imagined when I first discovered I was pregnant at age nineteen. I'd thought the sleepless nights with a newborn would be the most difficult months until the tantrums of the terrible twos came along, followed by the next stage in guiding our girls towards adulthood. I know Ben's right about setting a good example, but you only have one childhood and then you're a grown-up for a very long time. I want our girls to remember their childhood with more fondness than the memories I have of mine.

'What did you think of my suggestion?' I ask.

'I think you already do enough for this family,' he says, gently massaging my shoulders. 'An extra day at the library would leave you with even less free time, and that's always assuming Maxine would be able to offer it to you.'

I'm pretty confident my boss would wangle it somehow as she and I have an amazing relationship, but I appreciate what he means about having even less time for myself, particularly with having to walk a dog morning and evening.

'It'll be easier when Jade starts at senior school in September and I only have one lot of school drop-offs and collections to do. And the girls did promise they would help around the house more.'

'And you believe that?'

He has a point. We always start the new year off with lists of chores for them to help with at the weekend, and they are invariably abandoned with one excuse or another before we hit the end of January.

'If you want my honest opinion,' he continues, 'I think it would only work if you draw up a contract with the girls for chores they get paid for, and the money they earn would go straight into a dogfood collection box. Maybe set a three-month trial period and if they haven't stuck to it, they would only have themselves to blame.'

After months of refusing to even to discuss the possibility of getting a dog, this is a definite softening of attitude from Ben. I feel sorry for him sometimes; sharing a house with three women can't be easy, particularly when we all gang up on him. What I really want to do is punch the air. Instead, I make every effort not to sound triumphant when I say, 'Well, we could try your suggestion, I suppose.'

My husband knows me too well. 'You haven't won yet, Danni. I give the girls two weeks tops before they start finding excuses not to help out.'

I think he may have misjudged his daughters; they're desperate for a dog and I'm pretty sure we'll be visiting the local RSPCA at the start of the summer holidays. But I keep this thought to myself.

We can't have been asleep for very long when the shrill ring tone of our house phone shatters the night-time silence. I'm instantly alert, working out within a heartbeat what the noise is, and immediately panicking. Phone calls in the dead of night are rarely good news. I'm already halfway down the stairs before Ben has stirred. I can't think who it could be, unless my brother has got the time difference between the UK and New Zealand wrong. But Adam doesn't usually ring at all.

'Hello?' I say tentatively, trying to keep my voice low in the faint hope that the ringing hasn't disturbed Amber and Jade.

A female voice says, 'Is that Mrs Harper – Mrs Danielle Harper?'

The voice sounds official and very serious.

'Y-yes,' I stammer in response.

'This is the police. Your mother Diana gave us your phone number after we picked her up on the dual carriageway. Would you be able to come to her house please?'

My knees turn to jelly and I sink down onto the bottom step. What the hell has my mother been up to?

Ben's face appears over the bannister.

'Who is it?' he asks sleepily.

I place my hand over the receiver.

'It's the police,' I whisper. 'They're at my mum's and they want me to meet them there.'

'What?' he asks, clearly still struggling with his sleep-fuddled brain. 'When?'

'I think they mean now.'

I can hear the female police officer saying, 'Are you still there, Mrs Harper?'

I remove my hand from the mouthpiece and say, 'Yes.'

'We can send a car for you if that would help?'

'No… no, it's alright. It'll be quicker if I drive. What's happened?'

'I'd rather explain when you get here, if that's alright with you?' the police officer says.

'I'm on my way,' I reply, ending the call.

'What's going on, Danni?' Ben asks, sounding much more alert as I brush past him at the top of the stairs, heading into our bedroom to throw on a sweater and jeans.

'I'm not sure; they're going to explain everything when I get to Mum's.'

'I'm coming with you.'

'We can't leave the girls on their own,' I say, reaching for my trainers.

'I could ask Rachel to sit in with them.'

I'm pretty sure that our next-door neighbour would not be best pleased to be dragged from her bed in the middle of the night.

'There's no time, Ben, this sounds urgent. Turn your mobile on; I'll message you as soon as I find out what's happening,' I say, taking the stairs at a run, with him following.

'Are you sure you'll be alright?' he asks as I reach for my keys and unlock the front door.

I'm not sure of anything. I have no idea what I'm going to find at Mum's house and it's quite terrifying.

'Of course,' I say, pecking him on the cheek. 'Just stay by your phone.'

CHAPTER TWO
Tuesday, 3 April – 2 a.m.

My mind is racing on the drive over to my mum's, although my speed is a very sedate twenty-nine miles per hour. The policewoman said they'd picked Mum up on the dual carriageway. Maybe she was speeding and they pulled her over – which is why I'm making a conscious effort to keep below the limit, even though it makes the journey feel much longer than usual.

I say usual, but it's not a journey I do that often – once a month at the most. I've made an effort to have more contact with Mum since my brother packed his bags and headed off to New Zealand after he finished university almost two years ago. I thought it would be a good opportunity for her to get to know her granddaughters who she'd shown no interest in when Adam was around. The trouble is, our visits almost always end with her picking fault with something I've done and me getting upset, which confuses the girls. So those visits are less frequent than they could be. We're her only family, apart from her sister, my Aunt Susie, but she doesn't really count as the two of them haven't spoken since they were teenagers for some reason, and she's never bothered with friends, lavishing all her attention on Adam. I'm pretty sure Mum would have hated having to give the police my phone number, so the situation must be serious.

I pull up outside Mum's house and I haven't even turned the engine off before a police officer, who must have been on the lookout for me, approaches.

'Thanks for coming so quickly,' she says as I get out of my car. 'I'm PC Hammond. I'm sorry to have disturbed you in the middle of the night, but we didn't think your mother should be left on her own.'

'What's she done?' I ask.

I can't completely read PC Hammond's expression in the dimly lit street, but it appears to be a mix of surprise and concern.

'Why do you assume she's *done* something?' she asks, placing heavy emphasis on the word.

'Well, you said you picked her up on the dual carriageway. I thought she must have been speeding for you to pull her over. I can't imagine where she'd be going at this time of night.'

'She wasn't in her car.'

It's my turn to look surprised.

'We found her walking down the middle of the dual carriageway wearing nothing but her nightdress and slippers, after we received a call from a passing motorist.'

'What?' I say, my surprise turning to confusion.

'It's lucky that her nightdress was white, making her clearly visible and giving people enough time to avoid her. That said, it's nothing short of a miracle that she wasn't hit by a car on that stretch of road.'

I can hardly believe what I'm hearing. What on earth was Mum doing wandering down the dual carriageway in her night clothes, nearly two miles away from her home?

'I don't understand. What was she doing there?'

'I was hoping you might be able to shed some light on that for us. Was she on her way to your house?'

'No,' I say, shaking my head. 'We live in the opposite direction. Didn't you ask her where she was going?'

We've been walking up the path towards Mum's front door while we've been talking. The light is spilling out from her hallway, enabling me to see PC Hammond's puzzled expression as she turns to face me.

'When did you last see your mother, Mrs Harper?'

'Four or five weeks ago,' I reply. 'What does that have to do with what's happened tonight?'

She ignores my question and asks another, 'And you didn't notice anything strange about her behaviour?'

'No. Look, what's going on?' I demand.

'Once we had your mother safely in our car, she was able to give us her name and address, but when we asked her what she was doing on the dual carriageway and where she was going, she said she had no idea. I couldn't smell alcohol on her breath, and she didn't display any other outward signs of drunkenness, so her inability to explain why she was wandering the streets must be down to something else.' She pauses briefly. 'Has your mother ever been tested for any form of dementia?'

I can feel goose bumps forming on my arms. In my head, I think back to my visits, searching for anything I've missed over the past couple of years. Mum often got annoyed when she couldn't find her handbag or glasses and usually accused me of moving them; was that actually a sign of something more serious than ageing?

'I'd like to see her now,' I say.

PC Hammond steps to one side and I go through to Mum's lounge. She's sitting in her favourite chair, sipping a hot drink and chatting perfectly normally to another police officer as though she's invited him around for afternoon tea. She looks up as I enter the room.

'Danni? What are you doing here?' she asks.

I drop to my knees in front of her and take her free hand in mine before I ask, 'What were you doing on the dual carriageway, Mum?'

She snatches her hand away, as though she's been scalded by boiling water, and says defensively, 'I must have been sleepwalking.'

I exchange a glance with PC Hammond who is standing in the doorway. She shakes her head slightly. She clearly holds the opinion that someone walking in their sleep would not have strayed so far and in my heart, I fear she may be right.

'That's quite a long way from home,' I persist gently. 'How did you get there?'

'I don't know. I told you I must have been sleepwalking. Why is she here?' she demands of the male police officer she was talking to before my arrival.

'You gave us your daughter's number to call. We need to be going,' he says, putting his mug on the coffee table and getting to his feet. 'And we didn't think it was safe to leave you on your own.'

My mother makes a 'pah' sound. 'I'm always on my own. She couldn't care less about me. She'll be out of the door the moment you've gone.'

Her words are cruel, but what's even more hurtful is the thought that she might actually believe them.

'Mrs Harper?' PC Hammond says, forcing me to make eye contact. 'Will you be able to stay with her at least until the morning? Otherwise we'll have to take her back to the police station with us for her own safety.'

'Of course.' I hate to imagine what the police officers must be thinking. Mum is portraying me as an unloving and uncaring daughter, not to mention they already probably think I've missed changes in her behaviour that could indicate dementia.

'I don't need her here, and more to the point I don't want her here,' Mum says, glaring at me.

I bite my lip. Mum has always made it abundantly clear that she doesn't want me in her life, but she's never actually said it out loud before. I can feel the heat of blood rushing to my cheeks.

'It's your choice, Diana,' PC Hammond says. 'You can either stay here with your daughter or spend the night at the police station and we'll get in touch with social services in the morning.'

'Some choice,' she mutters. 'I'm not leaving here, so I guess I'm stuck with her babysitting me.'

After I've shown the two police officers out, assuring them that I will book an appointment for Mum to see the doctor as a matter of urgency, I take a deep breath and head back into the lounge.

'Come on, Mum,' I say, 'it's late, let's get you back to bed.'

Instead of the argument I'm expecting, she turns to look up at me with fear in her eyes. 'What's wrong with me, Danni? Am I losing my mind?'

I swallow hard as I pull her into a hug, which she makes no attempt to resist. Although I wouldn't have chosen those precise words, it's a pretty accurate description of the condition I'm afraid she may have.

'Let's not worry about that tonight. I don't know about you, but I'm pretty tired. We can talk about it in the morning,' I say, leading her towards the stairs and the safety of her bedroom.

Once she's climbed into bed, I pull her covers up and switch off her bedside lamp. As I'm pulling her door closed, I say, 'I'll be in the next room if you need me.'

She doesn't reply, but I hear a sniff and have a strong suspicion that she's crying. I hesitate, wondering if I should go back to try and comfort her, but I don't know how she will react. In the end, I close the door and head into the room next door – the room where I cried myself to sleep a hundred times or more when I was a child. It hasn't changed much: the same dark oak wardrobe and chest of drawers, and the floral-patterned curtains that I used to lie staring at, unable to understand why my mum had sent me to bed without any supper when I'd done nothing wrong. I used to try so hard to make her love me, saving up my pocket money to buy her little gifts and flowers, but nothing seemed to make any difference. In the end, I stopped trying and accepted that I would always be a disappointment to my mum, although I had no idea why.

I pick up my phone to text Ben about the situation, and then brush a tear from my eye before lying back on the lumpy pillow and attempting to get some sleep.

CHAPTER THREE
Tuesday, 24 April

It's been three weeks since the phone call in the middle of the night. I could only get an emergency appointment with Mum's GP surgery the morning after her nocturnal stroll once I'd told them that the police were involved and wanted to be kept informed. It wasn't exactly true, but it had the desired effect.

Mum was seen by the most senior of the practice doctors, Dr Morton. She ran through a series of standard questions to assess Mum's memory, problem-solving ability, language skills, maths skills and other abilities. At the end of the Folstein test, Dr Morton confirmed that there were some 'issues', as she put it, and said she would arrange an appointment for Mum to be seen by a specialist as soon as possible.

I suppose three weeks isn't long to wait when you think how rushed off their feet the NHS are most of the time, but it's been tricky dealing with Mum's moods. Some days she's been aggressive and belligerent, refusing to accept that there is anything wrong with her at all. She'll tell me to go away and leave her alone. Other days she has been tearful and needy. I've tried to call in and see her most days, but it hasn't been easy juggling my job and the two different school runs. Night-times have been the real problem though. I stayed with her for the first couple of nights after the police had found her on the dual carriageway, but it wasn't a long-term solution and I couldn't risk another episode of her wandering the streets in her nightie. She was lucky to escape unscathed last time. Not only did she run the risk of being knocked down, something much worse could have befallen her, which doesn't bear thinking about.

After talking to Martin, her kindly next-door neighbour, we devised a plan to lock everything at the front of the house, with me holding on to the keys, but to give Mum access to her back garden so that she wouldn't feel like a prisoner in her own home. She eventually agreed after I explained it would probably only be temporary and that it was for her safety. What we didn't tell Mum was that Martin came up with the idea of adjusting the angle of the motion-activated security lights at the back of his house to cover her back door as well as his own. The slightest movement and both of their gardens will be flooded with light meaning he can keep an eye on her if she wanders outside during the night. If I'm honest, I'd rather her not go outside at night but she told me that looking at the stars made her feel calm when she was anxious and it seems mean to take away small pleasures before we know for sure what we are dealing with. At least with everything at the front of the house locked up tighter than a drum, I know she can't get out onto the street, so I can sleep, safe in the knowledge that Martin will call if there's a problem.

Martin and his wife moved in next door to Mum and Dad when I was about nine, but they never socialised together as far as I can remember. His wife died soon after my dad left us and I've always suspected him of having a soft spot for my mum, not that she ever gave him any encouragement. I don't recall Mum having any male friends since my dad walked out the day after my twelfth birthday, but it never seemed to bother her. She had my brother, Adam, to lavish her attention on and apparently, he was the only male company she needed.

Looking at her now, sat opposite me in the hospital waiting room, I can't help wondering if she regrets not allowing anyone else into her heart – someone she could have grown old with and who would have taken care of her through the challenge that I strongly suspect lies ahead.

'Are you okay?' I mouth to her silently.

'Don't be stupid, Danielle,' she replies, her voice sharp and loud, cutting through the quiet nervous atmosphere like a knife. 'Why would I be okay about waiting to have a life sentence delivered? I wish you'd just go away and stop bothering me with your pathetic questions.'

The other outpatients are studying the floor and the receptionist, after an initial glance in our direction, goes back to whatever she is doing on her computer. I'm mortified. Mum often speaks to me like this in private and although I don't enjoy it, I just accept it, but it's quite different embarrassing me in public.

'Is that actually what you want, Mum?' I ask, struggling to keep my voice low and even.

Before she can answer, the receptionist raises her head again and says, 'The doctor will see you now, Mrs Jenson.'

Mum gets to her feet and stands, staring at me expectantly with her hands on her hips.

I have to take a moment to remind myself that maybe she can't help her behaviour; maybe it's the illness. I get slowly to my feet.

'Well, come on then if you're coming,' she says, marching off towards the door marked Dr Ranjid.

Mum is quiet on the drive back to her house. Dr Ranjid gave her another test similar to the one she had undergone at her GP surgery before saying he wanted her to have a psychiatric evaluation and a CT scan of her brain to rule out any other possible cause of the symptoms she was exhibiting, although he strongly suspected she had Alzheimer's disease. He told us there were different types of Alzheimer's which he would go into once Mum's diagnosis had been confirmed and that the scan would also give a fairly accurate indication of what stage Mum is at.

As we pull up outside her house, she says, 'I can always get a second opinion.'

I ought to feel sorry for my mum, clutching at straws when she knows she's been seen by the local expert in this field. She's clearly desperate for someone to arrive at a different conclusion.

What fills my mind instead are thoughts of what her future care might entail and whether or not she will allow me to look after her. Since Adam went overseas, I've invited her to our house for Christmas each year because I hate the idea of her being on her own, but she's refused to come. If she can't stand the thought of a few hours in my company one day a year, how will she react to having to rely on me as her primary carer? The sad truth is, there are no other options; I'm all Mum has.

CHAPTER FOUR
Thursday, 10 May

The only good thing to come out of Mum's diagnosis is that she is getting much closer to Amber and Jade. Without doubt, their Sunday visits are the highlight of her week. Ben and I reached the decision that they don't need to know why we've been seeing much more of their grandmother over recent weeks, but we've hinted that she's been lonely since their Uncle Adam left home. We would never out and out lie to our girls, but withholding the full truth seemed like the best option while we wait for an accurate prognosis. They're unaware that I spend Tuesdays and Thursdays – my days off from the library – with her while they're at school, but we've started getting her some shopping on Saturdays and dropping it off and then we all visit on Sundays, although Ben doesn't stay the whole time. He can't tolerate the way she speaks to me, especially as I'm doing so much for her at the moment.

None of the tests Mum has had have been encouraging, but the results we got yesterday have delivered the biggest blow. When we first saw Dr Ranjid, he explained about the seven different stages of Alzheimer's and that the various tests would discover what stage Mum was at so that she could receive the appropriate treatment. Yesterday, he broke the news that she is already at stage four, the moderate decline stage, which I must admit shocked me. Although I haven't been a particularly frequent visitor, she must have been hiding some of her symptoms from me whether or not she was aware that she was doing it. It made me wonder whether Adam had noticed anything odd about her behaviour while he was living with her before leaving for New Zealand. It's something I'm planning on asking him during our Skype call.

I'd been putting off telling him about Mum's diagnosis until we had the results of the latest test, but now he needs to know that her condition could deteriorate quite rapidly over the next couple of years. I'm hoping he might come home to see Mum, or better still stay and help with her care. It might seem churlish of me, but he's the one that has the most to repay her for after the love and attention she always showed him as a child. Ben doesn't think that Adam will be on the first plane home, but I'm crediting him with being a more thoughtful son and brother. That might be more hope than expectation as we've never enjoyed the best of relationships. I think my awareness of the closeness between my brother and our mum started the day she brought him home from the hospital.

I can still remember standing at the front door of our house, next to my grandmother who'd come to stay for a few days while Mum was in hospital. My mum walked up the driveway cradling Adam in her arms and said, 'At last I've got my son. No one can take him away from me.' Even as an eleven-year-old, I felt wounded by her words. Maybe she'd always wanted a boy and I'd been a huge disappointment to her no matter how hard I tried to make her love me. She hadn't allowed Grandma Sally to hold Adam at all and as a result Grandma had returned home early, saying she knew when she wasn't welcome. We'd never seen much of either of my grandparents but after that we saw them even less, apart from when I went to stay with them during the school holidays to give Mum a break. I don't recall Adam ever coming; Mum wouldn't allow her precious boy out of her sight.

Mum still idolises my brother despite him announcing that he was going to take a gap year with his girlfriend Zoe in New

Zealand, her home country, the moment he finished university. According to Mum, the relationship with Zoe ended earlier this year, but while Adam has fallen out of love with her, he loves the New Zealand lifestyle and is apparently in no hurry to come home. Maybe the situation with Mum will change that.

I check my watch before attempting the Skype call. Moments later my brother's face appears on my computer screen. He looks thinner than I remember, and tanned, but then it hasn't been long since the end of New Zealand's summer, so I expect he's been taking full advantage of the outdoors life.

'Hello, big sis,' he says. 'To what do I owe this pleasure?'

He's smiling, but there isn't a huge amount of warmth in his voice. We've rarely been in touch while he's been overseas, so he must have been surprised to receive an email from me suggesting the call. There's no point beating around the bush, he must suspect it isn't just a social call.

'I'm sorry to have to land this on you, Adam, but Mum's been undergoing some tests and they've discovered she has dementia.'

He flinches, and I regret being quite so brutal with the way I've broken it to him.

'Jesus, Danni, you could have softened the blow. That's awful news.'

It's too late to take back my previous words. 'I'm sorry, but there's really no easy way to tell someone this sort of thing.'

'When did you find out?'

'Mum had a bit of a funny episode a few weeks back,' I say, deciding not to elaborate on the details. 'It resulted in her having an MMSE test at the doctors which flagged up a couple of things, so she was referred to a specialist.'

'Hold on a minute; what's an MMSE test?' Adam says.

'It's the Mini-Mental State Examination which tests cognitive function; you know, things like memory, attention, language and maths skills, that sort of thing. I was going to ask you if you ever noticed Mum being forgetful when you were living with her?'

'I don't think so, but then I tried to be around her as little as possible once I'd started uni, so I might not have noticed.'

This takes me by surprise. 'I always thought you two were inseparable.'

'When I was little maybe, but once I got into my teens it wasn't so cool having a mum watching your every move. I only stayed at home throughout university because she'd get hysterical if I ever talked about moving into halls or into a student house.'

I can hardly believe what I'm hearing.

'Don't get me wrong,' he adds quickly. 'She's the best mum anyone could wish for.'

I shudder. Not from my point of view.

'It's just that sometimes she was a bit…' He pauses, struggling for the right word. 'Suffocating.'

I've spent so many years feeling envious of the unwavering love and attention Mum has lavished on Adam, I never stopped to consider how it might have felt from his point of view. In a funny sort of way, we're both victims of her inability to share her love equally between the two of us. Mum's obsession with her son drove us apart, but maybe I should have tried harder to reconnect with Adam once he was no longer living at home. It partly explains him running to the other side of the world as soon as he got the opportunity. It's a hard-won freedom that he's not likely to want to give up.

'How bad is she, Danni?' he asks.

'Well, she still recognises the people in her life. It's mostly just lapses in memory at the moment,' I say, softening my approach.

'So fairly early stages then?'

'Not exactly. According to the test results we received yesterday she's in the moderate decline phase, which is stage four in the seven stages. Dr Ranjid, her consultant, said if she is at the start of this phase, she could be in it for several years with very little change, but if she's towards the end of this stage, the decline becomes far more rapid.'

'Isn't there any treatment she can have?'

'She's going to start on some drugs which could potentially slow the decline, but they don't always work.'

'Okay. Well, keep me posted on how she's getting on.'

That sentence makes it clear that Adam isn't considering coming back to England to see Mum or help with her care. I decide to try and plant the thought in his mind.

'I don't suppose you'd be able to come home any time soon?' I ask.

He hesitates before speaking again. 'Not at the moment. Work commitments, I'm afraid. Maybe you could start sending me regular emails so that I can keep abreast of things?'

'Sure,' I say, trying to keep the disappointment out of my voice. 'Oh, and I'm sorry things didn't work out with Zoe,' I add.

'Mum told you?'

'Yes. Obviously, she didn't go into detail, she just said it was over, but you were staying on in New Zealand.'

'I love it here, Danni. It's a magical place, full of mountains and valleys. It's so different from flat old Lincolnshire. You should visit some time.'

My brother obviously doesn't know the financial pressure we're under and I've no intention of sharing it with him; it would only make me feel even more inferior. Instead, I just say, 'I'm glad you're happy. Let's do this again soon,' before I end the call. It's quite incredible to think that I've just had a longer conversation with my brother on the other side of the world than I ever had when he was living ten minutes down the road. It's also the first time I've considered that maybe his childhood wasn't as idyllic as I've always imagined.

CHAPTER FIVE
Thursday, 6 September

The late afternoon September sunshine is warmer than I realised and I'm regretting my choice of jeans and a sweater with nothing but my bra underneath. All around me, the other mums waiting at the school gate are stripping off cardigans and light jackets as they chat with their friends about the gym or the latest recipe they've tried. Although I already know quite a few of them because Amber has been at St Bede's for three years, I keep my distance. My mind is too full of thoughts about Mum and the deterioration in her condition to hold a conversation about dauphinoise potatoes.

Despite my work commitments and looking after Mum, picking my daughters up from school is something I've always done daily. It'll be easier now that they are both at the same school. Usually, I take the car, but today is special. It's Jade's first day at senior school and to celebrate I've decided to take them to Poppy's, their favourite café in the centre of town, for cake and a milkshake after school. It's easier to walk than drive as the parking can be a nightmare.

Of our two daughters, Jade is more like me both in looks and personality, but even I was surprised at how nervous she seemed this morning, repeatedly checking her uniform in the full-length mirror in our narrow hallway before plonking her hat on top of her unruly red curls. I doubt she'll wear the hat beyond her first week at St Bede's, but she wanted to make a good impression with the teachers on her first day so I encouraged her to wear Amber's mostly unworn one, telling her it looked very smart. Behind Jade's back, Amber had raised her eyebrows at me, as though to say 'smart' is not cool. Amber's hat didn't even last until the end of her first day. She'd tumbled out of the school gate with her newfound friends with it squashed into the top of her school bag. She's always been the more confident of the two of them, exactly like her dad.

I can see my girls walking towards me across the playground, arms linked and both smiling. I'm relieved. I know Amber will look out for her younger sister, just as she always has done, but Jade has to learn to stand on her own two feet and not rely on her so heavily.

'How was your first day?' I ask, when they're within earshot.

'Cool,' Jade says, her eyes sparkling with excitement.

She is hatless and I wonder whether that's from choice or whether she was teased about wearing it. Whichever; it doesn't seem to have bothered her. I need to stop worrying about my younger daughter, even though I see myself in her and remember the way I felt at her age. Nobody met me from my first day at senior school. Mum was heavily pregnant with Adam and had swollen ankles and my dad was working away from home. By the time I'd walked the mile or so to our house, the excited feeling had drained out of me. It was further quashed by the first thing Mum said when I unlocked the front door. Instead of, 'How was your day?' she demanded, 'Where have you been? I'm gagging for a cup of tea.' It was enough to burst anyone's bubble.

'Tell me all about it,' I say now, squeezing myself between my girls to link my arms through theirs and ushering them down the road in the opposite direction from where the car is usually parked.

'Where are we going?' Amber asks.

'It's a surprise; my little treat.'

'Poppy's?' Jade squeals excitedly.

I nod. I never have been very good at keeping secrets.

'Yes!' she says, fist-pumping the air with her free hand. 'Can I have a chocolate milkshake?'

'You can both have whatever you want; it's a special occasion,' I say making eye contact with Amber who gives me a smile of approval. She is much more aware of the situation with Mum and knows how stressed I've been since the tests confirmed that her nana is suffering from dementia, although we haven't gone into any details of what lies ahead. It will do us all good to escape reality for an hour or so. 'So, Jade,' I say, returning my attention to my younger daughter, 'what's your form teacher like? It's Mrs Lavery, isn't it?'

'Yes. She's really nice. I've got her for history too, and she says she hopes I'll be better at handing in my homework than Amber was when she was in her class.'

'Cheek!' Amber retorts. 'Although she has a point. History is so boring.'

By the time we've walked to Poppy's, ordered from the menu and sat down at a table near the window with our drinks and cake, I've heard about most of the girls in Jade's class: who she likes, who she's not so keen on and who she's intending on giving a wide berth to. It's Amber's turn now and she is filling us in on the two new girls in her class, Fay and Pippa, as well as the new PE teacher, Mr Ramsey.

'He's well fit,' she says, her cheeks colouring slightly.

'I'd hope so if he's a PE teacher,' I respond, but I think my tongue-in-cheek reply may be lost on her.

Amber hasn't really showed much of an interest in boys yet, but she'll be fifteen in a couple of months so I'm fully expecting that to change and with it the closeness of our relationship. I recently read in a magazine article that girls become closer to their dads in their mid-teens. She already has a strong bond with Ben, but until now she has always shared her secrets and insecurities with me. The thought of losing the closeness I never enjoyed with my own mum saddens me.

The slurping sound of Jade trying to suck the last drops of her milkshake up through her straw brings me back to the present.

'I think it's finished,' I say, as my phone starts to ring. 'I'll bet that's Dad wanting to know how your first day went.' But when I look at the screen, I feel the smile freeze on my face. It's not Ben, it's Martin, my mum's neighbour. I slip off my chair, telling the girls to stay where they are, and head outside to take the call.

'Is everything alright, Martin?'

'Um, well no, not really.'

I can feel the weight that had temporarily lifted off my shoulders while I was enjoying quality time with my daughters descending like a thunder cloud.

'What's wrong?' I ask, the pitch of my voice shriller than usual.

'Diana's okay, the paramedics are with her now, but the kitchen's a bit of a mess, I'm afraid.'

What the hell is he talking about? 'Paramedics?' My pulse is racing. 'Has she had a fall?'

'No, they're treating her for smoke inhalation,' Martin says. 'Apparently she'd put a pan of something on the stove to heat up and must have forgotten about it and gone upstairs to have a nap. I noticed the smoke billowing out of her kitchen window and rang the fire brigade. They were here in under ten minutes and it's a good job they were, because the smell of burning didn't wake her, and she was only semi-conscious when they found her in the bedroom.'

'Oh my God. I'm in town with the girls and I haven't got my car,' I say, panic preventing me from thinking clearly.

'You could jump in a taxi, Danni. I'll keep the girls round at my house if you'd rather not upset them by seeing their gran in a bit of a state.'

'Thank you, Martin, that sounds like a good plan. We'll be there as soon as we can.'

The paramedics were already lifting Mum's stretcher into the back of their ambulance when we arrived at her house less than fifteen minutes later. As promised, Martin took Amber and Jade to his house to wait for Ben.

I've been allowed to travel in the back of the ambulance with Mum and Sam, one of the paramedics who treated her at the scene. Mum can't speak to me because she has a mask over her mouth and nose, feeding her pure oxygen, but I've been squeezing her hand reassuringly trying to calm the panic in her eyes.

'You're going to be fine, Mum. Sam says they just want to keep you in hospital overnight to make sure the smoke hasn't done any lasting damage.' Mum nods and closes her eyes as though satisfied with my explanation. What I didn't tell her is that Sam had also asked me if we'd made any plans for the future as she didn't think Mum should be living on her own.

It's a conversation I've tried to have with Mum on several occasions, but she stubbornly refuses to say anything other than, 'The only way you'll get me away from this house is in a wooden box.' Ben and I have discussed the possibility of having a live-in carer for her but even with the income from my part-time job at the library, the sums simply don't add up. We haven't had the conversation recently as she seemed a bit better over the summer holidays – quite lucid, in fact, enjoying her time with Amber and Jade who made the effort to visit her almost every day. She's been showing them a few old photographs of me and Adam as children and has promised to look for some more because the girls enjoyed having a laugh at our old-fashioned clothes. When she mentioned how sad she was that she couldn't listen to her old music because it was all on records or cassette tapes and she didn't have anything to play them on, Amber came up with the idea of making a playlist on her phone for her nana. They've been borrowing Ben's portable speaker to take with them every visit and there would often be music from the 1970s or '80s blaring out when I arrived to take them home. I suppose I should have realised there would be some kind of negative reaction to not seeing the girls on a daily basis, but I wasn't expecting it so soon and in such dramatic fashion.

The ambulance jolts to a stop and Mum's eyes fly open, the anxiety intensified. Until her tests for dementia earlier in the year, she hadn't set foot in a hospital since the traumatic experience of giving birth to Adam, and he's almost twenty-four. He was a breech baby and the cord was wrapped around his neck, so he couldn't breathe for the first few minutes of his life. Although Mum has never spoken to me about it, I remember my dad telling me when he arrived home from the hospital, ashen-faced, that it had been touch and go as to whether or not Adam would survive. Maybe that's why Mum was so besotted with my brother and pushed me and Dad away.

Sam flings the back doors open and lowers the step to give her driver, Annie, access.

'Come on then, Diana, let's go and get you checked over,' Sam says, releasing the gurney from its locked position and expertly guiding it towards the doors.

Mum twists her head to maintain eye contact with me, panic starting to build.

'It's okay, Mum, I'm not going to leave you, I promise.'

CHAPTER SIX
Friday, 7 September

I'm not doing a great job of making breakfast. Ben made me tea and crumpets when I finally got back from the hospital last night and I forgot to adjust the dial on the toaster this morning, resulting in four slices of cremated toast and the smoke alarm going off – acting as a reminder that we should have been more vigilant in checking that Mum's was working properly. She'd told one of the firemen at the scene that she'd removed the battery in hers because it kept emitting a shrill beep. Apparently, she thought it was malfunctioning but had forgotten to mention it to me.

I'm wafting the tea towel around manically, trying to disperse the smoke in order to stop the deafening noise, when two arms reach around my waist, scaring the life out of me. It's Amber. I didn't hear her come into the kitchen.

'Is there anything I can do to help, Mum?' she asks, shouting to be heard above the din.

I pass her the hand towel from the rail by the sink and we both continue flapping around in some weird ritual dance until eventually the piercing noise stops completely.

'I'm glad my alarm isn't that loud,' Amber says, taking the tea towel off me and putting both of the cloths back on the rail.

'It's a shame Jade's isn't, because it looks like she's slept through hers *and* the smoke alarm. Go and give her a call for me, will you, and I'll put some more toast on. It wouldn't do to be late to school on the second morning of term.'

'Actually, Jade is awake. I stuck my head in on my way downstairs and she was sitting up in bed staring into space. She said she doesn't feel like going to school today.'

My heart plummets. I don't know why I thought our girls would just brush aside what happened to their nana yesterday.

'I'll go up and talk to her.'

Jade is still sitting in bed when I open her door after knocking. Her eyes are red; she's been crying.

'Hey,' I say, going over to her, 'try not to get upset about Nana. The hospital said she's fine and she should be allowed home later today.'

'But she's not fine, is she, Mum?' Jade sniffs. 'I'm not a baby; I know there's something wrong with her memory. She keeps calling me Danni.'

I swallow hard. It seems Jade is more aware of what is going on than I've given her credit for.

'Oh, sweetheart. Why didn't you talk to me if it was worrying you?'

'Amber said you were already really upset and it would only make it worse if you had to explain everything to me.'

'Well, for once your big sister is wrong,' I say, perching next to her on the bed and putting my arm around her shoulders. 'You know what I think about being honest with each other.'

'Then why didn't you tell me what was happening with Nana?'

'I wanted to, but with you starting at your new school I didn't want you getting upset. I was waiting for the right moment, but it never seemed to come along and now circumstances have beaten me to it. I'm sorry, sweetheart, I should have told you, but we'll talk things through when you and Amber are back from school and your dad's back from work, okay?'

'Do I have to go to school? I don't really feel like it,' Jade says, dropping her head against my chest.

I remember her happy, smiling face when I met them at the school gates yesterday. She was so upbeat about the girls she was hoping to form friendships with. If she misses today, maybe some of the girls will pair up and she'll be left out in the cold. Much as I want to tell her she can have a duvet-day, I know that won't be in her best interests.

'Look, it's Friday today and then you've got the weekend. We'll be able to go and see Nana; you know how much that cheers her up. Just get through today and we'll have a pizza after our family talk. How does that sound?'

Call me a bad mother, but I'd always resorted to mild forms of bribery to persuade my children to do things they didn't really want to.

'Okay, but I'm not sure I'll be able to concentrate on my lessons.'

'Good girl. I'll ring the school and let them know we've had a bit of a drama; I'm sure your teachers will understand. Now get dressed and I'll go and make you some toast.'

'Try not to burn it this time, Mum,' Jade says, managing a watery smile as she throws her bed covers back and slips her feet into her slippers.

After dropping Amber and Jade at school, I drive to the library. I usually work from nine until four on Mondays, Wednesdays and Fridays, but I'll only be able to do a couple of hours this morning as the doctor's rounds at the hospital are between eleven-thirty and twelve-thirty and I want to be with Mum to hear what he has to say.

I was delighted when Maxine offered me the position of part-time library assistant despite my lack of qualifications. I hadn't needed to provide any evidence of my love of books as I've been a regular at Woldington Library since I was old enough to read, which is about the same length of time as Maxine has worked there. My dad used to take me to return my books and choose new ones every Saturday morning, something I've continued into adulthood as I don't have the money to fund my solitary vice even when books are at knockdown prices in the supermarket.

'Morning Max,' I say, walking into the traditional Victorian building after hanging my coat up in the cloakroom. 'I'm so sorry, but I'll only be able to do a couple of hours today. My mum's in the hospital and I need to be there for doctor's rounds.'

'I'm sorry to hear that, love. Has she taken a turn for the worse?'

My boss knows all about my mum's dementia. I had to take some time off to ferry Mum around to various appointments, and when the diagnosis was confirmed I needed someone to talk to. As always, Maxine was there offering a supportive shoulder to cry on. It's funny really; in some ways she's been more of a mum to me than my actual mum. They're around the same age and Maxine has no family of her own so she's always treated me like the daughter she never had. Every year she buys Amber and Jade Christmas and birthday presents… books, of course.

'No,' I say with a sigh. 'She managed to set her kitchen alight yesterday and ended up in hospital being treated for smoke inhalation. I think they'll let her go home today, although she's not going to be able to cook until we can get it repaired on the insurance. I'm hoping her neighbour will do a few meals for her, although I hate to ask when he's already so generous.'

'Well, if you need to take any time off you only need to ask. I know you'll make the hours up when you can.'

'Thanks Max,' I say, turning away from her so that she can't see the tears forming in the corners of my eyes. She knows I'm on a tight budget and can't afford to take unpaid leave, so her kindness is much appreciated. 'I'll make a start on tidying the shelves in the children's section, shall I?'

*

The two hours pass in the blink of an eye. What's the saying? 'If you love your job, you'll never work a day in your life.' That's certainly true for me, I think, circling around the hospital car park for the third time looking for a parking space. I can see an elderly man approaching a VW Golf. I wind my window down.

'Are you going?' I ask, trying to keep the urgency out of my voice. It's 11.25 a.m. and it would be typical for the doctor to visit Mum first and for me to miss him.

'Yes, dear. If you wait a moment, I'll give you my ticket. I've paid until two o'clock, but I shan't be needing it now. Muriel passed away.'

I don't know who Muriel was, but I'm shocked at his lack of emotion. If someone I knew well enough to visit in hospital had just died, I'm pretty sure I wouldn't be holding it together that well. I swallow hard, thinking of Mum in the back of the ambulance and what might have happened if Martin hadn't been so alert. The man reaches for the white ticket on his dashboard and then brings it over to my car.

'There you go, dear, it'll make me feel as though I've had my money's worth.'

'That's very kind of you,' I reply, 'and I'm so sorry for your loss.'

'She was ready to go, has been for a couple of years. Damn dementia, she's barely recognised me for the past few months and we'd been married for fifty-eight years.'

It's all I can do to stop myself gasping as I realise he's speaking about his wife.

'Awful disease, taking the mind and leaving the body,' he continues. 'I wouldn't wish it on anyone. Take it from me, Muriel's better off dead.'

I'm relieved he's already making his way back to his car and doesn't see the effect of his words on me. Mum is already in the moderate decline stage of the disease and I know it's going to be a rocky road ahead, but even so, I can't imagine a time when I'd believe she would be 'better off dead', to use his phrase. The old man backs out of his parking space and raises a hand to wave to me as he drives off. What will life hold for him now? Will he feel like a weight has lifted off his shoulders and find someone else to share the remainder of his life with, or will the enormity of his loss break his heart? It's not uncommon for the long-time partner of someone who has died to give up the will to live. Pulling into the space he has just vacated, I can't help but wonder how I'll feel when Mum's dementia worsens to the point where she no longer knows who I am. We haven't had much opportunity to make happy memories, but if she'll let me, I'm going to try and make her feel loved for the time she has left.

CHAPTER SEVEN
Friday, 7 September

'Can you go and give your nana a call please, Amber?'

The timer has just gone off indicating that the shepherd's pie I've hastily rustled up for supper is ready to serve.

'Okay,' Amber says, closing her history textbook and returning it to her school bag, before uncoiling her legs from beneath her and padding across the room in stockinged feet.

'You need to stop what you're doing, too, Jade,' I add, reaching into the oven and withdrawing the rectangular dish with cheese bubbling furiously on the top. 'Can you lay the table for me please?'

'Where's Nana sitting?' she asks.

'You choose,' I reply, hoping that she'll put Mum between Amber and herself at the round dining table. Mum is much fonder of our girls than she has ever been of me and if she feels more comfortable, she's less likely to pick on me.

Our plans for the evening have radically changed. Although the doctor had been satisfied that Mum wasn't experiencing breathing difficulties after inhaling smoke from the fire and was willing to discharge her, the social care nurse raised objections. She wasn't happy for Mum to go back to a property that had no kitchen and was potentially unsafe. I tried to persuade her that it would be okay by offering Martin's help, in the hope that he wouldn't mind cooking the occasional meal for Mum while her kitchen was being repaired, but that didn't satisfy Pearl Wigley.

'Diana needs to be able to make herself a hot drink at the very least,' she said, 'and there's no way that's possible at the moment. She'll have to stay in the hospital for a few days until we can find a temporary place for her in a home.'

The conversation was conducted in hushed tones several paces away from the end of Mum's bed, but there is absolutely nothing wrong with Mum's hearing and she got the gist of what was being discussed.

'I'm not going into a home and that's final,' she said very loudly as though to emphasise the fact that we had been whispering. 'Once they get you in those places, you never get out alive.'

I couldn't help thinking she had a point.

'And I'm not staying here a moment longer than I have to,' she added. 'You can pick up all manner of things in hospital. Hazel Parker, at number twenty-five, only came in to have a hip replacement and they wheeled her out in a coffin ten days later after she got that MRSA thing.'

Pearl glanced at the very frail-looking, elderly women Mum was sharing the space with, concern etched on her face. Clearly, she was wishing my mum would keep her voice down so as not to upset the other patients.

'There is another temporary solution,' I offered, stressing the word temporary. Despite my resolution out in the car park to make Mum's life as good as it could be, the thought of having her living with us filled me with dread, but I couldn't see any other option. 'You could stay with us until your kitchen is cleaned up and we get you a new cooker. What do you think?'

For a moment, Mum looked like she was going to argue about it, but she apparently realised she had very few options.

'Just for a couple of days then,' she said ungraciously, 'and only to get me out of here.'

Pearl shot me a sympathetic look but seemed happy with the compromise.

'Can I go now then?' Mum demanded.

'As soon as the doctor signs your discharge papers,' Pearl replied, turning on her heel, evidently glad to be seeing the back of such a troublesome patient.

'That told her,' Mum said, 'thinking she could boss me around.'

'She was only looking out for your welfare, Mum,' I responded, wishing my mum could have been a little less aggressive and shown a bit of gratitude that I'd managed to rescue the situation.

Instead she said, 'Well, it's about time someone did,' totally oblivious of the crushing effect those words had on me.

Our takeaway pizza plans were shelved. Mum doesn't eat 'disgusting foreign muck' as she calls it, although if anyone quizzed her about it, they would soon realise she has no right to form an opinion on whether or not it's disgusting as she's never tried anything from further afield than Cornwall. We settled on shepherd's pie on the drive home from the hospital and I'd popped out to get the ingredients from the supermarket once we'd collected the girls from school. There was no way I was going to leave Mum alone in our house after the carnage she had created in her own.

The girls were genuinely pleased to see their nana in the car with me outside the school and delighted at the prospect of having her to stay. Amber didn't object to moving in with Jade for a few nights when I rang her in the school lunch break. Amber's room is slightly bigger and has a double bed so was the obvious one to give Mum, to make her as comfortable as possible. I changed the sheets while Mum was having a cup of tea in front of the television watching *Countdown*. She's surprisingly good at making words out of the nine random letters considering how confused she can get about other things, but that's the tragedy of dementia: some things are clear and obvious while others become shrouded in a grey fog.

As I'm dishing up, I hear the front door slam. I'm not going to lie; I'm relieved Ben is home as he will be able to deflect some of the harsh comments Mum is bound to fire in my direction over the meal. It will be too hot, too salty, the potato will be lumpy and the cheese tasteless, but at least I'm expecting the criticism, so it won't come as a surprise.

'Hello Diana,' he says, addressing Mum. 'Are you feeling a bit better?'

'Better than what? I'm not ill, you know, I just forgot I'd put the soup on to warm up while I went for a lie-down,' Mum replies defensively.

Ben and I exchange a glance. Mum knows full well that she has been diagnosed as having dementia, but at times she chooses to ignore it. 'Why do they have to put a label on everything these days?' she'd said when we'd emerged from Dr Ranjid's office and I'd asked her if she was okay. 'Everybody gets a bit forgetful as they get older; I guess our brains just get tired with all the things we've learned in our lifetime.' There was no point in arguing with her, and I didn't want to upset her any further after being on the receiving end of such devastating news.

'I meant after all the smoke you breathed in,' Ben says, attempting to defuse the situation.

'I'm not sure I believe you,' she snipes, 'but if you did mean that I'm absolutely fine.'

Here we go. Thank goodness it will only be for a few days.

'Something smells good,' Ben says loudly, ignoring Mum's comment about believing him.

'Shepherd's pie. Mum's choice,' I say, laying one plate in front of Mum and another in front of Jade.

'There's far too much there for me,' Mum says. 'No wonder people these days are so fat; everyone eats way too much.'

It's one barbed remark that she can't aim at me – if anything, I have the opposite problem in that I can't seem to add any weight at all no matter how much I eat – but I notice Amber flinch. She's going through a slightly plump phase, which will no doubt be followed by a growth spurt. She's almost as tall as me already and judging by her size-seven feet she could well end up dwarfing me. I bite my lip. I'm not going to rise to it and make Amber feel even more uncomfortable. I'll have a quiet word with her later instead.

'Just eat what you can, Mum,' I say, returning to the kitchen for Ben and Amber's plates, before finally fetching my own, by which time Mum is positively shovelling food into her mouth as though she hasn't eaten in a week. Maybe she hasn't; maybe she's been forgetting mealtimes. At least while she's under our roof I'll be able to keep an eye on that side of things.

With her mouth full of meat, gravy and mash, Mum asks, 'So, Jade, how was your first day at senior school?'

My heart contracts. She never asked me that; in fact, she never showed any interest in me at all from the moment she gave birth to Adam.

Following our Skype call back in May, when I first told my brother about Mum's dementia diagnosis, I now have a better understanding of things from his perspective, which I didn't have when I was younger. All I could see back then was that Adam had replaced me in my mother's affections, not that she had ever been particularly affectionate towards me. It was just about bearable while my dad still lived with us, but when he left, telling me that just existing was no way to live a life, Mum turned from being apathetic towards me to openly hostile. She completely doted on my brother, spending all the money Dad sent her for our upkeep on Adam. He had new clothes and shoes and all the 'must-have' toys, while I faced the humiliation of going to school with holes in my tights and the soles of my shoes, and frayed cuffs on my coat where I had unpicked the hem in an effort to make the sleeves longer. None of my school blouses fitted properly and I was constantly being told off for my skirt being too short. In the end, Mum was summoned to school by the head teacher and offered some second-hand clothes for me, because he assumed that Mum was in financial difficulty. She was furious with me for embarrassing her, but at least it was a bit of a wake-up call and after the incident she made sure that at the very least I had clothes that fitted me. It wasn't the material things Adam received which really upset me though; no, it was the love she lavished on him that really hurt. I now realise he must have felt more smothered than mothered, but it wasn't how I viewed things as a young teenager. I've lost count of the number of times I lay on my bed in my room wondering what exactly I'd done to make my mother so disinterested in me. I've never been able to fathom it, but maybe I did something when I was too young to remember that she never forgave me for.

'Can we, Mum?' Amber is asking.

Four pairs of eyes are trained on me and I have no idea what they have been talking about. I turn to look at Ben for help. 'What does Dad think?'

My husband knows me well enough to realise that I haven't been following the conversation.

'I think it's fine for you three to go up to Nana's room and listen to some music,' he says, filling me in on the original question.

'So long as it's not too loud,' I chip in. 'We wouldn't want to upset the neighbours.'

Once they've left the room, Ben says, 'You didn't have a clue what they were asking for, did you?'

'No,' I confess. 'Mum asking Jade how her first day at senior school went reminded me of just how little she cared about mine.'

'It's history, Danni, the past can't be rewritten,' he says, placing his hand over mine where it's resting next to my half-eaten plate of food. 'You should just be grateful that she's decided, for whatever reason, to take an interest in her granddaughters.'

I smile up at him. I'm so thankful to have Ben in my life. He fills the gaping hole left by my mother's lack of love for me and the absence of my father who never came back for me.

'You don't need Diana; not her love nor her approval. And despite having her as a role model, you're a fantastic mother to our girls; I'm so proud of who you have become,' Ben says, dropping a kiss onto my forehead.

I can't be sure, but I think there is a tear forming in the corner of his eye and I always think of myself as the emotional one in our relationship.

'Come on,' he says, pushing his chair back from the table. 'Let's get these dishes done and then we can watch a film; just the two of us.'

'Sounds good,' I say, 'after I've emailed Adam to tell him what's been going on.'

'Are you sure that's a good idea? It won't change his mind about coming home and he might just think you're trying to make him feel guilty.'

I mull it over for a moment. I now contact Adam at regular intervals to give him updates on Mum's condition and always tell him how much she misses him. It all seems to fall on deaf ears. I'll have to email him tonight to let him know about this latest development, but I won't hold my breath for a change of heart.

'I think I'd want to know if the situation was reversed.'

'And would you come back?'

Without a moment of hesitation, I say, 'You know I would; I'm a sucker for punishment.'

'Not true; you've just got a kind heart. You go and write your email while I clear up and then choose us a film – something light-hearted,' he adds, heading into the kitchen, plates in hand.

CHAPTER EIGHT
Tuesday, 6 November

I'm not a fan of hospital waiting rooms, but they're so much worse when the person you are with really doesn't want to be there. When I went to pick Mum up at her house this morning, she said she could feel a cold coming on and didn't think she should go spreading her germs around a hospital full of sick people. When that excuse didn't wash with me, she said didn't need to go for a check-up because she'd been feeling much better lately.

In fairness, in the weeks following the fire in her kitchen, Mum has seemed to be going through a very positive period, but that's no reason for her to miss her assessment. I explained to her that appointments were hard to come by and if she missed this one it might be several months before they could reschedule. From the initial diagnosis back in April, one thing had been emphasised again and again: it was important to track the illness at regular intervals. By monitoring and administering treatment, the disease could be managed to a degree. We had a long conversation about it at the time and although I don't stand up to Mum on many things, I really dug my heels in on this. 'The best way to maintain your independence,' I told her, 'is to know how quickly the disease is progressing.' Her face crumpled slightly, then she jutted her chin forward and said, 'I keep telling you, I'm not sick, just a bit forgetful.' I had to turn away at that point so that she couldn't see the tears welling in my eyes.

Although Mum and I aren't especially close, it was heart-breaking to witness her abject refusal to accept what the experts had told her. 'There is no cure, Diana,' Dr Ranjid said, 'but if we keep a close eye on you there's every possibility that you will have plenty of quality time ahead of you.' I found his use of the words 'quality time' pretty upsetting. What he actually meant was time when Diana still recognised and responded to her family. Ben and I knew the fight that lay ahead for us all; even Attila the Hun would have lost a battle with dementia. It's no respecter of who you are or how you've looked after yourself. It randomly chooses its victim, digs its claws in and insidiously creeps into their brain stealing memories as it goes.

Mum made one final attempt at not attending her hospital appointment. Walking down the drive, she rolled over on her ankle and insisted she'd sprained it so she wouldn't be able to walk from the car park to the outpatients' department. I knelt down pretending to examine it.

'Oh, it does look like it's swelling, Mum. We'd better get you to the hospital and have it looked at.'

She knew then that I'd won the battle, but she claimed a small victory by refusing to allow me into the doctor's office with her when we eventually got to the hospital. It wasn't an issue; as her principal carer, I knew the doctor would be discussing things with me later, and if it gave her satisfaction feeling that she had got one over on me, who was I to take that away from her? We've both mellowed in our attitude towards each other since she stayed with us after the fire.

Mum was with us for a week and a half in the end, during which time we got the approval through to have the damage to her kitchen repaired and the house re-painted throughout. I placed an order with a next-day delivery electrical retailer for a new cooker which Mum actually got involved in choosing, much to my surprise. It was far superior to the cooker that had been destroyed, but to be honest, anything would have been. According to Mum, her parents had gifted the 'top-of-the-range' model to her and Dad as a wedding present, but it was already over ten years old at that point, so it was impressive that it had still been working at all. I'm pretty sure very few of today's white goods would last fifty years. Ben and I have a theory that most electrical products are designed to fail approximately six months after the five-year warranty expires.

It felt surprisingly good having Mum under our roof. Maybe it was because she was so shaken by what could have happened if it hadn't been for Martin's quick thinking, but she seemed much less critical of me than she usually is, so I was more relaxed around her. I had to take a week off from the library as I couldn't trust her to be alone in case she had one of her memory-lapse episodes, which meant we spent several hours a day with just the two of us. We didn't talk much, we never really have, but we watched daytime television together in companionable silence and managed not to argue over trivial things at lunchtimes.

The only thing I did haul her up on was her remarks about fat people, pointing out that it had made Amber feel uncomfortable. Mum instantly bristled at being reprimanded but then her attitude softened, and she apologised, saying she hadn't realised how thoughtless and hurtful her comment had been. You could have knocked me over with a feather; my mother apologising for something she'd said was virtually unheard of. She also made an effort to smooth things over with Amber, telling her that I'd been exactly the same in my teenage years, filling out before shooting up. It wasn't entirely true as I'd always been on the slim side, but maybe she had a vague recollection of me bursting out of my clothes because I was still wearing things for a ten-year-old when I was fourteen. Whatever, it did the trick with Amber and the two of them seem closer than ever after their little chat. In fact, things were going so well that I even suggested to Ben that we consider having Mum live with us on a more permanent basis – but he didn't react well.

'You are joking,' he'd said, an incredulous look on his face. 'This is like the honeymoon period in a relationship. It won't take too long before she slips back into her old ways, and if she starts being cranky with you, the kids and I will bear the brunt of it. It wouldn't be fair on any of us – Diana included.'

I knew he was right, but it didn't stop me worrying about what we were going to do when Mum's condition worsened to the point where she would no longer be capable of taking care of herself. It's something I really need to discuss at length with my brother, but Adam still seems to be sticking his head in the sand over the whole situation.

After emailing him following Mum setting fire to the house, I eventually got a response a few days later:

Hi Danni

Thanks for letting me know about Mum's latest drama. There is a bit of me that suspects she is playing on the dementia thing, pretending it's worse than it is just to get me to come home. I've read up on her condition online, and it usually takes much longer from the early forgetfulness stage to accidentally setting fire to your home. Are you sure she's as bad as she's making out and not just playing you because she knows you tell me everything?

Maybe we could do a Skype call or something so I can see how bad she really is? What do you think?

Adam x

I mentioned the Skype idea to Mum and then had to explain what it was because she's definitely not joined the twenty-first century in terms of technology. She was really excited at the prospect of seeing Adam, even if it was only virtually. We set it up for the Sunday evening before Mum moved back into her house on the Monday, but Adam texted me that morning and said he couldn't make it because he was away for the weekend in the depths of the countryside and had no Wi-Fi and a very unreliable mobile signal. When I told Mum, there was a flicker of disappointment in her eyes, but she still defended Adam saying that having no Wi-Fi coverage wasn't his fault. I'd had to bite my lip. True, the Wi-Fi issue wasn't his fault, but did he have to go away to the countryside knowing that he'd arranged the Skype call with us all? Don't get me wrong; I'm growing more tolerant of my brother now that I understand his childhood wasn't without its issues, but he does pull some stunts at times. The girls were disappointed too as they'd been looking forward to chatting with their Uncle Adam, so it put a real dampener on Mum's last evening with us.

'Do you think he deliberately made himself unavailable?' I asked Ben as I snuggled into bed beside him later that night.

'It certainly looks that way,' he replied.

'But why? I don't understand; it was his suggestion after all.'

Ben took my face in his hands. 'Maybe he's been able to convince himself that Diana is not as poorly as you've led him to believe and he was worried that if he saw her it would be abundantly clear that he should make the effort to come back to England, even if it's only for a visit. He's not a cruel person, Danni. He must be torn between wanting to see his mum, who he knows adores him, and enjoying his freedom out of her clutches. It's a tricky one, but in my opinion, he'll eventually realise the choice he has to make.'

In Adam's defence, he has been in touch via email even more frequently since the cancelled Skype call, so it's obviously been playing on his mind.

The door to the doctor's office opens, but instead of my mum coming out, the nurse beckons me in. I gather up our coats and my handbag and make my way over, a knot of anxiety forming in my stomach. Why is Dr Ranjid calling me into his office? I take the spare seat at the side of Mum, whose eyes are studiously examining the floor.

'I'm sorry, Mrs Harper,' Dr Ranjid says, 'I'm afraid we have some worrying news. It seems your mother has noticed a lump in her breast.'

My world tilts; it's as though the rug has been pulled from beneath my feet. For a few seconds, which feels like hours, I just stare at Dr Ranjid unable to process the information. Eventually, I drag my eyes away from him to look at my mother who is still staring at the floor.

'Mum? What's Dr Ranjid talking about? Why didn't you mention it to me?' I ask, making an effort to sound concerned rather than annoyed. There have been a few times since her diagnosis when Mum has forgotten to tell me stuff, such as missed appointments because they didn't make it on to the wall chart in her kitchen or taking the batteries out of her smoke detector because it kept beeping, but this is on another level.

'I didn't want to worry you,' she mumbles, refusing to meet my gaze. 'It was only the size of a pea and I could barely feel it to start with.'

'How long have you had it?' I persist.

Mum is still silent, so Dr Ranjid answers for her.

'It seems your mother first felt a small lump in her left breast over a year ago but didn't think anything of it. While we were talking, I noticed she seemed a little uncomfortable and that's when she told me about it – it's recently got a lot bigger and has begun to hurt.'

I can feel heat in my cheeks and blood pumping around my body. I can't believe Mum hasn't mentioned it to me.

'Under the circumstances,' he continues, 'I've rung a colleague who works in the breast screening department and they've managed to squeeze your mother in this afternoon for a scan and if necessary, a needle biopsy, if that's alright with you?'

I nod. 'Yes – yes, of course, it's alright,' I manage to stammer.

'It could be nothing, just a large collection of cysts, but it's better to be safe than sorry,' Dr Ranjid says, attempting to reassure us both, although his voice lacks conviction.

'Thank you for arranging for the tests to be done while we're here,' I say, reaching for Mum's hand.

Finally, she raises her eyes to meet mine and says, 'I'm sorry to be such a burden. You'd be better off without me.'

Those words will be forever etched on my heart. Diana hasn't been the archetypal loving, caring, supportive mother that I hope I am to my children, but she's my flesh and blood. I make a vow there and then in Dr Ranjid's office that whatever the results of the tests and however much time she has left we'll do everything we can to make her as happy and comfortable as possible.

CHAPTER NINE
Tuesday, 13 November

Mum's scan showed a large mass in her left breast, which the technician decided needed further investigation. I rang the hospital yesterday and was told that a letter had been sent first-class so should be arriving in the post this morning. I didn't want Mum to be on her own when she opened it, so I headed over to hers after dropping the girls at school.

We've been sitting in the lounge making small talk over a cup of tea for the past half hour. The metallic sound of the letterbox flap springing back into place catches us both by surprise, even though it's what we have both been listening out for.

'You get it, Danni,' she says, the merest tremor in her voice.

It's the only letter on the door mat, sitting there taunting me as I stoop to pick it up. I carry it into the lounge and offer it to Mum.

'You read it,' she says.

I can feel my pulse rate increasing as I slide my finger under the flap and tear across the top of the envelope. There's a weird noise in my ears, a bit like rushing water as my eyes scan the four lines on the page.

'Are you going to tell me what it says or not?'

I raise my eyes to hers. I'm not sure what I thought I would see there – fear maybe? Instead there is resignation as though she already knows what to expect.

'You don't need to read the whole thing,' Mum adds, irritation creeping into her voice. 'Just tell me whether or not I have breast cancer and how bad it is.'

I concentrate on the page I'm holding, making a determined effort not to cry.

'It doesn't actually say, but they want you to make an immediate appointment with Mr Goldsmith to discuss the results of your needle biopsy. They say, given your existing health condition, they're prepared to do a phone consultation rather than you having to attend hospital,' I say, trying to keep my voice steady.

Although the letter doesn't confirm that Mum has breast cancer, the use of the word immediate suggests that she does and that it is potentially at quite an advanced stage. I can't help wondering why they couldn't arrange the telephone consultation when I called them yesterday instead of making us wait to receive the letter; hospital protocol, I guess.

'Well, let's get on with it then. Is there a number?'

I reach for the phone and dial the consultant's secretary's number. After explaining who I am, she takes Mum's number and says she will have Mr Goldsmith call as soon as he is free. Ten minutes later, the phone rings and I snatch it up off the coffee table where it had been sitting between Mum and me.

'This is Mr Goldsmith from the Royal Infirmary. Is that Mrs Jenson?'

'No, it's her daughter, Danielle Harper.'

'Ah yes, you came to the appointment with her last week. It's not good news afraid. Is your mother available to speak to?'

'Yes, just hold on a moment. Mum,' I say, holding the phone out to her with a shaking hand. 'Mr Goldsmith wants to speak to you.'

She snatches the phone from me saying, 'For God's sake, Danni, stop being so bloody dramatic.'

I can't bear to witness the realisation of her worst fears, so I avoid eye contact with her for the duration of the call, noticing instead her grip tightening on the arm of the chair. She doesn't say much, just the occasional 'right', 'I see' and 'I'll let you know'. The call is over in a few minutes.

'Well?' I venture.

'I have stage four breast cancer which he says is inoperable,' she announces in a matter-of-fact tone.

I can feel my heart thudding in my chest.

'He wants me to start on some chemotherapy drugs which he says may help slow the spread of the cancer,' she continues in the same tone.

'Right. Good,' I say, relieved that there is a glimmer of hope.

'I told him I'll let him know.'

'You have to give them a try, Mum.'

'What's the point, Danni? If the breast cancer doesn't get me the dementia will. I'm done for.'

'Don't say that, Mum. You can't just give up. You've got to try and fight this.'

'I haven't got any fight left in me. I'm dying; it's just a case of when.' She hauls herself slowly to her feet and heads for the stairs. 'I'm going for a lie-down and I don't expect you to be here when I wake up.'

'But I want to look after you, Mum. I want to be here for you to help you face what lies ahead.'

She pauses halfway up the stairs and, looking me straight in the eye, says, 'I don't need you, Danielle; I never have.'

I'm shocked into silence as I watch her slowly climb the rest of the stairs. A tear trickles from the corner of my eye followed by another and then I'm unable to stop the flow. From the way she looked at me when she spoke, I could tell it wasn't the dementia talking. Mum knew what she was saying; her cruel words were meant to hurt me. When the bedroom door closes it's as though she is shutting me out of her life all over again, just as she did when Adam was born. It's him she really wants at her side, not me.

*

Usually it takes a couple of days for my brother to email me back, but I get a response from him within minutes asking if he can call me. Before I've even had a chance to reply my phone starts to ring.

'Hi Adam,' I say. 'I'm sorry to be the bearer of such bad news.'

'Jesus, Danni, what the hell's going on? How come you haven't mentioned the breast cancer before?' he demands, clearly agitated.

'I only found out she had a lump last week and then only because her dementia consultant noticed her wincing in pain.'

'So why wait a week before telling me?'

'I didn't want to worry you needlessly until we knew what we were dealing with. You've been pretty sceptical about the dementia being as bad as it is. I didn't want you to think I was trying to pile on the pressure to force you to come home, but she really needs you, Adam. I'm trying my best but it's you she wants, not me.'

'Shit,' he mumbles from the other end of the phone line.

'Is everything okay, Adam?'

There's a pause before he says, 'No, everything's not okay. It's not that I don't want to come home, I can't afford to.' There's another shorter pause before he continues. 'I lost my job just after I split up with Zoe and couldn't afford to pay the rent on the apartment on my own. For the past nine months I've been sleeping on friends' couches while I waited for a job to come along. It hasn't; the job market is really depressed here at the moment.'

I now feel really awful. The times I've moaned to Ben that Adam couldn't be bothered to come home to visit his sick mother because he was enjoying his freedom too much. It turns out it wasn't by choice; he simply couldn't afford the airfare.

'I wish you'd told me, Adam.'

'What would have been the point? Mum was always going on about you and Ben not having much money. I didn't want you to feel guilty because you couldn't help when it's not your fault.'

Far from being embarrassed that Adam knows what a tight budget we're on, or feeling angry with Mum for telling him, my immediate reaction is to wonder whether selling my car would raise enough money for his airfare. I dismiss the thought almost immediately. I need the car to get to work and ferry Mum and the girls around and besides, I'm not sure that my ancient Fiesta would raise enough for a train ticket to London, let alone a flight from the other side of the world.

'Can any of your friends lend you the money?' I ask. 'It would be so lovely if you could make it back for Christmas. I wasn't being dramatic in my email when I said it's likely to be Mum's last one.'

'Unfortunately, most of my friends are as skint as me. No, I'll just forget waiting for my next step on the career ladder to drop into my lap and get myself a job in a bar or waiting tables. If I save every spare penny, with a bit of luck, I should have enough to buy a plane ticket early next year,' he says. 'She'll make it to then, won't she?'

The fear in his voice is evident, even from thousands of miles away. I have no way of knowing whether or not Mum will make it to the new year, but that's not what my brother wants to hear.

'She'll make it,' I say, sounding more confident than I feel, 'particularly when I tell her you're coming home.'

'Don't tell her yet, sis. I need to know I'll be able to save enough before I go making promises. I can't bear the thought of her being disappointed with me.'

I know exactly what Adam means because Mum has been disappointed in me my whole life.

CHAPTER TEN
Friday, 7 December

'Well, that was a success,' Maxine says, closing and locking the library doors. 'Thank you for staying late to help me out, I couldn't have managed without you.'

It had been my idea to invite Geraldine Bradley, a local author, to give a talk about her latest detective novel. The event had been fully booked within a few hours of the announcement and the library's percentage of book sales brought in some much-needed cash. It was just what we needed to demonstrate to the local council that Woldington Library was at the heart of our community and should be allowed to remain open. There have been several closures in neighbouring towns, but so far, in large part due to Maxine's commitment to stay late in the evening and host events, we've escaped the dreaded axe. I hate to think what will happen when Maxine retires, which can't be too far away as she recently celebrated her sixty-fifth birthday.

'It's the least I could do after all the times you've let me leave early to go to the appointments with Mum,' I say, giving her a watery smile.

'How's she doing?'

'Not great,' I admit. 'She hadn't fully accepted the dementia diagnosis, so this has hit her really hard and the drugs they've got her on to try and halt the cancer spreading are making her quite depressed.'

'Do you want to talk about it, love?' Maxine says. 'I can make us both a hot drink and there are a few biscuits left over from the event.'

I glance at my watch. It's half past nine and I really should be getting home, particularly as the forecast is snow and I hate driving in it.

'Only if you want to, of course,' she adds. 'It sometimes helps to talk.'

I nod, not trusting myself to speak, and follow her through to the compact kitchen where we take our breaks during quieter periods in the library. I watch her fill the kettle, flick the switch and get our mugs down from the cupboard. I don't know what I would have done without Maxine over the past few months since Dr Ranjid dropped his bombshell.

'Here you go, love,' Maxine says a few minutes later, handing me a cup of tea and sitting down on the chair opposite. 'I know you don't normally take sugar, but I slipped a spoonful in cos you look like you could do with it.'

I smile gratefully and take a sip of the scalding liquid.

'In your own time,' she prompts, dipping a custard cream into her mug of tea.

'I don't know where to start, Max,' I say, placing my mug on the table and dropping my head into my hands. 'I thought I was coping okay and Mum's been really positive once she got over the initial shock, talking about beating the cancer and getting back to normal. But this past week, her dementia seems to have got worse. In the past, she's occasionally made mistakes and called Jade by my name, but I suppose that's understandable because she looks so much like I did when I was young. But last weekend when we went to see her, she seemed to have a complete mental block.' I think back to the vacant expression on Mum's face when we went into her lounge. 'She stared at us all blankly and then started whimpering like a puppy who'd just been kicked. It was as though she was scared of us. It only lasted for a few minutes, but it really upset the girls, especially Jade. She's been having trouble sleeping ever since. I don't know what to do. I don't want to stop the girls spending time with their nana, but on the other hand it's obviously distressing for them to see her like that,' I say, feeling the tension relax in my shoulders simply by telling someone one step removed from my family.

'How much have you told the girls about dementia?'

'Not a lot,' I admit. 'It was much easier to explain Mum's physical illness than her mental one. Amber's class has already been taught about examining their breasts for anything unusual, and she was able to explain it in simple terms to Jade. All I've really said about the dementia is that their nana forgets things sometimes.'

'I think maybe the time has come to explain it a bit better, Danni. Being informed about something scary often makes it seem less frightening.'

I know she's right, but how do you go about explaining the complexities of a brain disorder to two young teenagers? Max seems to read what I'm thinking.

'Maybe you could compare it to a light switch? You could say that our heads are like a house with lots of different rooms and that sometimes Diana can't reach all the switches to turn on the light in every room. When she makes an extra effort and reaches the switch everything is illuminated and her memories coming flooding back, but you should probably add that eventually, even if she has managed to reach the switch, the light bulb will have blown, and that room will stay in darkness forever.'

I shiver at the thought of her final words but have to admit it could be a good way for me to describe what was happening in Mum's head, particularly to Jade. It's so much easier to understand things when a picture is painted. Why hadn't I thought of it like that?

'You know, that might just work. I think you've missed your calling, Max. Maybe you should have been some sort of counsellor rather than being stuck in a dusty old library surrounded by books.'

'I love the books; they're like old friends. Besides, where do you think I get my ideas from? None of them are original, I just read a lot in the hope that the information I absorb will be of use to someone at some stage.'

'I'm going to try it,' I say, pushing my chair back and walking over to the sink to tip the remainder of my tea down it. I've suddenly got an overwhelming urge to get home to my girls and try to explain Mum's condition in the way Maxine suggested. 'Would you like a lift?'

'Thanks for offering, but I think I'll walk. It's the first fresh air I'll have had since half past eight this morning.'

'Well, make sure you wrap up warm,' I say, winding my knitted scarf around my neck as I open the side door to the library to be met by a blast of icy air. 'It's bitter out there.'

'Don't you worry about me; you've got enough on your plate.'

'At least the threatened snow hasn't arrived yet. I'll see you on Monday.'

By the time I get home, Jade and Amber have already gone up to bed, but judging by the sliver of light showing from beneath their doors neither of them is asleep. Ben wanted to make me something to eat, but food is the last thing on my mind. Instead I ask him to come upstairs with me to talk to the girls as I think a united front of both parents in agreement is always a more positive experience. I knock on Jade's door first. I can hear the sound of a book being closed before she says, 'I was just finishing a chapter, I'll turn my light off now.' I push the door open sufficiently to pop my head around it.

'Actually, sweetheart, I want to talk to you and Amber for a few minutes.'

I realise I could have framed my words differently when I see the look of panic in her eyes and her bottom lip starts to tremble. 'It's Nana, isn't it?'

I could kick myself for my insensitivity. 'Nana's fine, well, as fine as can be expected,' I say, pushing into the room and crossing over to Jade's bed to put a comforting arm around her. 'But it is her I want to talk about. Put your dressing gown on and pull your covers up to keep the warmth in your bed and then come and climb in with Amber.'

Ben has already knocked at Amber's door and I can hear the low hum of conversation as I cross the landing to her room.

'What's wrong, Mum?' she says, the moment I appear in her doorway. 'Has Nana taken a turn for the worse?'

I'm so proud of our girls. Ben and I set out to raise kind and caring human beings and it would appear we've done an okay job. Jade has followed me and is climbing into bed next to her sister.

'No, there's no change as far as I know. I've been at an event at the library tonight, but I'm sure Martin would have let me know if there was a problem.'

Martin has been an absolute gem. To say he was devasted when I told him about Mum's latest diagnosis doesn't come close. He'd really shocked me by saying, 'I don't believe there is a God, how can there be? It's as though Diana's being punished for something.' I know it sounds awful, but that thought had crept into my mind. Maybe it was some form of ghastly retribution for the way Mum behaved towards Dad and me after Adam was born. Even as I'd had the thought, I hated myself for it. Nobody deserves the life sentence that dementia brings. Fleetingly, I'd remembered the man in the hospital car park and his words on losing his wife, Muriel. In a weird way, the breast cancer would deliver Mum from the inhumanity of the condition.

My girls are looking at me expectantly. I believe that part of my job as a mother is to be as honest with them as I can, unless the truth would cause them too much pain. I've always had the feeling that my mum was keeping some kind of secret from me, which is why honesty in my relationship with our girls is so important to me. Maybe now that Mum is being forced to rely on me more, she might open up to me. Who knows, there may even be something I can do to put whatever came between us right.

I take a deep breath and launch into Maxine's explanation of dementia.

CHAPTER ELEVEN
Monday, 24 December

'Mum, it's nearly time,' Amber calls from the lounge.

I'm in the kitchen carefully spreading thick royal icing over the marzipan I covered our Christmas cake with yesterday. Every year since Ben and I first moved in together, I've always made our Christmas cake rather than buying one. I found the recipe in a magazine and was keen to show I could be a proper homemaker. It turned out really well and I've used the same recipe ever since – it has never failed me.

I wet the palette knife with warm water and sweep it across the top of the cake in a lazy curve to create a path through the peaks I've just made. Taking a step back, I can't help but admire my creation. On the work surface next to the cake are little figures of snowmen, animals and fake snow-dusted trees, along with a chubby Santa Claus complete with rosy cheeks. They have adorned all our Christmas cakes since the very first one.

'Okay, girls, you can come and do the decorations now before the icing sets.'

This has been a family tradition since Amber was old enough to hold the figures in her chubby toddler hands. Having had no traditions to carry on from my own childhood, I've done my best to create as many as I can so that our girls will have something to continue when they have families of their own.

Jade appears in the doorway holding her nana's hand. No one was more surprised than me when Mum agreed to come to ours for Christmas after being asked a couple of weeks ago. It was shortly after Ben and I had our chat with the girls about Mum's dementia, which ended with the girls pleading with us to invite her for Christmas. Ben and I talked it over before falling asleep, eventually deciding that not only would it be good for Mum to be surrounded by her family rather than being alone as she usually was, it would also be the right thing for Amber and Jade. We woke the next morning to two feet of snow which prevented us from seeing her for a few days as the roads were impassable. I didn't want to broach the subject on the phone as it would be much easier for her to decline and I really wanted her to say yes, as much for the girls as for me.

As usual, Martin was an angel. He rang me at least three times each day that we were snowed in because he knew how stressed I would be that we couldn't visit. Mum is unaware that he's been staying over at hers because he didn't want to risk her wandering outside and slipping on the snow and ice. Apparently, he waits until Mum puts her bedroom light off before settling down on her sofa in the lounge and has a story prepared about dozing off if she comes downstairs and discovers him. It seems such a shame that Mum wouldn't allow him into her life after his wife, Audrey died. All he wanted was someone to love and care for.

On the fourth day after the heavy snowfall, we dug Ben's car out and tentatively drove to Mum's, a journey that took twice as long as usual in the treacherous conditions. The girls went in ahead of us while we shovelled the snow off Mum's driveway so that we could park our car. By the time we went inside, hands numb from the cold, Mum and the girls were sipping hot chocolate drinks and Christmas songs filled the air, courtesy of Ben's portable speaker. She looked so relaxed and happy and normal; how sad that it couldn't always have been like this. I seized the moment while she was in such a good mood and asked her about coming to ours for Christmas.

'The girls already mentioned it,' she said, smiling indulgently at them.

'And she said yes,' Jade said, high-fiving her sister.

'Just for a few days though; I don't want to outstay my welcome.'

I wondered how it was all going to work as I'm always so busy in the run-up to the big day with shopping and cooking and present-wrapping, but with a little forward-planning and a fairly big reliance on our girls to keep their nana entertained it was all going swimmingly so far.

'Can Nana help decorate the cake?' Jade asks.

'Of course, if she wants to.'

'She does,' Amber says, following them into the kitchen. 'Anyway, we've only got five minutes until the Skype call with Uncle Adam and it will be quicker if we do it together.'

My heart swells as I watch the three of them gather around the cake then, moments later, step back to admire their handiwork. Because it's always the same decorations, it looks virtually the same as it does every year, but it feels extra special because Mum has had a hand in it when previously she has refused to be part of our family celebration. I briefly wonder if she regrets all the opportunities she has missed to be a more important part of our lives. Her ill health has thrown us together this Christmas which will most likely be her last. I can feel a lump forming in my throat. All those wasted years; it's a crying shame really.

'Let me get a picture of you all with the cake,' I say, reaching for my phone. The girls pull silly faces and Mum looks uncomfortable posing, but I'm determined to preserve the moment.

'I'm connecting,' Ben calls through from the lounge. 'Come on girls.'

We hurry through to the front room and take our places on the sofa in front of Ben's computer just as a picture of my brother's face fills the screen. He looks different, much older and more worldly-wise than when I saw him on-screen back in May. He's grown a beard, something Mum latches on to immediately.

'Adam? Is that really you?' Mum says, peering at the screen. 'I can't tell with all that fuzz all over your face,' she adds, making no attempt to disguise the distaste in her voice.

I expected her to be quite emotional laying eyes on her prodigal son for the first time in two and a half years, but old habits die hard and she's always been one to say the first thing that comes into her head, even before the dementia dulled her ability to filter her thoughts.

'Hi Mum. Yes, it's me. I could say I've grown a beard to be fashionable, but the truth is I can't be bothered to shave. How are you doing? Danielle tells me you're a bit under the weather,' he says, his voice slightly muffled and his lips moving out of sync with what we are hearing.

That's not the turn of phrase I used when filling Adam in on Mum's dementia and subsequent breast cancer diagnosis, but I guess it's better than saying 'She told me you're terminally ill.'

Mum shoots me a look as though to say, *Why did you have to tell Adam I'm sick?* I can see it's thrown her off balance. Surely, she must realise that I've been keeping him informed.

Before she can say anything else, Jade chips in, 'Is it already Christmas where you are Uncle Adam? Have you opened your presents yet?'

I'm doubtful that Adam will be receiving many presents, if any at all. If he's saving all his money to buy a ticket to fly home, he probably won't be buying any and will have told his friends as much.

'Who's that?' Adam says.

'Me, Jade,' she says jumping up and dancing in front of the computer's camera. 'Can you see me?'

'Blimey sis, it's like looking at a mini version of you. Is Amber there too?'

'Hi Uncle Adam,' Amber says in response. 'What time is it in New Zealand?'

For a moment, I allow myself to imagine we're all on one of those television shows where the families think they are being connected via the worldwide web and then suddenly the studio doors open and the long-lost relative strides in, having travelled from the other side of the globe, and everyone hugs and cries in a massive reunion. If only. Adam and I have never been overly close, but right now I could do with a brotherly hug.

'Hey there, Amber. It's quarter past eight and I've already been out for a walk because it'll be too hot later in the day.'

'It's quarter past eight here too, but it's pitch black outside and freezing cold,' she says, pretending to shiver.

'Are you having roast turkey and stuffing for lunch?' Jade chips in.

'Probably not. I'm staying with friends at the moment and I think the plan is to have a barbecue,' Adam says. 'We might have barbecued chicken though, if that counts.'

'It must be funny to celebrate Christmas in the summertime.'

'I guess I've got used to it now. This is my third one.'

'Adam, when are you coming home?' Mum has found her voice again. 'I don't want to die without ever laying eyes on you again.'

The mood, which was light-hearted and festive, is suddenly dragged back to the awful reality of the situation. The only reason we're all together at our house doing a Skype call with my brother is because this is likely to be Mum's last Christmas and we want to make it special for her.

Mum is crying now, and our girls are watching her with tense, fearful expressions on their faces.

I can't be sure because of the bad connection, but it sounds as though Adam too is on the point of tears when he says, 'As soon as I get to the end of this project, Mum, I'll be on the first plane home.'

Only Ben and I know that the project is to save enough money for the flight.

'Do you promise, Adam? Have you forgiven me for trying to stop you leaving?'

'There's nothing to forgive, Mum. And yes, I promise I'll be home as soon as it's humanly possible. I love you, Mum.'

'And I love you too, son, more than you'll ever know.'

I don't experience the pang of jealousy a younger me would have on witnessing the love between my mother and her son. Instead I'm finding it difficult to breathe, I'm so choked with emotion.

'Look after her for me, sis,' Adam says, before ending the call.

Silence fills the room, heavy and oppressive. I don't know what to say to break it. Ben comes to the rescue as he has so many times before.

'It's time to hang the new baubles,' he says, reaching beneath the Christmas tree and extracting three parcels from the pile.

This is another of the traditions I've started which I hope my girls will continue for generations to come. Each year, since Amber was five years old and asked for a sparkly shocking-pink bauble while we were at the garden centre purchasing our Christmas tree, we've bought the girls a new bauble to hang on the tree. My idea is that when they leave home and have their own Christmas trees, decorating it with familiar baubles will banish any feelings of loneliness. Our tree is already laden with the baubles from previous years, but we always find room for two more.

'We got one for you too, Diana,' Ben says, handing over the parcel wrapped in colourful paper.

Mum looks at the package in her hands for a moment, before carefully unpeeling the tape holding the edges of the paper together and removing the layers of tissue paper beneath. She gazes down at the clear glass bauble with crystal beads and a white feather inside it and the word *believe* delicately painted on the outside. She raises her gaze to look me in the eye.

'Thank you,' she says, a slight tremble in her voice.

Those two words melt my heart. The bauble isn't new; I saw it in a post-Christmas sale the year after Amber was born. I remember holding it my hands just as Mum is now, closing my eyes and offering up a little prayer that one day my mother would want to get to know her granddaughter. It has hung on our Christmas tree every year since and I've had to wait a long time for that prayer to be answered, but now that it has, that small inanimate object has another job to do.

'You need to make a wish and then believe that it will come true, Mum,' I say. 'It worked for me and it will work for you.'

I watch as she closes her eyes. It doesn't take a genius to work out what Mum wants more than anything in the world. I don't feel jealous, just a little sad that I've never had the relationship with her that Adam did. I want Mum to see my brother in the flesh again at least one more time if it means she will die happy. What I've given her is the gift of hope.

CHAPTER TWELVE
Christmas Day

I should have known it was too good to last. The Skype call with Adam the previous evening unsettled Mum and she went to bed early claiming she had a headache. I took a mug of warm milk upstairs for her to take her medication with, but she barely spoke to me. She seemed distant, almost as though she was struggling to retrieve something from the depths of her memory. I squeezed her hand then turned off the bedside light and tiptoed towards the door, thinking she'd already fallen asleep. As I pulled the door closed behind me, I thought I heard her say, 'I would have loved him too if they'd let me.' I pushed the door back open a fraction and watched her for a few minutes, but she didn't move, and she said nothing else.

I had no idea what she meant and half-wondered if she was talking in her sleep. Her sentence made no sense; she lavished love on Adam to the exclusion of everyone else until he left to go to New Zealand. Mum has only recently allowed Amber and Jade into a small corner of her heart and although her love for them has grown, it's still nowhere close to the excessive adoration she's always heaped on my brother.

I mentioned her words to Ben when we finally climbed into bed after loading the girls' presents into their hessian Christmas sacks and leaving a plate with mince pie crumbs and a half-eaten carrot next to the fireplace. It's crazy we still do this as the girls have long-since stopped believing in Santa and his reindeer, but it seems to start Christmas morning off in the right way with us all pretending that Santa has magically squeezed himself down our chimney, navigating past the wood-burning stove on his way.

Ben snuggled into my back and said, 'Diana has dementia; she gets easily confused. I wouldn't worry about it,' before promptly falling asleep.

Although I felt completely shattered, sleep eluded me – a fairly common occurrence these days with all the worry about Mum. I lay staring into the dark for what felt like hours wondering what my life would have been like if Mum hadn't been so obsessed with Adam. I was never allowed to feed him his bottled formula, or rock him when he was crying; in fact, I couldn't recall ever being allowed to hold my brother when he was a baby. My mum had a willing helper in me, but she didn't want my help, at least not when it came to Adam. I wasn't allowed to do anything for him, but I *was* expected to clean and cook and put the bins out, all things an adult should have been responsible for. I wasn't allowed to take my brother for a walk in his pram when he was a baby or meet him at the school gates when he started in the kindergarten class even though it was on my route home. Mum tried and eventually succeeded in shutting me out from their cosy little relationship.

After a while I stopped offering to help because I knew my offer would be rebuffed. I'd get home from school and go straight up to my room to do my homework or read my latest book from the library. In my mid-teens I even stopped eating my meals with them as I'd always been made to feel like an intruder at their table. So, what on earth had Mum meant when she'd said, 'I would have loved him too if they'd let me'? She couldn't have loved him any more if she'd tried. And who were the *'they'* she'd referred to? And then it struck me. Maybe I misheard and she said *her* not *him*; 'I would have loved *her* too if they'd let me.' And perhaps *they* were demons in her head.

Was Mum trying to tell me she was sorry for not loving me? Had something happened when I was very young that I had no recollection of, but she had been unable to get past? Was it my fault that Mum couldn't love me the way she wanted to? Maybe if I could show her that I care about her, we could have a more loving relationship. It would never be the closeness I have with my daughters, but it's not too late to forgive and forget and make the most of the time we have left to us. With that thought in my mind, I finally fell asleep.

Although the girls no longer believe in Santa Claus, it doesn't stop them getting up pre-dawn on Christmas morning and coming into our room to wake us up. It feels like I've barely slept when I hear the tap on our bedroom door. I force my eyes open and plaster a fake smile on my face. Jade is standing at the foot of our bed, but instead of her usual smiles and excitement on her favourite day of the year, she looks frightened. I'm immediately alert and I shake Ben to wake him.

'What is it, Jade? What's wrong?'

'You need to come downstairs, Mum. Nana's hurt herself.'

I'm out of bed and in my dressing gown in two seconds flat. The room feels cold, and I realise it's earlier than I thought.

'Where's Amber?' I say, following my younger daughter down the stairs. She doesn't need to answer. The door to the lounge is open and I can see the back of Amber's purple fleecy dressing gown as she's bent forward over something. At first glance, I think she's rummaging in her hessian sack for her presents, but as I move further into the room, I can see two very pale legs stretched out along the hearth. I stifle a scream as Amber twists to face me, revealing the checked grey and white towel from the kitchen across which a red stain is spreading. For the first time I am aware of a low moaning sound.

'What happened?' I ask, moving swiftly across the room and bending down to relieve Amber of my mother's weight leaning against her. As I put my arm around Mum, I can see fragments of glass surrounded by crystal beads and off to one side a white feather. Mum tilts her face up to look at me, a vacant look in her eyes.

'I think she must have overbalanced when she took her bauble off the tree,' Amber says, getting to her feet and leaning against her dad's chest for comfort. 'I heard a noise, so I woke Jade and we came down to investigate. I was really scared when I saw Nana just lying there. I'm sorry about the towel, but there was blood dripping off the end of her fingers, so I told Jade to get me something to wrap around it before fetching you.'

'That was okay, wasn't it, Mum?' Jade says, clinging to Ben's other side.

'Yes, of course, you both did exactly the right things.' I give my husband a meaningful look. 'Ben, why don't you and the girls go into the kitchen and make Nana a cup of hot sweet tea while I take a look at the cut. Maybe bring me the first-aid box while the kettle's boiling,' I add to his retreating back.

Carefully I start to unwrap the towel from Mum's lower arm, not knowing what I'm going to find. She's stopped moaning now and her expression has changed from blank to puzzled.

'It's okay, Mum,' I say in a soothing voice, 'we'll soon have you sorted.'

Although there is a lot of blood on the towel, the bleeding appears to have stopped. The gash isn't on her wrist, but on the palm of her hand, suggesting that she might have fallen onto the ornament, backing up Amber's theory.

'What happened? Did you fall?'

Mum shook her head. 'I must have squeezed it too hard. I just wanted to make the magic work. But now it's broken,' she says, looking forlornly at the shattered glass. Suddenly, as though someone has flicked a switch, she demands, 'Why did you buy me that stupid trinket and tell me it would make all my dreams come true? You lied to me, your own mother. I should never have trusted you; you've always been a disappointment.'

Her voice is rising in volume and loaded with venom. I can feel a weight pressing down on my chest making it hard for me to breathe. I sometimes wonder if the reaction I have to my mother is some form of panic attack. She seems oblivious to the distress she is causing me and carries on with the verbal assault.

'You're just so jealous of your little brother. You couldn't bear the thought of me wanting Adam more than I want you, so you came up with this stupid bauble idea knowing that if I held it too hard it would shatter. Well, I hope you're satisfied.'

I wanted to give her something tangible to focus on, to believe in, but as usual Mum has managed to twist my good intentions. She isn't done with me yet.

'I'll go to my death bed without ever seeing my son again and it's all because of you,' she shrieks.

Each of her verbal blows connects sharply, like a boxer striking his opponent in the ring. My tender flesh feels bruised and battered, as I wait with trepidation for her knockout punch. It doesn't come. Ben is back in the room holding the green first-aid box; he must have heard the whole tirade.

'You do the tea, Danni and I'll deal with Diana,' he says, taking charge of the situation before it can escalate any further.

I get to my feet shakily.

'Make sure you wash the cut thoroughly to get all the shards of glass out,' I manage to say as I head to the kitchen. I can almost feel the heat from my mother's glowering look burning a hole between my shoulder blades.

After patching Mum up, we all go back to bed, not that I'm expecting to get any sleep. It was only just after 4 a.m. when Jade first came into our room, so it's too early for us to stay up even on Christmas morning. Besides which, we are all pretty shocked after what happened, so both Ben and I decide it would be better to try and start the day afresh after some sleep. Amber and Jade must have heard some, if not all, of my mum's verbal attack, but I brush it off by saying it was the dementia talking when I settle them back in their beds while Ben is in the bathroom dealing with Mum's cut. After leaving the girls, I stand outside the bathroom door debating whether or not I should go in and take over from Ben. I don't want Mum to get all upset again but she is my mum and it isn't really fair to expect Ben to deal with her. I listen for a few moments, trying to decide what to do for the best. I don't hear Mum speak, but I can hear Ben gently reassuring her. In the end, I leave well alone and head back to our room. A few minutes later Ben comes in, quietly closing the door behind him. Instead of climbing between the sheets, he sits next to me on my side of the bed.

'Thank you. I'm sorry you had to deal with that.'

'Look Danni,' he says, stroking the back of my hand, 'I know it was an accident and she was obviously upset, but I'm not having her talk to you like that.'

I start to speak, but he interrupts me.

'If she can't show you the love and appreciation you deserve after the way you've looked after her these past few months, she's not welcome in this house. I mean it, Danni, I won't have her upsetting you like this, dementia or not. It isn't fair on any of us, but especially you. We'll see how the rest of today pans out, but one more episode like that and I'm taking her straight home.'

I want to say something to defend Mum, to repeat what I said to the girls about it being her illness that made her behave that way towards me, but in my heart I can't be sure it is. I stay quiet and let Ben climb back into bed. He drops off to sleep straightaway and is snoring within a couple of minutes. How is it that men have the ability to do that? And why must they snore? Normally,

I'd dig him in the ribs and hiss at him to turn over, but I don't want to disturb him.

I lie staring into the inky darkness thinking about Ben's words. I know he said what he did because he loves me. He was the one who had to teach me what love was after a childhood where I'd been deprived of it, and I adore him for it, but he's put me in a difficult position. If Mum does get angry with me again and he carries out his threat to take her home, the girls will blame me. They don't know why she wasn't in their lives when they were younger because I haven't told them. For all they know, I was the one who kept her at arm's length because I was jealous of the relationship she had with Adam. To push her away now, when they know how ill she is, would appear unspeakably cruel in their eyes. My last thought before I finally fall into a fitful sleep is that I'm relieved Maxine is coming to have Christmas lunch with us. I'll try and get a few minutes alone with her at some point and ask her for advice.

CHAPTER THIRTEEN
Christmas Day

'Well, this all looks lovely,' Maxine says, a broad smile lighting up her face.

I have to admit that between us we've done a great job with the Christmas lunch table. There is just enough room around the circular dining table for the six of us and we've arranged alternating red and gold crackers and napkins. Ben sliced the turkey in the kitchen and divided it up onto our plates along with the sage and onion stuffing, but everything else is on the table in festive serving dishes for people to help themselves. Mum declined wine, which is probably sensible with all the medication she is taking, so she and Jade are having a non-alcoholic treat of sparkling elderflower water, but Amber is joining the adults in a glass of Sauvignon Blanc.

Our elder daughter hasn't shown a great deal of interest in alcohol yet, and flatly refused a glass of sherry while we were opening our presents earlier after trying a sip of mine. The words, 'Gross,' and 'How can you drink that?' accompanied a face that could easily have won a gurning competition. The wine, however, seemed more palatable when she tasted it, so it's a glass of that which Amber raises to join in with the Merry Christmas toast before we cross arms to pull the crackers.

True to form, I end up with two cracker ends and no middle section, but fortunately I'm sat next to Maxine and she has my middle bit so is happy to return it. As I'm unfurling my paper hat and forcing it down onto my auburn curls, where I know it won't stay for more than five minutes, I risk a glance at Mum who is sitting directly opposite me. We've pretty much kept out of each other's way this morning, which is probably for the best. She hasn't apologised for the hurtful things she said to me in the early hours of the morning, but I wasn't expecting her to.

Amber and Jade took her breakfast in bed this morning and stayed with her while she ate it before they came downstairs to make a start on opening their presents while Mum had a bath. She'd only just finished when Maxine arrived and although she's never met her before, they hit it off like a house on fire; probably a poor choice of words on my part. I wasn't surprised; everybody loves Maxine. She's a real people person, which often makes me wonder why she chooses to live alone. Maybe she gets exhausted by the face she presents to the public in the library on a daily basis and just needs her own time.

While Amber and Jade showed their nana the books that Maxine bought for them, the two of us headed into the kitchen to help Ben with the vegetables. He was already elbow-deep in peeling potatoes, so we started on the parsnips and carrots. Once they'd joined the turkey in the oven, I suggested that Ben should go and help the girls entertain their nana while Maxine and I prepared the sprouts. He knew to take the hint, winking on his way out of the kitchen.

'So, how's it been going with your mum?' Maxine said in a low voice the moment the kitchen door closed behind him.

Despite my best efforts, Maxine had obviously detected a slight atmosphere; she didn't miss a trick.

'Well, it *had* been going pretty well; in fact, I'd go so far as to say swimmingly. But she woke in the early hours last night and came downstairs to get the bauble.' I'd told Maxine about the bauble when I first had the idea to gift it to Mum. 'She… she must have squeezed it too hard, because the next thing I know

Jade is waking me up to come and see to Mum who has a bloody towel around her hand.'

'So, just an unfortunate accident then?' Maxine said, cutting a cross in the bottom of the final sprout and adding it to the steamer pan.

I've always preferred steamed sprouts to boiled ones, they hold their texture and flavour better.

'Yes, it was,' I agreed. 'And at first she was a little confused by what had happened. Then she turned on me, saying it was all my fault and because of me, her wish for Adam to come home wouldn't come true. Her words were unkind, but it was the look in her eyes that really hurt. I saw hatred there, Max, pure unadulterated hatred,' I added, a wobble in my voice. Maxine put her hand over mine and squeezed lightly.

She knows about the issues Mum and I have and has come up with various theories down the years as to why she treats me so badly, but neither of us really understand her behaviour. It isn't new; she's always been like it. It seems that I'm her punchbag and I can either soak up the punches and keep putting myself within arm's reach for more or stay out of her way completely. There doesn't seem to be any middle ground, and now that she's so sick and needs looking after, distancing myself from her is no longer an option.

'Well, let's see if we can get through today without any more drama as a starting point,' she said. 'When is she due to go back home?'

'On the 27th, but Ben told me last night that he'll take her straight home if she turns on me again.'

'Would he do that, do you think?'

'Absolutely. He gets to see the exhausted side of me after I've been running around after Mum without a word of thanks. Not that I expect any; she's my mum and I'll do anything I can to make her last few months as happy as they can be.' Just saying those words made me feel shaky. Ours is not a particularly loving relationship, but it's hard to imagine life without her in it at all. 'Ben accepts the lack of thanks, but he won't tolerate her vindictiveness, blaming me for anything and everything that goes wrong. He feels sorry for her situation, but he's done with allowing her to take it out on me.'

'You've got a good one there,' Maxine said, filling the saucepan with water before sitting the steamer pan of sprouts on the top and covering with the glass lid. 'There aren't many like Ben around.'

There was a hint of sadness in her voice which made me wonder if maybe she hadn't chosen to live a solitary life after all. It's funny how little we know about the people we spend many hours a day with.

'Actually, Max, I'm glad we've got this time together because I want to ask your advice about something.'

'Fire away. I'm happy to offer an opinion, but it won't necessarily be the right one.'

'It's the girls,' I said, perching on one of the stools by the wide shelf that we rather grandly call a breakfast bar. 'They heard the way Mum spoke to me last night even if they didn't catch all the actual words.' I fiddled with the buttons on my shirt. It was more difficult putting this into words than I'd thought it was going to be.

Maxine didn't push me, she just waited for me to carry on, knowing I'd get there in my own good time.

'I've never explained why they didn't see much of their nana when they were younger because when they weren't seeing her it wasn't really relevant. But since Adam left and she's taken an interest in them I guess they must be wondering about the lack of closeness.'

'Has either of them asked you about it?'

'Not yet, but that's my dilemma. Do I broach the subject with them, or do I wait for them to raise it? They've only just got their nana in their lives and I think they are both quite traumatised at the thought of losing her. Is it worth the upset of telling them the truth, that she simply wasn't interested in them because all her attention was focused on Adam? It might change the way they feel about her, which would be such a shame as they've become really close, particularly over this past year,' I said with a sigh.

'But if you don't give them any information, they'll form their own conclusions which might not be the right ones.'

I knew she was right, but I still wasn't convinced that anything would be gained by telling them the whole truth.

'Listen, love. Harsh as it sounds, your mum is dying. She'll only be around for a few more months but you guys have a lifetime together.' She paused for a minute to let that sink in. 'If it was me, I think I'd have the conversation with Amber and Jade, making it clear that they can ask as many questions as they want. They're not babies anymore, Danni,' she said, patting my arm. 'Sometimes the truth hurts, but it's better than them seeing your mum through rose-tinted glasses. Eventually, that could lead them to blaming you for depriving them of spending more time with their nana.'

I knew asking Maxine's opinion was the right thing to do. I decided right then to speak to Amber and Jade once Christmas was over.

Lunch has gone down well. Every serving dish is empty, and every plate cleared of food. I hate to think how many thousands of calories I've already consumed and that's before cheese and biscuits and Christmas cake later on. It's also not taking into account the alcohol. Ben and I don't drink much as a rule, but I won't be letting today end without a generous glass of cream liqueur on the rocks when everyone but the two of us is safely tucked up in bed. It's the quiet moments at the end of Christmas Day, sitting in near darkness cuddled up to Ben with only the Christmas tree lights on, when I can truly relax and reflect on how lucky I am to be surrounded by people who love me. It will be a bit different this evening because I'm not sure that Mum does love me – not after what she said last night. I need to talk to her about it. If I start the conversation, it might be easier for her to find the right words to explain why she's always had such difficulty in showing me affection.

'Right, let's get the table cleared and then we can go out for our walk,' Ben says, pushing his chair back from the table and picking up the two serving dishes closest to him.

Our post-Christmas-lunch walk is another of the traditions Ben and I established in the very early days of our relationship. Whether it's snowing or raining, dull or bright, we always wrap up in winter woollies, usually ones we've opened as gifts earlier in the day, and head out to stretch our legs for half an hour or so.

'I'm not coming,' Mum says.

It's the way she says it that's irritating. Not, 'I think I'll pass,' or 'I'm not sure I can manage it,' just a blunt refusal. Although Ben has his back to me, I can see his shoulders tense up. There's no way we can leave Mum here alone, particularly after last night's incident, which means one of us is going to have to break with tradition and stay behind to look after her; no prizes for guessing who that's going to be.

I try to hide my disappointment as I say, 'I'll stay here with you, Mum. There's probably a good film on if you fancy it.'

'You'll do no such thing,' she says. There's an edge to her voice and I'm worried things are about to spiral in a downwards direction. 'I'm not a child, you know. I can look after myself; I do most of the time, after all.'

The girls exchange a glance, perhaps wondering if they should have offered to stay home instead of me.

'Actually, Danni, my ankle's been playing up a bit, so I'd rather not go if that's alright with you,' Maxine says. 'I can stay here with Diana; we can keep each other company.'

Ben is back in the room. He's watching Diana, almost willing her to argue. But to his surprise, and mine, she smiles and says, 'I'd like that. It'll be nice to have a bit of company of my own age.'

Before I can speak, Maxine says, 'Well, that's settled then. Off you go, you lot, while it's still light. Diana and I will clear the table and do the dishes since you made us such a delicious meal.'

Mum looks like she might be about to object, but thinks better of it. Instead she pushes her chair back from the table and carries her plate – and only her plate – through to the kitchen, oblivious to the wink in my direction from Maxine.

CHAPTER FOURTEEN
Christmas Day

If I'm honest, I prefer it a little colder for our Christmas Day walks, but since the snow of a fortnight ago the temperatures have got milder and the weather forecast rated the chance of a 'white' Christmas as zero. Having wrapped up in our coats, hats, scarves and gloves, we are all sweating profusely when we return to the house some forty-five minutes later.

'We're back,' I call out, as we all crowd into the hallway to disrobe.

'In here,' I hear Maxine's voice say.

I pop my head around the door to see Maxine sitting on the sofa alone, flicking through a magazine. I feel embarrassed. I invited her round to our house so she wouldn't be spending Christmas on her own and here she is alone and not even with her own home comforts.

'Where's Mum?' I ask, scanning the lounge and listening out for a chink of china from the kitchen, thinking maybe she'd gone to make them both a cup of tea.

'She went upstairs for a lie-down.'

'She did help you with the washing up, didn't she?' Ben asks, coming into the room behind me, his face flushed and with beads of sweat around his nose. I'm not sure how much longer his 'Rudolph the red-nosed reindeer' jumper will last before he strips down to his T-shirt.

'Yes. I washed and she dried as she didn't want to get her bandage wet. I wasn't sure where anything went, so it's all stacked up on the work surfaces waiting for someone to put it away.'

'And she was okay with that?' I probe. 'Not complaining?'

'Not at all. I think she was glad to feel useful.'

I don't know why that surprises me, but it does. Mum's never been particularly house-proud. I've often gone around to hers to find the sink overflowing with dirty dishes which I then set to and wash for her. Maybe that's the point; she knows I'll do it because I'm always trying to please her. She does it with Martin too. I've known him vacuum the carpets and even give the bathroom a wipe round if it's looking a bit grubby. I feel a bit bad about not inviting Martin to ours for Christmas lunch after all he does for Mum, but when I suggested it, she said if he came, she wouldn't. I'm intending to give him a ring later on and make Mum wish him Merry Christmas; it's the least she can do.

'Can I get you a drink of something, Max? Tea, coffee, something stronger?'

'Tea would be nice,' she says. 'And are we allowed to tuck into that delicious-looking Christmas cake?'

'That's what it's there for,' I say, heading into the kitchen to put the kettle on. 'Girls, can you come and put the dishes away and then maybe we can have a game before Maxine has to head home.'

She'd already told me when she accepted the invitation that she would want to be home by six and it was almost four o'clock now.

'Can we play Chase the Ace?' Jade says.

It's a card game where the players swap low-denomination cards with their nearest neighbour so as not to lose a life. I don't know why Jade is always so keen to play it. She doesn't have much of a poker face and almost always ends up with a dog's life hand because she's out first.

'Sounds good to me,' Ben says, heading towards the cupboard next to the fireplace where we keep all the board games and playing cards.

While the kettle is boiling, I take a sharp knife and slice into the cake, avoiding snowmen and reindeer as best I can. The sweet heady aroma of brandy is released as I remove the first slice and lay it on a side plate. Brandy is my secret weapon when it comes to keeping my Christmas cake moist. I don't 'feed' it over a number of weeks in the run-up to the big day; I just ladle several tablespoons of it over the cake once it's cooled and then wrap it up and leave it to mature. I've sometimes wondered if the girls should be having quite such large slices of it at their ages, but they've always gone to bed happy and had no ill effects in the morning, so I'm guessing it doesn't do them any harm.

The rest of the afternoon seems to pass very quickly with no sight or sound of Mum until just before six o clock when Maxine and I are in the hallway as she puts her coat on to leave.

'Thanks for coming, Max,' I say. 'I hope you've enjoyed yourself.'

'I most certainly have. And thank you again for the bracelet,' she says, fingering the delicate silver chain with a moon and stars charm suspended from it. 'I shall treasure it.'

As I lean in for a hug, my mobile phone starts to ring in my coat pocket. I realise I must have left it in there after taking it out on our walk. I retrieve it and glance at the screen.

'It's Martin,' I say. 'I was going to call him when you'd gone, but he's beaten me to it.'

'What does he want?' Mum says aggressively from her position at the top of the stairs. She startles me as I didn't realise she was awake. I'm guessing she's been eavesdropping on Maxine and my conversation, so it's a good job we weren't discussing her.

'He probably just wants to wish you a Merry Christmas, Mum,' I say, my finger hovering over the 'accept call' icon.

'Well, I wish he hadn't bothered. He can be a very irritating man, always hanging around. He's like a stalker.'

I pause for a second, not sure whether to answer the call, and then change my mind, tapping the screen of my phone flamboyantly.

'Martin,' I say, with forced cheerfulness, 'Merry Christmas! Mum and I were just about to call you; yes, she's here if you want a few words with her.'

Mum glares at me for a moment and then looks beyond me to where Maxine is standing. Her expression softens and she plods down the stairs with an air of acceptance. She takes the phone from my hand and heads into the lounge. I turn to look at Maxine who shrugs her shoulders.

'She must have had a change of heart. Right, I'll be heading off,' she says, lifting the deadlock and opening the door. 'Thanks again for a lovely day.'

'Thank you for coming, you really have made it extra special.'

I watch her climb into her battered old Mini and pull away from the kerb before I close and lock the door. I can't help wondering what she and Mum talked about while we were out walking and whether it contributed to Mum changing her mind about speaking to Martin on the phone; I'm guessing it did.

CHAPTER FIFTEEN
Wednesday, 26 December

There were one or two tense moments on Christmas Day, but Boxing Day is a different story, again making me think that Maxine might have had a word with Mum about trying to show more appreciation.

After a morning playing Monopoly with no tantrums, followed by dominoes and a light lunch, Ben has gone out with his friend Mark. Neither of them are huge football fans, but Mark's firm invariably take an executive box for the Boxing Day game if it's a home fixture, and he always invites Ben along as his plus one. Wine and beer will be flowing freely all afternoon, so Ben will be a little worse for wear when he gets home around six. Some people get aggressive when they've had too much to drink, but Ben is the polar opposite. He goes all giggly, a bit like a teenage girl on a first date.

I don't mind him going out. Firstly, I'm not a football fan so I have no interest in attending the match myself. I can't see the point in a bunch of men running up and down a pitch kicking a ball about; and the eye-watering sums of money they are paid to do it just seem obscene to me. Secondly, by lunchtime on Boxing Day I'm totally wiped out after all the preparation and excitement of the previous day. It always seems such an anti-climax with everyone in a weird kind of limbo, waiting for real life to start again.

My plan, after clearing away the lunch things, is to sit with my girls and watch a film on television. We don't have any of the expensive additional channels, or one of those smart TVs that let you watch things when you want, so it was a relief when I discovered that this afternoon's offering on BBC One is *March of the Penguins*. I've seen it once before and just know Amber and Jade will love it.

I'm waiting for Mum to excuse herself to go for her afternoon nap, but she surprises me by saying she'd like to stay down and watch the film with us if we don't mind. If we don't mind? When did my mother become so considerate? It adds more fuel to the fire suggesting that Maxine had a good old heart to heart with her yesterday. The girls, of course, are delighted and snuggle up on the sofa on either side of their nana while I pop through to the kitchen to fetch a bowl of crisps and a plate of chocolate biscuits. More calories, but hey, it's Christmas, so who's counting!

It's such a pleasurable couple of hours. The film is every bit as good as I remember. It warms my heart to see those majestic creatures waddling in their ungainly way, covering huge distances in order to bring food back for their young. And while they are away hunting, the other parent is protecting the egg and then the hatchling by folding their tummy down over it to shield against the sub-zero temperatures. It's this teamwork that gives the young the best chance of survival and I can't help thinking that it is also true in human families.

From the age of twelve, my family life, which had always been less than ideal, disintegrated in spectacular fashion. My absent father and uncaring mother probably halved my chances of growing into a normal adult. There wasn't even any extended family to fall back on. Mum and her only sibling, my Aunt Susie, had quarrelled in their teens and had never been able to reconcile their differences, and although my grandparents occasionally had me to stay at their bungalow in Mablethorpe, they couldn't be described as warm and loving. If I'd been a penguin baby, I would definitely have perished after being pushed out of the huddle to make room for my brother.

I hate to think what would have become of me if I hadn't met Ben. Funnily enough, it was a chance encounter that might never have happened if Melanie, the girl I was sharing a flat with at the time, hadn't got cold feet about a blind date. She was a really nice girl and hadn't wanted to simply stand the poor bloke up, so had begged me to go and make her excuses for her. So I went, reluctantly, but I didn't make excuses for her. The moment I laid eyes on Ben I had a feeling that I'd never experienced before: it really was love at first sight, for me anyway. I'd let him call me Melanie for the first few dates we'd gone on before coming clean about the situation before things got too involved. That night was the first time we were intimate, and also the night Amber was conceived. Neither of us ever contemplated a termination; instead, we planned our wedding for a few weeks later. It was a very small affair that my mum, and therefore Adam, refused to attend. I hadn't been able to contact my dad, so I'll never know if he would have come or not.

'I think I'll go for a lie-down if that's alright with you, Danni?' my mum says, hauling me back to the present.

I glance at my watch. It's ten to five. 'Are you sure, Mum?' I say. 'It's a bit late really. It might stop you sleeping tonight.'

'I just need a short nap. I can barely keep my eyes open. I'm not used to all this excitement,' she says, giving the girls an affectionate squeeze before getting to her feet. 'Can you give me a call around six?'

'Will do,' I say, again marvelling at her change in attitude towards me.

Ben arrives home at quarter to six, predictably slightly the worse for wear. I make him a strong black coffee and send him through to the lounge to watch television with Amber and Jade. As the kettle has just boiled, I make a cup of tea for Mum and take it upstairs. I knock on the bedroom door and wait for a moment. There's no response, so I knock again. Still nothing. A cold fear creeps into my heart. Have we exhausted Mum? Has it all been too much for her with her ill health and all the medication? With a shaking hand, I press down on the handle and ease the door open, fearful of what I might find. The light spills into the room from the landing revealing her outline under the covers. She doesn't stir.

'Mum,' I say, my mouth feeling dry with apprehension. 'Are you awake?'

There is a slight movement and the tight feeling in my chest eases. I cross the room and perch on the edge of the bed, putting her cup of tea down on the bedside table.

'It's almost six, so I'm giving you a call like you asked.'

Slowly she rolls onto her back. I can see her eyes are open but there is no hint of recognition in them even though she is looking straight at me. She furrows her brow as though trying to remember something.

'Where did they take him?' she asks.

I'm not sure how to respond. I don't know who Mum is talking about and I don't want to upset her by saying the wrong thing, so I stay quiet.

'It's alright, I won't go looking for him,' she says, her voice shaky.

The light is quite dim, and I can't be certain, but I think her cheeks are wet. Has Mum been having some kind of nightmare and she's not properly awake yet? In the back of my mind, I remember that you're not supposed to wake people when they are talking in their sleep. Or is that when they're walking in their sleep? I'm not sure, but I might have to risk it because Mum is starting to get quite upset.

'Please tell me,' she pleads. 'I'll keep my promise because I know you're right and he'll be better off without me. I just want to say goodbye.'

She's sobbing now, her face contorted with pain. I have to try and wake her whatever the consequences.

'Mum, it's me, Danni,' I say, gently shaking her shoulders to try and wake her. 'You're having a bad dream.'

She recoils from my touch as though a thousand volts of electricity have gone through her. Her eyes still have that vacant look I've seen before when the dementia is preventing her from recognising people she knows. Maybe she's not asleep after all.

I try again. 'It's okay, I'm here. It's Danni, your daughter.'

'No, it wasn't a girl,' Mum says shaking her head. 'It was a boy. That's what the nurse said. I remember she asked me if I had a name for my son before she took him away.'

I'm a bit confused, but I want to try and help. It seems likely that the Skype call with Adam has had more of an impact than we thought it would. She must be reliving the trauma of the medical team taking my brother away to resuscitate him after he was born with the cord around his neck. That's why she's in such a state.

'And you did,' I say in a soothing tone of voice. 'Adam's a lovely name.'

'No!' she shouts, sitting bolt upright in bed. 'Don't lie; his name's Jason.'

I hear footsteps on the stairs and turn to see Ben silhouetted in the doorway.

'What's going on?' he asks, no hint of slurring in his voice. It's amazing how quickly shock can sober you up.

'Jason?' my mum says. 'Is that really you? They told me you died, but I didn't believe them and now here you are.'

Tears are streaming down her face and she's making a guttural noise through her sobs as she attempts to breathe. I've never seen Mum remotely this bad before and it's frightening.

'Come to me, Jason,' Mum begs, 'let me see you.'

I shake my head at Ben. I have no idea how to handle what's happening, but nothing will be gained by Ben pretending to be someone he's not.

'You're mistaken, Mum. That's Ben – my husband.'

For the first time since I came to wake her almost ten minutes ago, I see a flicker of recognition in my mum's eyes as she turns to look at me. It's quickly replaced by bewilderment and fear. I don't think she has any recollection of what has just taken place. I motion for Ben to come closer.

'You see, Mum, it's just Ben. You didn't recognise him with the light behind him.'

She takes a few moments, clearly trying to process the information before saying, 'Yes, Ben, of course. You're Amber and Jade's dad.'

'You had a bit of a funny turn, Diana,' he says moving to the other side of the bed. 'Are you feeling better now?'

'I'm fine. What time is it?'

'Six o clock,' I reply. 'You asked me to wake you at six.'

'Yes, I know, otherwise I won't be able to sleep tonight. I'm not stupid. I do remember the conversation,' she adds with a hint of irritation in her voice.

I swallow down the temptation to react.

'I brought you a cup of tea up, but would you rather have it downstairs? It might need a drop of hot water now.'

'Yes, let's go downstairs, it's a bit claustrophobic in here. I don't understand why they make the rooms in modern houses so small.'

It might sound strange, but it's good to hear her moan. At least I've got Mum back, but for how long? I don't know if it's the combination of the cancer and dementia drugs or whether her dementia has moved on to the next stage, but the whole episode has scared me. It's also left me with a question running through my mind. Who is or was Jason? Is he real or imagined?

CHAPTER SIXTEEN
Wednesday, 2 January 2019

It's my first day back at work today since the Christmas break and also the girls' first day back at school. I'm running a bit late because, after dropping them off, I had to pick Mum's prescription up. I hate being late for anything, but especially for work when I take into account how understanding Maxine is as a boss.

She re-opened the library on the 28th December and then only closed for one day at New Year, but she insisted she could manage on her own as she didn't think it would be too busy. I was doubtful about that. It's funny how families who spend the whole year saying they wished they had more time together, get to Christmas and within a couple of days are sick of the sight of each other. The library is a great place to escape to for a few hours and it's free.

The real reason for Maxine's generosity in allowing me a few more days off is that she knows it's always a bit tricky for me during the school holidays. Amber is fifteen, following her birthday in November, and is responsible enough to be left in charge of her sister, but the girls have been under a lot of stress lately and I don't want to add to it. The other consideration is them wanting to visit their nana every day.

In the summer holidays, I'd frequently dropped the girls off with Mum for the day and then picked them up after work without giving it a second thought. They'd all really enjoyed each other's company and having the girls around had certainly helped Mum. Since then, her dementia has become markedly worse with more frequent lapses in memory including the one on Boxing Day. I haven't had the opportunity to ask her any questions about Jason yet, but I'm planning to when it's just the two of us.

Ben took Mum home on the 27th and I've taken Amber and Jade to spend time with her every day since, but I've stopped leaving them there without me in case she turns aggressive. I managed to get in touch with Dr Ranjid a couple of days ago and he was able to bring Mum's next appointment forward, so we are seeing him next week. On the phone, I told him what had happened and what my concerns are for the future, so top of the list of things to discuss is how much longer she will be capable of living on her own.

I'm not looking forward to the conversation that will inevitably follow. Mum has been absolutely adamant about staying in her own house, but we are fast approaching the point where that simply won't be viable even if we could afford daily carers, which we can't. Although we coped pretty well over Christmas having her at our house, that was only for a few days and I worry about the effect the memory lapses and outbursts might have on the girls. Ben and I agree it's not a workable long-term solution, although it may not be that long-term if her breast cancer prognosis is to be believed. So, the only option left to us will be to move her into a care home – and to be able to afford that we are going to have to put her house on the market and hope it sells quickly.

I pull into my parking space behind the library and hurry up the steps, anxious to get in out of the cold. After the mild Christmas, it's turned very wintery again with heavy overnight frosts and the threat of more snow. Some of the long-range weather forecasts are predicting three months of arctic conditions, the coldest winter for several years, apparently. Even the thought of it makes me shiver.

I hang my coat up, change from my furry boots into my ballet pumps and go in search of Maxine to apologise for my lateness.

A few parents have congregated at the school gates while they wait for their children, but the majority of us have sensibly stayed in our cars, not willing to brave the weather to show off the coat or boots we got for Christmas. I didn't have either as a present this year. Ben and I agreed that we would keep our spend on each other at twenty-five pounds as we'd be spending more on food than usual with Mum coming to stay and Maxine joining us for Christmas lunch. Although I managed to get three days of meals out of the turkey, I was horrified when Ben had arrived home with it and told me it had cost forty-nine pounds!

We made sure the girls had plenty of presents to unwrap though, so hopefully they were unaware that we were doing Christmas on a budget, and I did splash out a bit on Maxine's bracelet, because she's been such an incredible friend to me. I also treated Mum to a luxuriously soft viscose and wool blend shawl. It had been difficult choosing a present for her that wouldn't seem pointless, but she seems to be really appreciating her gift. Every time we've visited during the school holidays, she's had it draped around her shoulders over whatever she's wearing, and she always comments about how cosy she feels wearing it.

It's freezing, with a biting easterly wind which I discovered when I popped out at lunchtime to get some cakes from Poppy's as a treat to take to Mum's. We're heading there when the girls show up. I couldn't quite run to a sit-down visit to the café, as we'd done on the first day of last term, but I thought that the cakes were a good compromise. I got an extra one to take back for Maxine as an apology for being late. Typically, she'd grabbed two plates from the cupboard in our library kitchen and cut the iced doughnut in half. The world would be a much nicer place if there were more Maxines in it.

I'm just thinking that the girls seem to be taking their time today, probably catching up on all the gossip with their friends, when my phone starts to ring. For a moment I have a horrible feeling that it might be Martin ringing to tell me of some disaster at Mum's, but when I glance at the screen, I can see it's Ben.

'Hiya,' I say. 'Are you missing me so much that you needed to call?'

'Well, that as well, but I thought you should know that I popped into one of the estate agents earlier to ask what they thought we might be able to ask for Diana's house when it goes on the market.'

I catch my breath. I'm not sure how I feel about him doing this. Yes, we've talked generally about the need to sell Mum's house, but we haven't discussed specifics and we certainly haven't talked about approaching estate agents. Besides which, I'm pretty sure we'll have to have something in writing from Mum before the house can go on the market.

'Are you there, Danni?' he says, when I don't speak.

'Sorry, yes, just distracted by the girls waving to me,' I fib.

'Oh right. Say hi to them for me. Anyway, Janet from Ballard and Ross has just rung me to say they put a few feelers out from their list of registered clients, and they think they might have a potential buyer.'

I can hear the excitement in Ben's voice which is fuelling the bubble of irritation I'm feeling that he has taken this step without asking me.

'Apparently,' he continues, 'this couple have been looking for something in that area for ages and are very interested to view. That's good news, isn't it? They might even make an offer without the need for putting a For Sale board up, and that's one of the things you said you were worried about.'

He's right. I've been dreading Mum's reaction to a sign going up outside the house where she's lived her entire life. I should probably be pleased that he's taken the initiative on this and got the ball rolling, but I'm not. I'm cross that he's gone behind my back and approached an estate agent without telling me he was going to do it. It feels like it's all moving too fast, maybe because it signals the beginning of the end for my mum. I swallow down my annoyance. I don't want to have an argument with him about it, particularly on the phone, so I choose my words carefully.

'I think we need to take a step back, Ben. It's not our house to sell. There's no desperate rush and we need to speak to Mum about it before getting estate agents involved.

'Oh, right,' he says. I can hear the disappointment in his voice. 'I thought you'd be pleased that I'm trying to help when you've got so much on your plate.'

'I am,' I say, 'it's just come as a bit of a surprise. Look, can we talk about it later when the girls have gone to bed. They're nearly at the car and I don't want to discuss it in front of them.' I'm telling the truth this time; Amber and Jade are walking along the pavement towards the car both with massive grins on their faces.

His one-word answer – 'okay' – before hanging up, signals that he's annoyed I wasn't more enthusiastic.

'Hi girls,' I say, adjusting my features into a welcoming smile, as Amber opens the door on the passenger side and pulls the seat forward to allow Jade to clamber into the back. 'That was Dad on the phone. He says hi. How was your day?'

CHAPTER SEVENTEEN
Wednesday, 2 January

On the short drive to Mum's, I'm regretting being so negative on the phone with Ben. He was only trying to help because he knows how overwhelming I'm finding the speed with which my mum's mental health is deteriorating. When we arrive, I settle the girls with their nana, who is once again wearing her new shawl draped over her shoulders, and head in to the kitchen to put the kettle on and get some plates out for the cakes. The girls have both got iced doughnuts, but I got egg custard tarts for me and Mum because they are her favourite. It also gives me the opportunity to drop Ben a quick text message:

Sorry for the lack of enthusiasm – I guess it just brought everything home to me that Mum won't be able to cope alone for much longer. I've decided to stay and have dinner with her tonight so that we can have a talk about it, so can you pick the girls up from here on your way home? Maybe call into the chippy if you don't fancy cooking, or there are sausages in the fridge for bangers and mash. Love you xx

Before the kettle has boiled, he messages back:

Good idea – a horrible situation but it has to be faced… together x I'll do bangers and mash. Love you too xx

Amber and Jade are chattering away excitedly to Mum when I go through to the lounge with her cup of tea in one hand and the plates for the cakes in the other. The box containing our treats is sitting on the coffee table, tied up with a ribbon, and I tell the girls to dish them out while I fetch the rest of the hot drinks. When I go back through, I'm surprised to see that Jade has got a custard tart in front of her rather than her usual favourite. I raise my eyebrows in question.

'Is it okay if I have the same as Nana?' she asks.

'Of course,' I reply, reaching for my plate. I sink my teeth into the spongey doughnut but am finding it difficult to swallow because of the tightness in my throat. However hard losing my mum is going to be for me, it's going to be twice as hard for my girls. I put the cake back on the coffee table and take a swig of tea to try and wash it down. It does the trick.

'How do you like your custard tart?' Mum asks.

'It's really nice,' Jade replies. 'I've never had one before because I didn't like the look of them much.'

'You can't judge a book by its cover,' Mum says. 'That's an important life lesson for both of you.'

'Next time we have cakes from Poppy's I'm going to try one,' Amber says.

The funny thing is, I'm not really a fan. I only bought it to keep Mum company.

'I was thinking of inviting myself to dinner tonight if you're up for it, Mum,' I say, waiting for the inevitable pleading from the girls; I have my answer already prepared.

'Can we stay too?' they chorus.

'Sorry girls, not on a school night. I'm pretty sure you've both got homework to do?'

They look disappointed, but to their credit they don't argue. We spend the next hour or so talking about their respective days at school and what their friends had for Christmas. Despite most of them having had way more extravagant gifts than Amber and Jade, they don't seem bothered by it because they knew how much thought went into what they received. All the time they are talking, Mum is stroking her shawl as if to underline that it's the thought that counts.

Ben picks the girls up at quarter past six and after waving them off, Mum and I head to the kitchen to see if she has anything in her small freezer for us to have for dinner. Mum doesn't go shopping anymore and she doesn't own a computer so can't do online shopping, but between us, Martin and I try to keep her stocked up with things she likes to eat. That said, there isn't a lot in the freezer unless we want Yorkshire pudding with mixed vegetables – not very appetising.

'What were you planning on having tonight?' I ask.

'I've got some chunky vegetable soup in the cupboard. I was either going to do that or scrambled eggs. Martin usually shops for me on a Wednesday, but I shouted at him and told him to leave me alone this morning, and for once he has,' she says, shrugging her shoulders.

'Mum,' I say, unable to keep the exasperation out of my voice, 'why would you do that? He's only trying to be helpful.'

She has a sheepish expression on her face.

'What exactly did you say to him?'

'I told him to piss off and leave me alone or I'd call the police and have him arrested for molesting me.'

I'm shocked. Firstly, I've never previously heard my mother swear; and secondly, I don't understand how she can treat Martin so appallingly after all he does for her. It must be the dementia making her behave this way.

'Right, well, while I'm warming the soup for us, I suggest you ring Martin and apologise. That was a horrible thing to say.'

She's glaring at me and for a minute I think she's going to refuse, then she strokes her shawl in what can only be described as a soothing manner and heads off to the lounge to use the pay as you go mobile phone I bought her earlier in the year after the incident on the dual carriageway. It's one that doesn't require a pin code, so in the unlikely event that I should forget to lock up properly and she wandered out into the street, whoever found her would be able to call me. I can hear her talking while I open the tin and tip the gloopy contents into a saucepan. I can't say I'm looking forward to my meal. At least I had the foresight to buy her a crusty loaf of bread in Poppy's, so that will make it more palatable, not that I'm here for the quality of the food. I break the bread into chunks and put them on a plate in the middle of her small kitchen table before getting two bowls down from the cupboard. I'm just ladling the hot soup out when she comes back into the room.

'Well,' I say, 'has he forgiven you?'

'He said he'll do my shopping tomorrow. He was going to come around for a shopping list, but I told him not to bother because you were here,' she says, sitting down at the table and taking a chunk of the bread to dip in her soup.

'Mum!' I say, exasperated with her thoughtlessness towards him. 'You can't treat him like that. If it wasn't for Martin's good nature and kind heart you wouldn't be able to live here on your own.'

Her spoon was halfway to her mouth, but she lowers it back to her bowl. She has me fixed with a steely stare. To be honest, this is not how I'd intended to broach the subject of her having to move out of her home, but I'm just so upset by her attitude towards Martin, treating him like a doormat.

'What do you mean?' she demands.

The lid is off the can of worms now. There's no point in putting it off any longer.

'What I mean, Mum, is that I'm not sure how much longer you're going to be able to live here alone given the state of your health.'

She's still staring at me but unless I'm imagining it, her expression seems less hostile. I think I was expecting her to rant and rave and shout about what a terrible daughter I am, but she's just looking at me.

'Mum?'

'I can't leave here, Danni,' she says, her voice measured and calm. 'What if he comes looking for me? I've stayed here all these years in case he comes looking for me.'

For a moment, I wonder if she's talking about my dad. This was our family home until he upped and left the day after my twelfth birthday. Has she really been hoping all these years that he would come back to her? Surely not. I've never thought she was that bothered about him leaving us and anyway, she was the one who told me he'd got married again and moved to Spain with his new family. But if not my dad, who is she talking about?

'If who comes looking for you, Mum?' I say gently, reaching for her hand across the table.

Her eyes have a faraway look, but it's not the same as when she's struggling to recognise me.

'Jason. They told me he died, but I never believed them really. I'd have known, wouldn't I?' she says, her voice little more than a whisper and her eyes searching mine for confirmation. 'A mother would know if her child died, wouldn't she?'

My breathing is shallow, and my face feels tingly. Ever since she mentioned the name on Boxing Day, I've wanted to ask her about Jason, but the opportunity hasn't arisen. If I'm understanding her correctly, she's saying she gave birth to a stillborn baby. Why on earth has she never mentioned it before?

'Tell me about Jason, Mum,' I gently coax.

'He was my baby. They wanted me to get rid of him, to have an abortion, but I said no. I loved him so much, the thought of losing him physically hurt, but it was nothing compared to the pain I went through to give him life. I knew I wouldn't be allowed to keep him; they told me I couldn't.' She's crying now, the tears streaming down her cheeks and dripping off her chin into the abandoned bowl of soup. She grips my hands tightly, her knuckles white with the effort. 'I had to promise to give him up. But I wanted to see him, just once, to tell him how much I loved him and that I would always love him. They wouldn't let me; they told me he died without ever taking a breath.'

Tears are welling in my eyes now. I have no way of knowing if what I'm hearing is real or imagined, but clearly Mum believes it to be true and I can almost hear her heart breaking as she talks. If it is true and she gave birth to a stillborn baby, why wasn't she allowed to hold him for a few precious moments? I can remember the excruciating pain of bringing my two into the world, and I'm shocked that she wasn't given time to grieve with her child before he was taken away. Maybe this goes some way to explaining why she found it so difficult to love me, although I'm not entirely convinced what she's saying is true. In the confusion of her illness, she could have unwittingly concocted the whole story and now has no idea herself whether it's real or imagined. Or she could be simply be making it all up as Dr Ranjid had warned me some dementia patients do. I need more information.

'When did all this happen, Mum?'

She looks puzzled, her face screwed up with concentration as though trying to drag something from the back of her mind. She gives a little shake of the head.

'A long time ago,' is all she says.

I need more, so I persist.

'Before I was born?'

'Yes, of course,' she says, as though I'm stupid to ask.

'And when you say *they*, who do you mean exactly?' I find it difficult to believe that my dad would suggest that Mum should have a termination, but of course I'm not aware of the circumstances. For all I know, one of the scans might have detected abnormalities. Maybe they suspected the baby wouldn't survive and wanted to spare her the pain of delivering at full term.

'My mum and dad. They said I'd brought shame on the family by having an illegitimate child.'

It's like a sucker punch. I wasn't expecting that. I assumed that Mum had already been married to my dad, but it seems that's not the case.

'Do you remember how old you were when this all happened, Mum?' I ask, trying to compose my thoughts and taking a slightly different approach.

'Sixteen,' she says with absolute conviction. 'I remember because I was supposed to have a birthday party, but it was cancelled when they found out I was pregnant. I'd managed to hide it at first,' she says, her tone conspiratorial, 'but two weeks before my birthday, Susan walked in on me in the bathroom and saw my swollen belly. She went and told Mum straightaway, even though I begged her not to. I was five months pregnant, but they still wanted me to have an abortion. I couldn't do it. I'd already felt Jason kick; he was already a little human being.'

I'm listening to Mum, but my thoughts have drifted to Amber. She's only a year younger than Mum was when she gave birth. How would I react to finding out my daughter was pregnant? It's impossible to say for sure, but I like to think I'd be more tolerant and supportive. Thinking back, Mum didn't suggest that I should have a termination when I rang to tell her I was getting married to Ben because I was pregnant. She called me stupid, but she never mentioned adoption or getting rid of my baby. Now I know why, if what Mum is telling me is true. I can't imagine what it must have been like for her, feeling her baby growing inside her while all the time knowing she wouldn't be allowed to keep him. It's unbearably sad.

'They should have let me say goodbye, Danni. Things might have been so different if they'd let me say goodbye.'

Mum's tears have stopped now and she's gazing off into space, but mine have just started. It's like a dam has burst. All those years of trying to please her and I now realise I could never have succeeded. Everything seems clear to me now: she didn't want a girl, she wanted a boy to replace the son she lost. If only she had told me about Jason before. It's the most natural thing in the world to mourn a stillborn baby – to place flowers on the grave every birthday. We could have done it together. All those wasted years for both of us, and now we have so little time left to try and right the wrongs of the past. I feel utterly devastated. I get up from my side of the table and move round to hers, throwing my arms around her needing to feel her close to me.

'What are you doing?' she cries, pushing me away. 'Have you gone mad?'

I stagger backwards, just managing to keep my balance.

'I – I thought maybe we could try and make the most of the time you have left,' I say, stunned by her reaction to my hug and surprised at the strength of the push. 'Now that I know about Jason, I think I understand why you've always been so distant with me.'

'What are you talking about?' she says, looking at me as though I'm speaking in a foreign language. 'Who's Jason?'

Mum complained that her soup was cold, so I reheated hers for her. Mine went in the bin. I couldn't eat; my head was still spinning, wondering if what she had told me was the truth or a total fabrication.

While she's in the bathroom brushing her teeth before bed, I ring Martin to ask him to sleep over on her couch. One thing is very clear: her dementia is reaching the point where I don't feel safe with her being on her own.

After saying goodnight to Mum and whispering my thanks to Martin who has just arrived from next door, I let myself out into the cold night air. I'm still feeling shaken by the apparent revelation that I'm not my mum's firstborn child – or am I? I just don't know what to believe.

CHAPTER EIGHTEEN
Friday, 4 January

I've been parked outside a large Victorian detached villa in an upmarket part of Woldington for the past ten minutes, trying to pluck up the courage to walk up the tiled pathway and knock on the imposing front door. It isn't as though I'm not expected, I am; it's just that I'm feeling very nervous about coming face to face with my Aunt Susie for the first time.

It was Ben's idea to try and trace her after I got home from Mum's two nights ago and broke down in tears telling him Mum's story about Jason. He held me and listened while I poured my heart out and when I'd finished, he gave me the choice between a cup of tea and a gin and tonic. For once, I chose the gin and tonic. He fixed himself one too, then came and sat next to me on the sofa and we talked late into the night.

We agreed that it was important to know if Jason was real or a figment of Mum's imagination and as both my grandparents are dead, the obvious next course of action was to try and make contact with Mum's sister, Susie. They haven't spoken for over forty years, having fallen out about something in their teenage years, and it's not beyond the realms of possibility that the 'something' was Mum's pregnancy. I didn't want to ask Mum if she had an address for Aunt Susie, it would only have aggravated or upset her. Besides, I figured it was pretty unlikely that she would still be living where she was when the two of them were last in contact.

The only actual information I had to go on was her maiden name, Willetts, but I did know that she was married because I remembered seeing her wedding photo when I'd stayed with my grandparents in Mablethorpe.

The following morning, once I'd dropped the girls at St Bede's, I called in to see Maxine at the library. After I explained that I needed to contact my mum's sister, Maxine sent me off to make a cup of tea while she checked the marriage register. She enjoys a bit of sleuthing, and less than an hour later she had come across the marriage of Susan Willetts to Colin Kingman in the summer of 1978. We then checked the local newspaper from that week and sure enough, there was the same photo of my aunt and uncle that had graced my grandparents' sideboard. The next stop was the telephone directory where there were three C. Kingmans listed. With shaking hands, I dialled the first one and my aunt Susie had answered the phone.

I wasn't completely honest as to why I was reaching out, which is probably why I'm feeling so nervous. *You're being ridiculous*, I tell myself. *She's probably as interested to meet you as you are to meet her.* With that little pep talk, I climb out of my car and head up the path noticing the curtains twitch as I do. I've barely even raised my hand to the brass door knocker before a generously proportioned lady with a slightly purple tinge to her silver hair swings the door open.

'You must be Danielle,' she says, beaming broadly. 'I would never have recognised you, you look nothing like Diana. Come on in, I've got the coffee ready to go.'

I follow her into the hallway, which is bigger than our lounge. The centre point of the high ceiling is marked with a chandelier hanging from an ornate plaster rose and underfoot are striking black and white tiles. Everything about this house screams wealth and opulence and I'm only just through the front door.

'I thought we could sit in the conservatory,' Aunt Susie says. 'Don't worry, it's not cold in there, it's triple-glazed and we've got underfloor heating. Shall I take your coat?'

I haven't really been planning on staying long. Fridays are work days for me, but Maxine has given me a couple of hours off.

'Um, thanks,' I say handing her my wool blend coat, the one I usually keep for meals out or the occasional trip to the theatre in Oakbridge. I felt the need to dress smartly after Maxine had described Aunt Susie's address as being in 'millionaire's row'. At the time, I thought she was exaggerating, but now I'm not so sure.

'How do you take your coffee?' she asks.

'Strong with a dash of milk, please.'

'No sugar?'

'No thanks.'

'That'll be why you're so skinny,' she says, leading the way through to the conservatory completely oblivious to the fact that she might have caused offence.

It's funny how people never show the same level of sensitivity with slim people as they do with those carrying more weight.

'Take a pew,' she says, indicating an overstuffed sofa, 'and I'll pop downstairs to the kitchen to get our coffees. Make yourself at home.'

She's only gone a few minutes, but it gives me time to collect my thoughts. This is not going to be easy. What I'd told her on the phone was that Mum was seriously ill and wanted to make her peace before she died, which is some way off the truth. I'm here under false pretences, so I have to tread carefully. I can hear the rattling of china and Aunt Susie enters the room pushing a trolley laden with all manner of sweet treats. Aunt Susie said the kitchen was downstairs, so how did she get up here with a trolley unless her house has a lift! And with all that food, she's either trying to impress me or fatten me up. I can't really refuse as she hands me a plate and then offers me a choice of Bakewell tart or Battenberg cake. I haven't had either for years, so I take a slice of each to keep her sweet.

'This is a beautiful house,' I say. 'Have you lived here long?'

'It belonged to my husband's parents, but it was in a bit of a state when we inherited it: crumbling plaster, and all the original fireplaces boarded up from the abomination that was the 1970s. Fortunately, most of the original features had just been covered up rather than being ripped out so we were able to restore it to its former glory. Cost an arm and a leg, mind you. Where do you live, Danielle?'

'Danni, please call me Danni. We're on Westfield Close, about a ten-minute drive from your parents' old house,' I say, taking a bite of the Battenberg cake which looks much nicer than it tastes.

Aunt Susie is still smiling, but I detect a bit of tension at the mention of her old home. Maybe she doesn't like being reminded of her humble beginnings, or maybe she's aware that I'm about to steer the conversation in the direction of my mum. She takes a sip of her coffee so that she doesn't have to comment.

'Mum still lives there,' I say, taking a sip of my own coffee to allow the information to register.

'Yes, she's always had a weird fascination with that house. She virtually forced our mother and father to sell it to her when they moved to the coast. You said she's quite poorly?'

There doesn't seem much point in sugar-coating the pill.

'She's dying,' I say.

My words don't provoke the emotional response I expect – even if the sisters *haven't* set eyes on each other for years.

Her voice is non-committal as she asks, 'What's wrong with her, if you don't mind me asking?'

'Well, what's killing her is breast cancer, but she's also been diagnosed with Alzheimer's disease.'

Aunt Susie puts her plate and cup and saucer down. At least that revelation has prompted a reaction.

'I'm sorry to hear that, Danni, really I am. She hasn't been the best sister, but I wouldn't wish either of those things on anyone. How bad is she, with the Alzheimer's, I mean? Does she still recognise you?'

'Most of the time, but she does have periods when she seems to go completely blank, as though a light switch has turned off in her brain,' I say, once again using Maxine's analogy.

'Do you think she would recognise me if I were to go and visit her?'

I'd expected Aunt Susie to ask this after I'd suggested Mum wanted to make her peace. 'Would you like to see her?' I ask. 'You two have been strangers for so long, I wasn't sure if it would be that important to you.'

'She hasn't told you, has she? Is that why you're here? You want to know what happened all those years ago to force two sisters apart.'

I nod, dropping my eyes to my plate and concentrating on my Bakewell tart.

Aunt Susie clears her throat. 'Stupidly, it was over a boy.'

My head snaps up. That was not what I was expecting to hear. I'd more or less come to the conclusion that Mum was telling the truth about baby Jason and that it was the stigma of her sister's underage pregnancy that had forced a wedge between the two of them.

'Really?' I say. 'You let a boy come between you and the feud lasted all these years?'

'It's not as simple as that,' she says in a resigned manner. 'I'd been dating my boyfriend, Kevin, for nearly two years. He was two years older than me but acted much more grown up than his nineteen years. He didn't have a particularly happy home life, so he was always round at ours. Sometimes Mum would let him listen to music in my room while he waited for me to get home from school. We'd talked about getting engaged when I left school, married even, and then she went and spoiled it all.'

'You mean my mum?'

'Yes. You know, in a funny sort of way, I should thank Diana. If I'd married Kevin my life would have been nothing like this,' she says, indicating with her hand and casting her eyes around her. 'I know money isn't everything, but it has its compensations and apparently Kevin is now on his third wife.'

I'm trying to imagine what my mum could have done to come between Kevin and Susie in such spectacular fashion. I'm aware of Aunt Susie watching me. She's probably wondering if I know anything of the story at all.

'There was a baby,' she says, taking a sip of coffee as though to calm herself. 'Your mother was fifteen, didn't have a boyfriend and yet somehow managed to get herself pregnant.'

I can feel my hackles rise. Nobody 'gets themself pregnant', there has to be another party involved. But it appears Mum was telling the truth about the baby. That was what I came here to find out, and Aunt Susie has confirmed it.

'I know. She told me,' I say in clipped tones which I hope portray how annoyed I am with her comment. 'She said that she begged you not to tell your mum, but you did anyway.'

'They'd have found out soon enough. She'd been hiding it successfully for the first few months, but she'd started to show,' my aunt says, studiously looking into her cup. She seems to be deep in contemplation. She places her cup and saucer down and looks me full in the eyes. 'Diana accused Kevin of being the baby's father.'

I gasp. I can hardly believe what I'm hearing. My mum had sex with her sister's boyfriend. What sort of a person does that? I came to Aunt Susie's house wanting to place the blame on her for the falling out, but it seems I may be off the mark.

'You say Mum *accused* your boyfriend as though you don't really believe it. Why would she lie about something like that?'

'Who knows? Maybe to protect the baby's real father. Of course, Kevin strenuously denied everything and I wanted to believe him,' she says, 'but Diana had planted the seed of doubt in everyone's mind. Dad went ballistic and told Kevin that if he ever came near me again, he was going to report him to the police for having sex with a minor. Kevin wasn't prepared to take the risk, so he stayed away.'

'From both of you?'

She nods. A part of me is thinking that my aunt had a lucky escape. If Kevin hadn't done anything wrong, why wouldn't he try and prove his innocence? And if he was guilty, she was definitely better off without him.

'If he was the father, shouldn't he have been with my mother when the baby was born?'

'I already told you, our dad wouldn't allow him anywhere near either of us.'

'But she was sixteen. She must have been terrified.'

'Our mum was with her at Beechmede Hospital. Diana wasn't going to be allowed to keep the baby anyway, so it didn't really matter who the father was. They had adoptive parents all lined up, but then it was stillborn. Call me callous, but I've often thought it was for the best.'

Horrified doesn't come close to how I feel on hearing Aunt Susie say that. How can she think that the baby didn't deserve its chance at life regardless of how it was conceived?

'You can't mean that,' I blurt out.

'Actually, I do. Despite having agreed to the adoption, Diana didn't really want to give the baby up. She wanted to keep it. Imagine that: a sixteen-year-old schoolgirl bringing up a child on her own. How ridiculous. What kind of a life would they both have had?'

'Is it ridiculous? There are lots of teenage single mothers who make a better job of parenting than many couples.'

'These days maybe, but we're talking about the 1970s. Anyway, it's irrelevant. The baby was born dead.'

I'm desperate to get out of my aunt's house. I'm finding the way that she's talking about her dead nephew really difficult to deal with. But there is one more question I want to ask.

'Mum said that they wouldn't let her hold her baby. Do you know why?'

'No, why would I? I didn't ask what happened at the hospital, and our mother never spoke of the whole shameful episode again.'

The coldness in her voice astonishes me all over again. All I can think of is how I would have felt if either of my girls had been stillborn. I would have wanted to hold them, to cuddle them against my breast, to rail against the injustice of what had happened and tell them how much I loved them. I can feel tears pricking the back of my eyes at the thought. Poor Mum, what a state of utter despair she must have been in returning home to a family who were unsympathetic and despised her for the disgrace she had heaped on them.

'Would I be right in thinking you don't have children?' I say.

'Yes,' she replies, the corner of her mouth twitching. 'Unfortunately, Colin and I weren't blessed in that regard.'

So that's something else she blames her sister for. If there was the tiniest doubt that Kevin could have been the baby's father, she's probably never forgiven my mother for the children she was denied. I'm beginning to understand why the rift between them became a chasm that couldn't be bridged.

'I'm sorry,' I mumble, getting to my feet. 'I need to get back to work. Thank you for the coffee and cake and for your honesty.'

She stands too. 'I wish we could have met under better circumstances.'

'This is my number,' I say, pulling a scrap of paper with my mobile number on it out of my handbag and handing it to her, 'in case you want any updates on Mum.'

Back in my car, it takes a full five minutes for me to stop shaking. I've got what I came here for and discovered so much more. How sad that the events of over forty years ago have impacted so many lives, including Adam's and mine. I'm desperate to know if Mum was telling the truth about Kevin being baby Jason's father, but I'm not sure I should ask her for fear of stirring up too many unhappy memories. I know my aunt is watching from her window, but I don't turn to wave as I pull away from the kerb.

CHAPTER NINETEEN
Friday, 4 January

When I get back to the library just after 11.30, Maxine is busy helping an elderly man find the gardening book he is looking for in the 'leisure' section. I've already decided I will forego my lunchbreak in order to make up for the time I've been out. Fridays are often quite busy with people wanting something new to read over the weekend. It's the one day of the three that I work where Maxine and I seem to have very little chance to chat. It's a shame, because right now I could do with some of her worldly advice.

I'm in the children's section tidying up after the morning's young readers' session when Maxine finds me.

'What was she like?' she asks without preamble.

It's a tricky question. Aunt Susie was, after all, kind enough to invite me to her house and ply me with coffee and cake, but holding a lifelong grudge against a sixteen-year-old girl who has made a mistake, particularly when that girl is your sister, has not made me warm to her. In fact, neither my mum nor my aunt could be described as having a loving disposition, which could be attributed to their parents, my grandparents. I don't recall either of them being affectionate on my infrequent trips to Mablethorpe. I'm glad I've broken the mould, even if I do get a bit over-emotional sometimes.

'She was nice enough,' I say, shrugging.

'But? Come on, Danni, I know you better than that.'

'I was just a bit disappointed with her attitude.'

'Towards your mum, do you mean?' Maxine says, picking up the pile of books I've just gathered off the floor and making a start on putting them back on the shelves.

I'll have to tell Maxine about baby Jason if I'm going to ask her advice.

'I found out what they fell out over and it's pretty major.' I take a deep breath. 'Mum had an illegitimate baby and apparently she claimed her sister's boyfriend was the father.'

I've known Maxine a long time and I can honestly say I've never seen her jaw hit the floor the way it does now.

'You're not kidding about it being pretty major,' she says, once she regains her composure. 'That is huge.'

'The thing is, I sort of knew about the baby, because Mum has mentioned him by name a couple of times when she's been having her episodes, but I wasn't sure if he was real or a product of her imagination brought on by her illness. That's why I wanted to find Aunt Susie, not to try and get them to reconcile. I wanted to know if Jason existed.'

If Maxine's disappointed with me for not being honest with her, it certainly doesn't show on her face.

'So, where is he now, your half-brother?'

I hadn't even thought about Jason being my half-brother, but I guess that's because I know he's dead.

'He was stillborn.'

'Oh, my goodness,' Maxine says, her face filled with the compassion that was missing from Aunt Susie's. 'Poor Diana. No wonder she worshipped the ground Adam walked on. She must have been afraid of losing him, like she lost her first son. How strange she didn't mention him to you though. If that had been me, I'd have wanted you to know about him and possibly even visit his grave together.'

'Me too; but she can't. They took him away from her without ever letting her set eyes on him.'

'But the little mite must be buried somewhere. Surely she could have found out.'

My heart has started to pound in my chest. Why didn't I think of that?

'Oh my God, Max, you're a genius,' I say, wanting to hug her. 'If I can find out from Beechmede Hospital where Jason was buried, I could take Mum to lay flowers on his grave. Maybe it would finally give her some kind of closure.'

'There's no time like the present,' she says. 'You go through to the kitchen and give them a call while I finish up here.'

Initially, I wasn't able to get through to Beechmede. Each time I tried, it went straight through to voicemail and it wasn't the sort of thing I felt comfortable leaving a message about. After a few attempts, I went back into the library to give Maxine a hand with the lunch-time rush of people returning and signing out books. At 2 p.m., I decided to give it one more try; the call was picked up on the third ring.

'Beechmede Hospital, how can I direct your call?' said a pleasant female voice on the other end of the line.

'Oh, um, I'm not actually sure who I need to speak to. I'm making enquiries about a baby boy born in the hospital in late September or early October of 1974.'

I've been able to work out the month and year from the information Aunt Susie gave me.

'I'm sorry dear, we wouldn't be able to give out any information over the phone. Are you a relative?'

'Yes,' I say. 'The baby was my brother.'

There's the slightest of pauses before the woman says, 'Well, you'd need to be a bit more specific with the date if we're to find the birth you're asking about, and we'd need a name, but as I say we can't divulge information over the phone.'

'It's Jason. Jason Willetts,' I say. 'And the mother's name is Diana.'

'Diana Willetts, baby Jason,' she says slowly and clearly as though confirming she has the correct details. 'I've made a note of that and I can pass it on to the records office to look into for you but, like I said, they wouldn't release any information unless you come to the hospital in person with some proof of identity.'

'Oh, right,' I say, 'I was rather hoping it would just be a case of speaking to someone on the phone.'

'Oh no, data protection and all that, and I should also warn you that it can take several weeks, if not months when they are busy.'

My heart sinks. I might not have that much time if Mum's condition worsens. I'm wondering if I could drop into the hospital with my ID before I pick the girls up from school to at least get the ball rolling.

'What time does your records office close?' I ask.

'Four o'clock this afternoon and then they're not in over the weekend, so it would be Monday after that.'

I check my watch; it's only ten past two and I'm pretty sure Maxine won't have a problem with me going. She knows how important this is to me and Mum.

'I'll be there in twenty minutes. Thanks for your help,' I add. From past experience, people usually respond to politeness and there might be something the receptionist can do to speed my request through.

CHAPTER TWENTY
Friday, 4 January

The snow is starting to settle as I turn off the main road and into the driveway of Beechmede Hospital. It's on the outskirts of Wold-ington and is a much smaller hospital than the Royal Infirmary in Oakbridge where Mum is being seen for both her dementia and her breast cancer, although the grounds are extensive. After about a quarter of a mile, I follow the signs to the visitor car park and manage to find a space close to the front entrance. I pull the spare fold-up umbrella that I keep in the car out of the glove box and make a dash for the steps leading up to the front doors. I can't help picturing smiling young women cradling their newborns in their arms, waiting on the steps for the car to take them home to start the next phase of their lives. It would have been a very different journey home from hospital for my mum and the thought brings a lump to my throat. I push through the double doors, shaking the snow off my umbrella before I step into the small, brightly lit reception area. In front of me is a wooden desk, at which is sat a middle-aged woman who appears to be deep in conversation with another woman standing at her side. They both turn to look at me as I approach the desk.

'Miss Willetts, is it?' the receptionist asks.

I wonder how she knows it is me, but a quick glance around the empty reception area tells me that it's not a busy afternoon.

'Mrs Harper actually, but that was my mum's maiden name,' I say, smiling, pursuing my thought process from earlier that if I'm nice to the receptionist, whose name badge identifies her as Grace, she might be more inclined to be helpful.

'Well, you might be in luck,' she says. 'Linda here popped out to the desk to check on the whereabouts of her next patient who's late for her antenatal appointment. She saw your mother and brother's name on my notepad and thought she recognised them.'

I take a closer look at the woman standing at Grace's side. She's much older than the receptionist, around my mum's age, I would estimate. My heart starts to thud in my chest. Is it possible that she remembers Mum from all those years ago?

'Have you brought some form of identification with you?' Grace continues.

I reach into my bag for my purse containing my driving licence. As I hand it over, I see Grace's expression and realise it's useless as a form of ID. I've taken time off work to come all the way out here in the snow and my driving licence doesn't provide any connection between me and the Willetts family. Damn. If I hadn't been in such a rush, I would have realised that and could have gone home first to get my birth certificate.

'I'm sorry Mrs Harper, but I'm afraid this doesn't prove any familial connection. I don't suppose you've brought anything else with you?'

I shake my head.

It's looking as though it has been a wasted journey when Linda says, 'Before heading back out into the snow, why don't you get yourself a hot drink? I'll show you where the café is if you like.'

I'm just about to say that I should be getting off to pick my girls up from school, when I catch Grace shooting Linda what can only be described as a warning look. Maybe it is my lucky day after all.

'That's very kind of you. It's bitter out there and I could do with a bit of warming up. I'll come back on Monday with my birth certificate,' I say to Grace. 'That will have all the information you need about me.'

'I'll hold back from sending this through to records until Monday then,' she says, as I follow Linda through a half-glazed door to the right of the reception desk. We go along a short corridor before turning left, following the aroma of freshly brewed coffee. The café only has six small round tables and, like the reception area, is completely empty. There's no one serving behind the counter.

'Are you okay with a machine coffee, or would you prefer tea?' she says, indicating an urn of hot water.

'Coffee from the machine is fine,' I reply, wondering if I've got any coins left in my purse after paying for my parking. 'How much is it?'

'Don't worry, I'll put them both on my staff card. Black, flat white or cappuccino?'

'Flat white is fine,' I say distractedly, wondering what information Linda might have for me. I don't really need a coffee, but at least it would give validation if Grace were to pop her head into the café. 'Thanks,' I say, as she hands me a white mug and takes a seat across the table from me.

'I haven't got long, Mrs Harper,' Linda says.

'Please, call me Danni.'

'Danni it is,' she says smiling. 'My next appointment is due at three, always assuming they turn up in this weather,' she adds, indicating the window where the snowfall appears to be getting heavier. 'What is it you want to know about Diana and Jason?'

I take a deep breath. 'Grace said you thought you recognised the names. Were you working here back in 1974?'

'I'd just started my training as a student nurse. I'd only been here a month or so and the whole situation had such an impact on me. I remember wondering if I was cut out for a career in nursing,' Linda says. 'Can I ask why you're taking an interest in this now after all these years?'

'I've only just discovered I had a half-brother,' I answer truthfully. 'It's been a long-buried family secret, but now it's out in the open.'

'I did wonder if it was something along those lines. Illegitimate births were rather hushed up back in those days.'

I take a sip of coffee, hoping that Linda will fill the space by telling me what she knows; she obliges.

'I was so pleased to be placed on the maternity ward. Some areas of nursing didn't really appeal to me, but I loved the idea of being part of the joy of bringing new life into the world. How naïve was I?' she says, shaking her head. 'I quickly learned that childbirth doesn't always go to plan.'

I am aware of time constraints, so I offer, 'Jason being stillborn you mean?'

She nods. 'He was my first, although sadly of course not my last. But it wasn't just him being stillborn that stuck in my mind, it was the way Diana was treated by the woman who was with her; her mother I think?'

It's my turn to nod. It's a bit overwhelming to be talking to someone who had been with Mum as she suffered through the agony of childbirth.

'It wasn't an easy labour. Diana was admitted during my shift the night before, but didn't deliver Jason until early the following evening, almost twenty-four hours later. We'd struck up quite a bond; maybe because I was a similar age but more likely because her mother barely spoke to her and when she did, she just kept saying, "You've only got yourself to blame for getting into this mess in the first place. I hope you've learned your lesson."

I'm trying to breathe steadily to keep my emotions under control. I was appalled this morning to hear Aunt Susie speak of the situation in the way she did, but it's now apparent that my grandmother was the architect of those opinions. My poor mum had no family support at all, not even from her mother, which I find hard to comprehend. While I wouldn't want Amber or Jade to become pregnant outside a loving relationship, I certainly wouldn't turn my back on them.

'I remember feeling so sorry for Diana,' Linda continues. 'I tried to stay with her as much as possible, holding her hand and mopping her brow with a cold flannel, but despite her pleas, Sister Pullinger made me take my dinner break when Diana was in the really advanced stages of labour. When I returned to the delivery room half an hour later, Diana was lying flat on her back staring up at the ceiling, tears rolling out of the corners of her eyes. Although it was clear to see she was in a state of shock, her mother was saying, "Pull yourself together, you weren't going to be keeping him anyway. It's the adoptive parents I feel sorry for." That was the first I knew of the baby being stillborn.' She looks down at the contents of her cup and takes a couple of moments before continuing. 'It took a long while for me to forgive myself for leaving Diana when she needed me, but I was very junior, and in those days, we did as we were told. It was so distressing when she clung to my arm saying, "They wouldn't even let me hold my Jason." To this day, I'll never forget the look in her eyes, which is probably one of the reasons I remembered the names so clearly. The other was because she had given him a name even though she wasn't going to keep him. I found that heart-breaking.'

There is a crumb of comfort in knowing that Mum had someone so kind and caring with her just after Jason was taken from her, but that's all it is – a crumb.

'Do you know why she wasn't allowed to hold him, even for a few minutes to say her goodbyes, after all she'd been through with the labour?' I ask.

'It was hospital policy in those days with stillborn infants. I think it was believed that it might form some kind of bond which could lead to depression.'

'But surely they must have realised that the bond between mother and baby is formed while it's still in the womb,' I say, recalling all the times I laid my hands on my swelling belly and spoken lovingly to my daughters.

'We know that now, but everything was so different back then.'

'Do you know what happened to the stillborns after they were taken from their mothers?'

'Barbaric as it sounds, I believe some hospitals incinerated them.'

I shudder.

'At least we didn't do that at Beechmede. Our groundsman at the time, Ray Pullinger, Sister Pullinger's husband, made little wooden boxes, blue for the boy babies and pink for the girls, which he then buried in the grounds with little wooden crosses as markers.'

My pulse is quickening. It might not be much, but if we could find where Jason was buried, I could take Mum there.

'Do you think Ray might remember where he buried Jason?'

'I don't expect so,' Linda says. 'Sadly, infant mortality was much higher in those days, so there would have been quite a few of those pink and blue boxes. And we can't even ask him. If I remember correctly,' she says puckering her brow, 'he and his wife left Beechmede fairly soon after that, but I think Gary, the new groundsman, carried on the practice for a while. Of course, it's all different now. Stillborn babies get proper funerals if that's what the parents want. Mothers are actively encouraged to grieve.'

I know I've been clutching at straws somewhat, but it does feel as though the lifeline I've been thrown has suddenly been snatched away from me. With no Ray to ask, it would be an almost impossible task to try and locate Jason's grave, wouldn't it?

'Did Ray write the babies' names on the crosses, do you know?'

Linda glances at her watch and I find myself looking down at mine. It's almost three o clock, the time of her next appointment. I need to get going too if I'm going to get to St Bede's on time in the worsening conditions.

'I don't think so because most mothers didn't give their baby a name. He may have written the case numbers on the crosses, though,' she adds.

The glimmer of hope starts to bubble again. If Beechmede were to grant me permission to have a look in the grounds and I discovered where the babies were buried, I would need something to help me identify my half-brother's grave.

'The records office should be able to give you Jason's case number,' Linda says, pushing her chair back and standing up. 'I'm afraid I have to go now; my next appointment is due.' She goes to leave, then turns back. 'It might be best if you keep our conversation to yourself, in case I've told you more than I should. That said, if you give me your mobile number, I can call you if I remember anything else that I think might be relevant.'

'Thank you, Linda, for being so kind to my mum,' I say writing my number on a paper napkin and handing it to her.

'I came into nursing to be kind and to care for people,' she replies, tucking the napkin into the pocket of her uniform. 'I retire in a couple of years and I like to think I did my job well. I hope you find your brother's grave,' she says, exiting the café through a door marked private which I suspect bypasses the reception area. However friendly the two of them are, Linda is obviously worried that Grace might not approve of the information she has shared with me.

CHAPTER TWENTY-ONE
Tuesday, 8 January

Mum didn't make any excuses not to attend her appointment today, and as a consequence we're very early for her 11.30 with Dr Ranjid. So early, in fact, that we have popped into the hospital cafeteria for coffee and cake. I've sat her down at a table near the window while I queue up to get served. It's very different from the cosy hospital café at Beechmede where I'd sat chatting to Linda on Friday afternoon, but I suppose that's because it's at least four times the size.

I didn't see Linda when I called in at Beechmede with my birth certificate during my lunchbreak yesterday. Grace photocopied it and then handed the original back to me saying she would forward my query about Jason to the records office. I went over in my mind what I'd originally said to Grace and was pretty sure I wasn't landing Linda in trouble by being more specific about the information I wanted from them. All I really need to know is Jason's case number and in what part of the extensive grounds he may have been buried. I no longer needed confirmation that my mum's baby had never taken a breath. I also mentioned to Grace that Mum didn't have long to live and how I hoped to be able to show her where her baby was buried before she herself died. Grace didn't make any promises, but I saw compassion in her eyes and knew she would do her very best to hurry things along.

I pay for the cherry Bakewell tart, the slice of carrot cake and the two milky coffees and head in Mum's direction. She's had an amazingly lucid few days and has been in particularly good spirits having agreed to stop overnight at our house on Friday and Saturday. It had looked as though the snow was going to keep falling and settling, meaning we wouldn't have been able to go and visit her, so I suggested she should come and stay when we'd called in at hers on Friday after I'd picked the girls up from school. As it happens, the weather forecasters got it wrong and the snow stopped early on Sunday, so Ben was able to drop her home on Sunday evening after dinner.

I have to admit I was quite glad as although she'd been impeccably behaved, I've been finding it difficult not to tell her that I know she was telling the truth about having a baby. I want to wait until I've found out where he's buried so that we can go and visit the grave together. There is also the question over who the baby's father was. We've become so much closer over the past few months that I'm hoping she might tell me the truth about what happened all those years ago. Ben doesn't understand my need to know, which led to a minor disagreement on the whole subject.

'What on earth do you think will be gained by opening up old wounds?' he said, when he climbed into bed after dropping Mum home on Sunday night and I finally got the chance to tell him about my meeting with Aunt Susie and the subsequent visit to Beechmede Hospital, without fear of being overheard.

'I'm not opening them up, Ben, her illness has done that,' I tried to explain. 'Some days Mum can't remember what she had for breakfast, but her brain has dredged up this memory because it played such a huge part in her life. The wound has already been re-opened and if we don't do anything to treat it, it will keep festering.'

'Treat it how?' he asked obstinately. 'What are you hoping to gain?'

'Closure?' I replied quietly. 'If I can find where Jason was buried, I could take Mum there. Having an actual place to visualise when she thinks of him might encourage her to grieve and let go of the idea that one day he'll walk back into her life. It could even give her a degree of acceptance towards the people who forced her to make the decisions she did. Although my grandparents are long dead, I doubt if she ever truly forgave them and of course there's her sister, my Aunt Susie. They haven't spoken since what happened. Maybe the two of them could reconcile, for however long Mum has left.'

'You don't know enough about it.' Ben turned over in our bed so that he had his back to me. 'You could make matters worse. You've found out what you wanted to know. Your mum had an illegitimate baby called Jason, who sadly died at birth. If you want my opinion, I think you should leave things alone.'

I put Ben's attitude down to him being tired. Nevertheless, it upset me and there was a frostiness between us on Monday morning which still hasn't completely thawed. I know my mum isn't the easiest person to like, but what I've uncovered has helped me understand her a bit better. I'm also disappointed that Ben didn't give any consideration to how I might be feeling. If I'm honest, I don't know how I'm feeling. It's strange to think that I wasn't Mum's first child, but it's more than that: I feel sad that I was denied the opportunity to know Jason. Ben asked what I hope to gain by finding my half-brother's grave and now that I've had a couple of days to think it over, I know. I want to be able to grieve for the brother I never knew alongside my mum. I want to try and make the end of Mum's life happier than the majority of it has been. I've tried so hard to please her throughout my life, but nothing has ever been enough. Maybe doing this for her will finally win me the approval I've desperately craved. But all that aside, I truly believe what I'm doing is the right thing for both of us.

Placing the plates in the middle of our table, I ask, 'Which would you like, Mum?'

'You choose,' she replies, 'I like them both.'

I'm tempted to tell her to have them both. She looks so thin and old, way older than her sixty years, but that's what illness and chemotherapy drugs can do to a person. I take the carrot cake and she reaches for the cherry Bakewell. I watch as she sinks her teeth into the soft white icing, crumbs from the pastry dropping onto her plate. It's somehow appropriate; Adam returning from New Zealand would be the cherry on top of the happiness cake that I'm trying to bake for her.

I'm about to make a start on my carrot cake when I feel my phone vibrate in my pocket. I've got it on silent, ready for Mum's appointment with Dr Ranjid. I glance down and see it's a number I don't recognise, so I don't answer. I get really fed-up with all the calls that begin with, 'We hear you've been in an accident'. I've only managed one forkful of my cake when my phone vibrates again, this time with a text message;

Hello Danni, this is Linda from Beechmede hospital. Can you call me when you get a minute?

I'm pretty sure it's the same number that tried to call a few minutes ago, so clearly Linda is anxious to speak to me, but it's now quarter past eleven and I don't want to be late for Mum's appointment. Linda will have to wait until after I drop my mum back home even though I'm intrigued to know why she's calling. I hope I haven't got her into trouble with Grace.

CHAPTER TWENTY-TWO
Tuesday, 8 January

Mum was very quiet on the drive home. When she's lucid, it's easy to forget how worrying the bad days are. Dr Ranjid expressed his concern over the incident with the Christmas bauble, but explained that the cocktail of drugs she was now taking for both the dementia and her breast cancer might be exacerbating her confused episodes. He also pointed out that she could have come to some real harm if it had happened at her house without Ben and I on hand to look after her. Mum glared at me at that point, obviously furious that I'd told him about the incident, but I honestly believe it was for her own good. Dr Ranjid went on to gently suggest that the time had come for her to move into a care home where she could be monitored twenty-four/seven and her medication could be adjusted if necessary. I expected her to get really upset at the suggestion, angry even, but she sat in silence for the rest of the appointment.

Mum didn't say a word to me as we walked back to the car. She clutched the information booklets about the three establishments that Dr Ranjid had recommended, and stared out of the window as we travelled along the now familiar route back to her house from the hospital. It's only when we're within the confines of her kitchen and I'm heating up a tin of baked beans for us to have on toast, that she finally speaks.

'I've told you why I can't leave here,' she says very quietly.

I have my back to her, for which I am very grateful as it gives me a moment to remove the look of pity from my eyes. Mum has clung to the desperate belief that her son didn't die in childbirth and will one day come looking for her and I'm about to crush that belief forever. I turn the gas off from beneath the saucepan; something tells me neither of us will feel like eating any time soon. I turn towards her. The look on her face is a heart-breaking mix of hope and despair. It takes me another few moments before I can trust myself to speak.

'I've got something to tell you, Mum.' I sit down opposite her at the small kitchen table and reach for her hands. 'Ever since you mentioned Jason to me, I've wondered if he was real or whether your illness had made you confused and Jason was someone else's baby, or maybe never existed at all.' I pause, waiting for some kind of reaction, but there is none, so I carry on. 'I… I decided to do a bit of investigating, starting with Aunt Susie.'

Mum's eyes widen, but she doesn't speak.

'I found out where she lives, and I went to see her last week.'

'You spoke to my sister?' she asks. 'Why? Why would you do that?'

She still seems quite calm, but I'm fully aware that I have to be careful in order to keep her that way.

'There was no one else to ask,' I reply. 'Grandma and Grandad are dead, and I figured your sister would be the only other person who might know about it.'

Mum's hands are trembling in my grasp and her shoulders have slumped forward, her head bowed between them.

'Aunt Susie told me what happened,' I say. Mum raises her gaze to look into my eyes, but I can't read her expression. 'At least, she told me her version of events.' I pause again. I want to give Mum the opportunity to tell me what happened in her own words, but she doesn't say anything, so I continue. 'Aunt Susie told me Jason was stillborn,' I say gently.

'Susan wasn't there; she only knows what our mother told her, and it was a lie.' My mum's voice is rising in volume, but she doesn't sound angry. It's more like she is trying to convince me that what she is saying is true. 'They wanted me to *believe* that Jason was dead when he was born,' she says, 'but I heard him whimper, I know I did.'

This is so much harder than I'd imagined it would be. It's likely that the sound Mum thought she heard came from her own lips after being told her baby was dead, but for more than forty-four years she has clung to the hope that her baby survived. Maybe Ben was right after all and I should never have started all this. It's too late now, I have, and she needs to know the truth so she can have the chance to grieve.

'It wasn't only Aunt Susie who told me your baby didn't survive.' Mum is staring at me and yet it feels as though she is looking straight through me. I don't want her to go into one of her forgetful episodes because I don't want to have to say any of this again; it's too painful. I plough on. 'I've been to Beechmede Hospital and I've spoken to the nurse who was with you for most of the labour. Her name was Linda. Do you remember her?'

The veil that seemed to be falling over her eyes appears to lift.

'Linda,' she says. 'That's it; I've tried to remember her name, but it wouldn't come. It was always just out of reach. Did Linda tell you the truth?'

I'm fighting back tears now. What I'm about to say will end all hope that Jason survived. Honestly, I don't know if I'm doing the right thing, but in my heart I think that if it was me, I would want to end the torture of hoping and praying that there might have been a mistake.

'Linda told me that Jason was laid to rest in a blue coffin in the grounds of the hospital,' I say, gripping her hands even more tightly.

The sound that fills the air is like nothing I have ever heard before – so raw and filled with anguish. I feel like a dagger has been plunged into my heart, so I can only imagine the agony my mum is experiencing. I don't know how to calm her down, but I have to try as her howling screams are terrifying. Over and over, as though all those years of pent up hope are exiting her body.

'Mum,' I say as loudly as I can without shouting while struggling to make myself heard over her continuous shrieking. 'We're going to find him. We'll find where he was laid to rest and we'll visit him together, I promise.'

CHAPTER TWENTY-THREE
Wednesday, 9 January

All morning I've been making valiant attempts to stifle the yawns brought on by a lack of sleep last night. I hope none of the patrons in the library have noticed the weird expressions I've been pulling as I've gone about my duties. Maxine hasn't said anything, but she did bring me a black coffee for my elevenses an hour ago, which she handed over with a knowing wink. I am so lucky to have such an understanding boss.

Wednesday is my favourite day of the week as we have Ella, a university student, come in from midday to help out. That means it's the one day that Maxine and I can sit down to lunch together. I can't wait for lunchtime to come as not only am I really hungry, having missed breakfast because I overslept and then had a mad rush to get the girls to school, there are also a few things I want to run past her today.

Eventually, 12.30 arrives and I leave Ella holding the fort while I head to the kitchen. Maxine already has the kettle on.

'More coffee?' she asks, raising her eyebrows. 'Or are you awake enough to have a tea now?'

I normally have only one or two cups of coffee a day so I'm feeling pretty wired after my third one. It's a relief to be able to switch to my usual beverage.

'Tea would be great,' I say. 'I think I can make it through the rest of the day without any further hits of caffeine.'

'There's caffeine in tea, you know,' she says, pulling the box of PG Tips out of the cupboard. 'Just not in the same quantity as coffee.'

'You'd be great to have on a pub quiz team with all the little snippets of information you store,' I say reaching into the fridge for our sandwiches. 'Not that Ben and I have been to the pub on quiz night lately, or any other night for that matter. Cheese and pickle or egg mayo, or shall we have one of each?'

'Happy to share if you are,' she says, in a tone of voice that suggests she's not only talking about the sandwiches.

I get two plates and divide the sandwiches out while Maxine adds milk to our teas and then we sit munching in comfortable silence for a couple of minutes before I take the plunge.

'This whole thing with Mum and her stillborn baby is moving at quite a pace now. Remember I told you that Grace, the receptionist at Beechmede Hospital, said the records office could take weeks or even months to look into things? Well, they rang yesterday as I was leaving Mum's to collect the girls from school and guess what?'

'Don't tell me they've found where Jason is buried?' Maxine says, pausing with her sandwich halfway to her mouth.

'Not exactly, but they have given me his hospital number and they also said that there was only one area that the groundsman used for burials because the rest of the hospital grounds are prone to flooding. Not only that, they've given me permission to go and look for his burial cross; I can hardly believe it.'

I'm pretty sure Maxine can hear the excitement in my voice. I wanted to go to the hospital to search for Jason straightaway yesterday, but the light was already fading by the time I'd picked Amber and Jade up and besides, I couldn't leave Mum on her own after the distressed state she'd been in earlier in the afternoon. Martin sat in with her while I did the school run and then I stayed until she went to bed last night. Once again, I'd had to impose on Martin's good nature and ask him to sleep over on the sofa.

'That's incredible,' Maxine says. 'What are you doing here when you could be up at Beechmede?'

'Ben doesn't want me to go alone and he couldn't get out of the training course he's on today.' The surprise is evident on Maxine's face and matches the way I felt when we spoke about it this morning. 'He claims it's because where the babies are buried is quite a remote part of the grounds, but I think he's more worried about how emotional I might get.'

He has a point. Everything is moving so fast and I've only had a few days to process the information that I had a baby brother. It's part of the reason that I couldn't sleep last night. Every time I closed my eyes, I kept seeing a baby's face with its eyes closed as though sleeping. The weirdest thing was that it was my younger brother Adam's face that I kept seeing. I haven't decided whether to tell Adam about Jason before he comes back from New Zealand; maybe that's why I'm seeing his face. My conscience is telling me he has a right to know too.

'So, we're going to go up there together tomorrow as long as it doesn't snow,' I say.

'Good. And for what it's worth, I think it would be very odd if you didn't feel emotional,' Maxine says. 'Have you told your mum about it yet?'

'No. She was terribly upset yesterday when I told her that I had spoken to Linda, and she had confirmed that Jason was stillborn.'

Mentioning Linda's name has made me realise that I forgot to return her call. It completely went out of my head after the call from the records office. I'll try her number once I've finished my lunch. Maybe she was ringing to tell me the good news that the records office already had some information for me.

'I want to find Jason's actual grave before we tell Mum, always assuming that his little cross is still there marking the spot. Her first impression of where Jason has lain all these years will be so important to her, so I also want to be able to tidy it up a bit if it's all overgrown. Apparently, that whole area is awash with bluebells in the spring, which makes me feel happy.'

'I'm sure you don't need me to tell you that you'll have to tread very carefully,' Maxine says.

I nod. Mum is increasingly fragile, but when she'd eventually calmed down after her hysterical outpouring yesterday, she'd said, 'Find him for me, Danni. I want to see my son's resting place before I'm laid to rest myself.' Maxine's right; I have a huge responsibility resting on my shoulders.

'I… I don't suppose you'd consider being with me when I tell Mum, would you? I know it's a big ask, but you seemed to really hit it off with her at Christmas. I'm still not sure what you said to her that seemed to keep her impatience with me at bay.'

Maxine smiles. 'She needed something tangible to remind her to be kind towards you. The softness of the shawl you bought her couldn't have been more apt. I just suggested that each time she felt herself getting cross or anxious, she should touch it to calm herself.'

I think back to Christmas and my mum stroking the shawl. I hadn't read anything into it at the time, just assuming she liked the feel of it, but now it makes perfect sense. Maxine is so intuitive; she seems able to judge every situation and act accordingly.

'I know it's a bit cheeky of me to ask, so please, say no, if you'd rather not.'

'I'm just wondering if it would be better for you to be with Ben when you tell her? He's had quite a lot to deal with over the past few months which must have put a strain on the closeness of your relationship,' she says, appearing to choose her words with care. 'It might be a good idea to show him how much you value his support?'

Although it's not exactly a criticism, Maxine's comment has caught me off guard. 'He knows how much I value everything he does for our family,' I say defensively.

'I'm sure he does, Danni, but you said yourself that you two haven't been out together much recently because you're spending every spare minute with your mum. But you don't want Ben to feel as though you are pushing him away. When Diana dies, you're going to need his love and support more than ever.'

Once again, I can't help thinking that Maxine would have made a wonderful counsellor. She has such a calm and measured way of making her point. And she's right; things have been a little more strained between Ben and me lately, particularly over the business of him contacting the estate agent. Following Mum's appointment with Dr Ranjid yesterday, I messaged Ben to ask him to call Ballard and Ross to see if the prospective purchasers were still interested in Mum's house. Fortunately, they are, so now I just have to persuade Mum to sign the document to allow us to put her house on the market. Once she's done that, we can organise a viewing for them when I next take Mum for a hospital appointment to minimise any distress at having strangers looking around her home.

'You're right,' I say. 'If we do find Jason's grave, it should be Ben by my side when I tell Mum.' Without thinking, I add, 'You'd have made an amazing mother, Max, you always give the best advice.'

'Motherhood isn't for everyone,' she says with a wistful smile.

I'm not sure what she means by that. Did she not want to have children, or did she never meet the right person to have children with? I decide not to pursue it. Instead, I gather up the plates and mugs from our lunch and carry them over to the sink to wash.

'Thanks for the sandwiches,' I say, adding a dash of washing-up liquid to the running water. When she doesn't reply, I glance back over my shoulder, but her chair is empty. I wish Maxine found it as easy to open up to me as I do to her.

After I've washed, dried and put away the crockery, I decide to call Linda at Beechmede Hospital, but it goes straight to voicemail. I leave a short message simply saying, 'I'll try again later.' Halfway through the afternoon my phone vibrates, and I can see it's a text message from her;

Hi Danni, I'm sorry I missed your call, but I have back-to-back appointments all day today. Mindful of how poorly your mum is and knowing how long the records office can take with things, I had a bit of a snoop around at work yesterday and managed to find a forwarding address for Ray Pullinger, the groundsman, although he may no longer live there as we are talking forty-four years ago. Let me know if you'd like me to send it to you. Diana and Jason have been constantly in my thoughts since our conversation on Friday. I so want her to find the peace she deserves. I hope this helps.

Linda x

What a kind and thoughtful thing to do, particularly as Linda could have got into trouble if she'd been caught looking at private files. I feel bad that she's put herself at risk when it wasn't necessary as the records office has already provided me with the information I need. I don't say that in my reply though:

Thanks so much, Linda. I'll have a think about it and I'll keep you posted on Mum's condition.

Danni xx

I shake my head, trying to rid myself of the thought that sprang into my mind as I was typing. *I should invite her to Mum's funeral.*

'Mum's not dead yet,' I mutter under my breath, as I continue organising the books.

CHAPTER TWENTY-FOUR
Thursday, 10 January

Ben has only managed to get the morning off work, but I'm hoping that will give us enough time to locate Jason's grave. Neither of us speak much on the drive over to Beechmede after dropping our girls at St Bede's. We reached the joint decision not to tell them about Jason as there doesn't seem any point in putting them under any further stress.

They've both coped pretty well with their grandmother's ill health, but it hasn't all been plain sailing, particularly the chat we had about why my mum and I had been so distant in the early part of their childhood. Growing up, they saw more of Ben's parents, who'd moved to the Isle of Skye when Ben had left home to go to university, than of my mother who lived in the same town. I didn't exactly tell them that their nana barely even recognised their existence until their Uncle Adam had left for New Zealand. No, I softened things a bit, saying that being a single parent wasn't easy and didn't leave much time for extended family.

They seemed to accept that as an explanation, but then Jade surprised me by asking why their nana always seemed to be so angry with me. She exchanged a look with her sister when she asked, suggesting that the two of them had talked about it between themselves. It was a tricky question for me to answer. I didn't want to blame it entirely on Mum's dementia so was truthful and said that I'd felt pushed out from the moment Adam was born because my mum had focussed all her attention on him. Amber said she was glad I've been able to share my love equally between them, which had resulted in the three of us having a group hug.

I can feel the pace of my heartbeat gradually increasing as we turn off the main driveway onto a narrow gravel trail. It leads to a little copse of trees which, according to hospital records, Ray Pullinger chose as a burial ground for the babies who had been denied life. Having given birth to two healthy babies myself, it's impossible for me to imagine the devastation of being told that the tiny being you've been nurturing inside you for nine months hasn't made the final hurdle. Part of me understands the reasoning behind whisking stillborn infants away from their mothers: the image of the tiny still being that should have been filling its lungs with air before filling the air with sound, would last a lifetime. But the other part of me thinks that at least they would have an image of their child, a memory to hold onto, almost as though their baby was sleeping peacefully. That's what Mum and other mothers like her had been denied and it just feels wrong.

Ben pulls the car to a halt as the trail peters out completely. He reaches for my gloved hand and gives it a squeeze.

'Are you sure you want to do this?' he asks.

I nod.

'Come on then, we'd better make a start,' he says, opening the door and stepping out onto grass still stiff from the overnight frost.

He's brought a torch, but I'm not sure we're going to need it. The skies are bright blue overhead, and the winter sun gives the impression of warmth until I step out of my side of the car and realise the trick mother nature has played on us. I'm grateful for my quilted coat and knitted bobble hat as I follow Ben along a very narrow path partially obscured by bracken. I almost bump into him when he stops abruptly.

'Over there,' he says, pointing to the right.

My eyes follow where his arm is indicating, and my heart skips a beat. Only just visible above the brown fronds of bracken is the top of a very low picket fence. It appears to be encircling an oak tree and looks as though at one time it might have been painted white. Years of neglect and the effect of being under the dappled shade of the trees have turned it green as the moss has been allowed to take hold. I don't know what I imagined, but it wasn't this. Maybe I'd thought it would be more random. From this distance, and because the bracken has been allowed to invade the area, none of the crosses are visible, but I know they are there and I feel certain we are going to find the one bearing Jason's number: 843.

'Okay?' Ben asks.

'Yes,' I reply. Although my voice is trembling, I know this is the right thing to do for both Mum and me. And when Adam arrives home from New Zealand, I'll bring him up here too when I tell him about Jason. I've been sending him regular emails, but have avoided calling him as I'm not sure I would feel right keeping the discovery that we had an elder brother from him in conversation. I want us to be together when he finds out.

Without me asking him to, Ben steps aside to let me lead the way. I'm glad he does that. He knows how important this is to me and it shows the level of understanding that has developed between us over fifteen and a half years of marriage. My legs feel a little wobbly as I move forward along the path towards the perimeter fence of this miniature graveyard. The closer we get, the more obvious it becomes that a great deal of thought had gone into the planning of this special place where the babies could rest in peace. Standing at the gap in the fence through which the path passes, I can see pieces of wood, lots of them, poking through the bracken. I assume they must be the tops of the crosses and although I'm not a religious person it feels right to drop my head and take a moment to remember all these lost souls, not only Jason.

After a few moments, Ben breaks the silence.

'There seems to be a bit of a pattern,' he says, looking around him. 'They appear to fan out from the base of the oak tree in three rows. Maybe we should check the numbers closest to the tree first to give us an idea of where to look for Jason.'

I nod and head towards the tree whose branches reach out over the graves as though offering them protection. When I'm close enough to touch the tree, whose trunk suggests it has stood on this spot for hundreds of years, I rest my hand on the gnarled bark in an attempt to gather strength for what I'm about to undertake. Ben is already down on his haunches, gently pulling back the undergrowth to peer at one of the crosses.

'It looks as though your groundsman has put more than just the case numbers on the crosses,' he says looking up at me. 'I think this one says, "Baby Welbeck" and in brackets it says girl, followed by the number 527. He's even carved the date underneath, March 1971. I wonder if he organised them by the numbers or the dates, or whether it's alphabetical?' He carefully moves his feet further from the path and starts to examine the next cross.

If Ray Pullinger organised the graves alphabetically, Jason might be lying very close to where I'm standing. It probably sounds pathetic, but I want to be the one to uncover my brother's grave, so I immediately bend down to examine the cross closest to the path on the left-hand side.

As I'm clearing the weeds away and gently rubbing at the moss with my gloved hand, Ben says, 'No, I think it's numerical. This one is "Baby Johnson", number 476. It looks like he buried them clockwise around the base of the tree and then started a second and third row when it became necessary.'

While he's speaking, I finally clear enough of the moss to be able to read the writing on the cross I'm examining. I catch my breath. The baby whose cross I'm looking at was given a name, just like Jason. This little boy was called Graham... Graham Pullinger.

A shiver runs through me. I've been wondering why Ray was so thoughtful, and now it's become clear. He and his wife must have experienced the devastation of losing a baby first-hand. I examine the cross again, looking for the date. April 1969. Maybe he originally buried their son in this peaceful location, which in the spring would be awash with bluebells, so that he and his wife had somewhere to visit. When the next stillborn infant was taken from its mother, he must have decided to treat it in the same way as his own child.

'Yes, definitely numerical,' Ben says. 'This one is 431. What was Jason's number again? I think we can probably move to the third row and start looking there to save us some time. Danni? Are you alright?' he asks when I don't answer.

I get to my feet and turn to face him.

'It looks as though the Pullingers had a stillborn baby too,' I say through my tears. 'This cross bears the name Graham Pullinger. I'll bet that's how this little graveyard came to be.'

Ben moves towards me as quickly as he dares, treading carefully between the crosses, and pulls me into a hug. I'm properly sobbing now. Although Graham never had a life, at least he had two parents who loved and wanted him so much that they created a special place for him to rest. My brother wasn't so lucky. He was laid to rest in his little blue box with no one to mourn him. I'd always known this would be emotional, but I don't think I had any idea how overwhelmed with grief I would feel.

Not long after we've established that there is a pattern to the burials, Ben discovers a second cross bearing Ray's surname. I am bending down to examine a cross, when Ben reads out the name 'Luke Pullinger'. According to the date carved, he was buried in September 1974, shortly before my brother. To lose one baby is devastating, but to lose a second must have been indescribably painful.

I'm still reeling from the discovery when I realise I've found my brother. Like the others, the cross bearing Jason's details is green with moss, but the carving is still intact. I take my gloves off, despite the freezing temperature, and run my fingers along first the letters, then the numbers and finally the date. Such care was taken by Ray Pullinger to ensure that these little humans left their mark on the world, despite never having experienced life. I'm going to get the address off Linda and write to him to express my gratitude.

For almost two hours, Ben and I clear the undergrowth away from the crosses and pathways inside the picket fence. Once we've finished, although it looks much more cared-for, I'm worried that we might not have done the right thing. What had been a secret place is now visible to anyone who happens to be walking through the little wood. There are some unpleasant people living in our world and I fervently hope that no one will desecrate this little sanctuary now that it has been unearthed.

'Do you think we should put a sign up saying "Trespassers will be prosecuted" or some such thing?' I say to Ben as we finally head back down the path towards his car.

'No, I think that would just draw more attention to it. Hopefully in the depths of winter there won't be too many people out walking, and by the time the spring comes the bluebells will be out and will disguise the crosses. When were you planning on bringing Diana up here?'

'I was wondering about Sunday morning. I thought we could both bring her, if you don't mind.'

'Of course I don't, we're in this together. But what about the girls? I'm not really keen on leaving them home alone at the moment.'

'I mentioned it to Maxine, and she's offered to pop around to ours to keep an eye on them.'

'Good plan. You're lucky to have her, you know. She's been like a surrogate mother to you.'

'I know; it's sad to think she never had any children of her own to share her wisdom with. It seems so unjust. There's my mum with an unplanned pregnancy and then a daughter who she really didn't want and never really loved.'

'I don't think that's true,' Ben says, holding the passenger door open for me to get in. 'She wanted a boy to replace the son she lost, and she never found a way to get past her disappointment. It doesn't mean she didn't love you; it just means she didn't know how to show it.'

He closes the door and I watch him walk around the back of the car in the rear-view mirror. He still makes me feel exactly the same as I did that first night when I pretended to be his blind date. He's my rock and I know that I don't tell him often enough how much I love him. He slides into the driver's seat and turns the engine on, turning the heater up to maximum.

'Are you going to tell Diana about finding Jason's grave, or should we just bring her out here?' he says.

'I don't know, what do you think?'

Ben is quiet for a moment as he concentrates on reversing his car back down the narrow trail towards the main Beechmede driveway. Once he's back on tarmac, he says, 'I think maybe bring her here and take her to the grave. If you tell her first, she won't rest until she's seen it. At least this way you'll have more control over things and we'll both be here to support her physically and emotionally.'

'Thank you,' I say, turning my head to look out of the window. I don't want Ben to see my eyes filling with tears yet again.

CHAPTER TWENTY-FIVE
Saturday, 12 January

To say things aren't exactly going to plan this morning would be a massive understatement.

I was about to leave the house with the girls to head over to Mum's while Ben did the supermarket shop, when my mobile rang. It was Martin.

'You need to get over here straightaway,' he said without any preamble. His voice sounded sharp and most unlike the Martin I knew.

'What's wrong?' I asked immediately, tensing up. 'Is Mum okay?'

'Not exactly; she's leaning out of her bedroom window screaming at the people who've come to view the house,' he said.

'View the house?' I repeated, parrot-fashion. 'That's not supposed to be happening yet.'

'So, the house is up for sale then?' he snapped. 'Were you planning on telling your mother, or me for that matter?'

'Oh, Martin, I'm so sorry. You weren't supposed to find out like this. I'll be there as quickly as I can.' I ended the call and rounded on Ben. 'What the hell's going on?' I demanded. 'Why is the estate agent at Mum's house for a viewing?'

For a moment, he looked as taken aback as me. Then he seemed to realise what might have happened. 'Ballard and Ross mentioned a possible viewing date of the 22nd to me once we've given them

Diana's written consent. I'm guessing someone thought it was a firm appointment and arranged the viewing for today after misreading the date.'

I stormed out of the house, telling Ben he'd have to take the girls supermarket shopping with him and threatening to get whoever had made the error at the estate agent's sacked for incompetence.

I'm a little calmer when I arrive at Mum's ten minutes later, but only because I know I need to be. As I pull into the kerb outside her house, I can see her at her bedroom window, which thankfully is now closed. Martin is waiting for me on the pavement outside her gate, hopping from foot to foot as though standing on burning coals. There's no one else around, although I'm pretty sure I notice a few curtains twitching in neighbouring houses as I get out of my car. Clearly, they've been watching the drama unfold. I wave in the vague direction of the neighbour who lives over the road from Mum which, childish as it may seem, gives me a small sense of satisfaction.

'Do you want to come in and tell me what happened, Martin?' I ask as I unlock the front gate.

He pushes past me, muttering, 'You've got a lot of explaining to do.'

By the time I've locked the gate and unlocked the front door, Mum is at the foot of her stairs glowering at me. I immediately notice she's not wearing her shawl, which she's had draped around her shoulders every day since Christmas.

'You're not welcome here,' she says. She's not shouting now; her voice is low and icy. 'How dare you put *my* house up for sale without asking me?'

'It's not up for sale yet, Mum, we wouldn't be able to do that without your consent, but we do need to talk about it,' I say, taking a step towards her.

'Don't come any closer,' she says, 'or I'll call the police, and have you arrested for trespassing.'

'Come on, Mum, you're being ridiculous. We both know what Dr Ranjid said on Tuesday. It's not safe for you to live on your own anymore, even with Martin's kind support. That's why he gave us the brochures, so that we can choose a care home where you will always have someone on hand to look after you.'

While I'm speaking, I notice she is clenching and unclenching her fists.

'You – don't – make – decisions – for – me,' she says, getting louder with each individual word. 'You don't care about me, so stop pretending that you do. All you want is to sell my house and take the money for yourself because you're broke. It's not my fault you got yourself pregnant and had to marry someone who doesn't earn enough money to support his family.'

If she'd slapped my face it would have stung less. Her accusations are horrible; we may not have much money, but Ben is one of the kindest, most loving people you could ever wish to meet, and I couldn't be more thankful that fate threw us together. Even making allowances for her dementia, how dare she speak about him in that way. And her comment about getting myself pregnant, using the exact same phrase that had so appalled me when Aunt Susie said it about my mum, is even more distasteful. If blood could actually boil, mine would be. I glance briefly at Martin. Cowering is probably the most accurate way to describe his posture as he stands in the doorway to the kitchen looking like a rabbit caught in headlights.

'Martin, would you be able to stay with Mum for a while?' I say, struggling to keep the wobble from my voice. 'I need to take a moment.'

'I don't need a bloody babysitter!' Mum shouts. 'I want you both to get out of my house, right now.'

Martin hesitates, looking from one to the other of us. 'I'll be next door if you need me, Diana,' he says withdrawing into the kitchen before letting himself out of the back door.

'Are you satisfied now?' I demand. Martin has put me in a difficult position; I don't want to leave Mum on her own while she's so agitated, but I need space to calm down and collect my thoughts – so I don't say something I'll later regret. 'I'm going to head off for a while. I'll bring the girls over later if you can promise to be civil to them,' I say, turning my back on her to unlock the front door in order to let myself out.

'Don't bother; I'm sick of the sight of them, particularly Jade. It's like looking at you all over again and God knows I never wanted that first time around.'

For a second, I'm too upset to speak and then something inside me just snaps. I've put up with my mother saying some awful things to me throughout my life, but I won't tolerate her speaking about my girls in that way. All the pent-up anger from years of Mum either ignoring me or criticising me, combined with the stress and emotion of caring for her, explode as I spin around to face her.

'You evil, ungrateful bitch,' I scream. 'Grandma was right when she said you brought everything on yourself. If you hadn't claimed your sister's boyfriend got you pregnant none of this would have happened. Jason deserved better than a mother like you.' I can see shock register on Mum's face, but she's opened the floodgates now and there is no way to stem the tide. 'I'm glad he died; he was luckier than me because he was spared having you as a parent!' I know I'm completely out of control, but I'm unable to stop myself. 'To think I've actually been feeling sorry for you. Well, I don't feel sorry for you anymore. You've got nothing more than you deserve. It's punishment for all the people you've hurt and all the lives you've ruined. I hope you rot in hell!'

The silence that follows my outburst is deafening, broken only by the thunderous pounding of my heart and the rhythmic ticking of the kitchen wall clock. I'm shaking like a leaf, such is my fury, and my cheeks are wet from the angry tears that I didn't realise I was crying. Almost in slow-motion Mum sinks onto the bottom step of the staircase. Her face is ashen. Immediately, I feel incredibly guilty over the things I've just shouted at this dying woman. I'm torn. Filled with remorse, I want to rush over to her and put my arms around her, begging to be forgiven, but I'm terrified my attempt will be rebuffed and if she pushes me away now, I don't think I'll ever set foot in this house again. I don't know what to do; I wish Ben or Maxine was here. I feel so inadequate.

'I had no idea you hated me quite so much,' she suddenly says, her voice tiny and almost childlike. 'I can't say I blame you; I haven't been a very good mother, have I?'

I don't speak. There's nothing I can say. She hasn't been a good mother; in fact, she's barely been a mother to me at all. I'm starting to unpick her history and understand the reasons why, but that doesn't make it any easier to accept that I was a disappointment to her from the moment she gave me life. The clock ticks on; seconds extend into minutes with her crumpled on the bottom step and me stood rigidly in her hallway not two feet away.

'You're wrong, you know,' she says, lifting her eyes to look into mine. All I can see there is pain; no confusion, no anger, just pure pain. 'I didn't tell them that Kevin was the baby's father, I just didn't deny it,' she adds, blinking rapidly.

Finally, I find my voice, 'Why not?'

'Because… because it was the truth,' she whispers, her whole body slumping forward as though the effort of finally saying those words out loud has drained her.

Aunt Susie hadn't wanted to believe that her boyfriend was the father of Mum's baby and had put doubt in my mind, but it was true. What on earth was Mum thinking having sex with her sister's boyfriend?

As though she's reading my mind, she says, 'It's not what you think, Danni.'

Something about the tone of her voice touches a nerve. I take a few deep breaths before saying, 'Do you want to tell me about it?'

She nods and reaches a hand out in my direction for me to help her to her feet. She's shaking, so I put my arm around her shoulders and usher her into the lounge. I sit her down in her favourite chair and pull up the small ottoman that she keeps her knitted blanket in so that I can be close to her. I hold her hands, waiting for her to start talking. I'm not confident that I'll get the whole story before her mind starts to play tricks on her, but if she feels safe there might be a better chance.

'So, what happened, Mum?' I gently prompt.

'Susan got the looks in our family and I got the brains. I always had my head in books studying while she preferred to be out with her friends at the Youth Club. That's where she met Kevin,' Mum says, her voice faltering. 'He was really good-looking and charming too, and my sister couldn't believe her luck when he asked her out on a date. Our mother liked him straightaway, but our father wasn't too keen on him at first because he was a couple of years older. Kevin gradually won him over though and he was soon spending so much time at our house, he was like part of the family.' Mum stops speaking, and for a moment I think she's lost her train of thought but then she continues. 'Susan used to tease me that I'd never attract boys if I didn't make an effort with my appearance, so one afternoon while she was at hockey practice I snuck into her room and tried on some of her clothes and make-up. I… I didn't hear him come in. Susan's skirt was really short, and when he touched my leg, I should have stopped him.'

My mouth feels dry. I can't believe what I'm hearing. Kevin took advantage of an innocent situation and my mum seems to think she was to blame for not stopping him.

'It wasn't your fault, Mum. He had no right to lay a finger on you.'

'But I could have stopped him, Danni, and I chose not to,' she says blinking rapidly again. 'The truth is, I didn't want him to stop. He made me feel special.'

I'm momentarily speechless, which Mum misunderstands.

'You must hate me even more, now that you know what I did.'

'*You* didn't do it, Mum, *he* did,' I say, trying to keep calm. 'Whether or not Kevin intended to have sex with you, he abused his position of trust in the most deplorable way. And yet it's you who's paid an enormous price. Whatever he said to try to convince you otherwise, it was his doing not yours.'

Mum is shaking her head. She doesn't want to accept that he was to blame.

'Even if you'd stripped naked and done a dance, he should have been able resist any temptation,' I persist. 'Please tell me you understand that what he did was wrong.'

It's as though she hasn't heard me when she continues speaking.

'After it was over, he told me he was sorry and that it would never happen again. He said he'd made a terrible mistake.' Mum's bottom lip is trembling. 'I felt dirty then. That's when I knew it was all my fault and that I had to keep it secret because my sister would never forgive me. But then I missed my period. I was so frightened; I didn't know what to do. I thought if I told people about what happened with Kevin, they wouldn't believe me because I'd said nothing at the time. I was afraid everyone would hate me for telling lies about him when he was so nice.'

'Stop it, Mum!' I shriek, unable to control my emotions. 'Anyone who can sleep with their girlfriend's sister isn't nice! He should have had the decency to own up to what he did and face the consequences instead of allowing a fifteen-year-old girl to shoulder the blame. His actions destroyed your family – *our* family.'

Mum removes her hands from mine and brings them up to her face, fingertips resting against her forehead with the heels of her palms pressing into her eyes.

'I didn't betray Kevin. My dad was ranting and raving. He wanted to know how I could be pregnant when the only boy they'd ever seen me talk to was Kevin. If only he hadn't said, "I suppose you're going to claim he's the father", I would have kept it a secret. But when he said that, I couldn't lie, so I just didn't say anything.'

'Let me get this straight. Your mum and dad had reason to believe that Kevin had slept with you, their underage daughter, and yet they didn't report him to the police. I'm sorry, Mum, but I'm struggling to understand why they believed him rather than you?'

'I'm not sure they did. They just wanted the whole mess to go away. They probably thought that the less fuss they made, the quicker people would forget about me having an illegitimate child. It didn't matter who the father was because I was never going to be allowed to keep him,' she says, wrapping her arms around herself in a hug and gently rocking backwards and forwards.

It's a pitiful sight. I want to throw my arms around her and hold her like I used to hold my girls when they'd had a bad dream, but I'm not sure that would help. Mum lived through this nightmare and it can't simply be hugged away.

'Jason was all I had. I used to talk to him, tell him how much I loved him, and I felt like he loved me back when everyone else was being so unkind. I thought they would let me hold him, Danni,' she says, reaching one of her hands out for mine and gripping it tightly. 'I knew I had to give him up, but I just wanted to see his face and hold his tiny hand for a few minutes. My boy; my Jason. I loved him so much.' Tears are now flowing freely down her cheeks. 'I hope they loved him as much as I did and gave him a good home.'

The last time I hugged my mum, she pushed me away, but I can't stop myself from dropping to my knees and enveloping this broken woman in my arms. I continue with the motion she started, rocking her gently as I used to do with my girls. Tears are streaming down my face too as I struggle with the decision I must make. Despite me telling her that both Aunt Susie and Linda have confirmed that baby Jason was stillborn, Mum obviously wants to believe that Jason survived. I know that's untrue; I've seen where his body was laid to rest. I thought I was doing the right thing by searching for the proof that Jason died in childbirth. I'd hoped that by taking Mum to his grave and letting her grieve for the baby she was never allowed to hold, it would close a chapter of her life that had been unfinished for over forty years, only now I'm not so sure. If the doctors are to be believed, Mum only has months to live so why not let her live out her days believing that her firstborn child had a happy life with his adoptive parents?

Because you know it's a lie, and there have already been too many lies.

'Mum,' I say, swallowing hard, 'there's something I need to tell you.'

She pulls away from my arms and slumps back in her chair.

'If it's about putting the house up for sale, we can talk about it later. I know it will have to be sold to pay the care home fees. Don't worry, I'll sign the paperwork giving you authority to act on my behalf.'

It's an enormous relief to hear her say that, but it's not what I want to talk about. 'Actually,' I say, 'there's something else.'

'Can it wait, Danni? I'm not feeling so good. This has all been a bit much for me. I think I need to have a lie-down.'

Mum looks pale. Revealing the truth has clearly taken its toll. I'm glad she's finally told me about Jason, but I'm feeling enormously guilty that I had to force it from her in the manner I did.

'I'm sorry I shouted at you, Mum,' I say, looking into her troubled eyes. 'I shouldn't have said such awful things.'

'It's me who should apologise,' she replies. 'I don't know why you bother with me when I've never been the mother I should have to you.' I start to speak, but she wearily raises her hand to stop me. 'Time and again you've given me the chance to show you how much you mean to me, and each time I've thrown it back in your face. I don't deserve you, Danni,' she says, reaching for my hand and holding it tightly as though her life depends on it.

Maybe I'm supposed to feel elated that she has admitted to never having been a proper mother to me, but I don't. All I feel is sadness that we have so little time left. Gently, I pull her to her feet. 'Come on,' I say, 'let's get you upstairs, you look completely shattered.'

Mum's eyes are barely open, and she leans heavily on me as we climb the stairs and I push open the door of her bedroom. I pull back the covers and she slips between the sheets; she closes her eyes the moment her head hits the pillow and within moments the even rise and fall of her chest indicates she is sleeping. I move around the bottom of her bed towards the window to draw the curtains. The shawl I bought her for Christmas is lying in a heap on the floor. That's why she wasn't wearing it; it must have slipped off her shoulders when she was shouting at the estate agent. I stoop to pick it up and am surprised to see a small piece of the beautiful fabric is in my hand, but the rest remains on the floor. For a brief moment I wonder if Mum caught it on something and a piece tore off. Then I notice the scissors lying on the floor next to the brightly coloured pile and quickly raise my hand to my mouth to prevent myself from exclaiming out loud. The shawl has been cut to shreds, the jagged and frayed edges suggesting it was in some kind of frenzied attack.

I glance over at Mum to make sure she is still sleeping before I slip the scissors into the pocket of my jeans and scoop up all the fabric pieces into my sweatshirt to carry downstairs and dispose of. If I can persuade Martin to come around and sit with Mum, I should just about have time to pop into the town centre and buy her a replacement before she wakes up. She's going to need the comfort of stroking her shawl when I take her to the burial site at Beechmede Hospital tomorrow.

CHAPTER TWENTY-SIX

Sunday, 13 January

It's another bitterly cold morning as I stand on our front doorstep waiting for Maxine to finish parking her Mini on the roadside. Unlike Thursday morning, when it was cold but bright, the sky has the kind of silvery-whiteness that threatens snow. I hope Mum won't want to stay at Jason's graveside for too long. Even wrapped up in her winter coat and with her shawl around her neck and shoulders, she could easily get a chill and that's the last thing her frail body needs.

It was a mad rush yesterday to drive into town, get parked along with all the other Saturday morning shoppers, buy the shawl and then meet up with Ben to transfer the girls to my car and get back to Mum's before she woke. After thanking Martin for keeping an ear open for her and promising to explain what had happened with the estate agent over the phone later in the day, I went upstairs to wake Mum, having sent the girls into the kitchen to warm some soup to have with the fresh bread I'd bought at Poppy's. She was already sitting up in bed. I handed over the bag containing the new shawl and she raised her eyes to meet mine when she realised what it was. Neither of us said anything, but for those few precious seconds we connected in a way we hadn't previously.

The afternoon passed happily. Mum, with her new shawl draped around her shoulders, sat with my girls listening to music while I washed up and then we all watched *The Sound of Music* on the television. Ben arrived at half past six with a fish and chip supper for us all and then he took the girls home with him while I stayed a bit longer to make sure Mum was settled for the evening. I've started making her a flask of warm milk to save her having to get the saucepan out. As I put it on the small table at the side of her favourite chair, she reached out her hand and rested it on my arm.

'Did we talk this morning?' she asked tentatively.

That's the thing with Mum's illness; she's often unsure whether she has said something out loud or whether it has all been in her head.

'About what, Mum?' I asked in return.

'Jason's father.'

'Yes, we talked. I know it was Kevin and if it's alright with you, I'm going to tell Aunt Susie what actually happened.'

Her eyes widened fearfully. 'Must you tell her?'

'I think she should know that her wonderful boyfriend forced himself on her kid sister and then denied it.'

'Do you think she'll be able to forgive me?'

I wasn't sure whether to feel angry or sad. Mum still felt guilty for the terrible thing Kevin had done despite my efforts to convince her otherwise.

'Maybe it needs to be mutual,' I said.

She didn't reply but sat for a few moments, stroking her shawl and nodding her head as though she was mulling it over.

'Girls, Maxine's here,' I call up the stairs now as Maxine walks up the path towards me. 'I hope you're both ready!'

We've told them that we are taking Mum for a drive in the country and they accepted it without question.

'Coming,' they shout in unison.

There are a few minor bangs and crashes before the two of them come thundering down the stairs, both with big smiles on their faces.

'Have you got your pocket-money?' I ask.

Amber raises her eyebrows. 'Allowance, Mum, nobody of our age calls it pocket-money.'

'Yeah, Mum, that's for little kids,' Jade chips in.

'Whatever,' I say. 'Have you got money to spend is the question? I don't want to hear that Maxine treated you to anything after offering to take you.'

I mouth thank you at Maxine before she heads off down the path with them. They're all laughing as they get into her Mini and I just catch the words, 'she won't know if we don't tell her', as the car doors slam shut.

'Phase one complete,' Ben says, startling me. I didn't realise he'd crept up behind me. 'We'd better make tracks if we're going to beat the snow.'

I've sat in the back seat of Ben's car with Mum on the journey. I want to keep her occupied when we approach the turn-off from the main road. It's been over twenty years since she was last at Beechmede for Adam's birth, so I'm fairly confident she won't recognise her surroundings once we're on the hospital drive. The risk is of her seeing signs for the hospital as we get closer, so I make sure I'm pointing things out on a map at the relevant time. Ben swinging the car off the drive onto the narrow gravel path attracts her attention.

'Have you taken a wrong turn?' she asks. 'This looks like a dead-end. Unless you've brought me out here to bump me off and bury me in among those trees,' she says, smiling as she indicates Jason's copse up ahead. When I don't say anything, she adds, 'You haven't, have you?'

'No, Mum,' I say, reaching for her hand and gently squeezing it. 'But we are going to that little copse.'

'What's going on?' she says, panic building in her voice. 'Ben, what are we doing here?'

He's just pulled the car to a halt. He switches the engine off and turns in his seat to face her.

'We've brought you to see Jason,' he says.

The happy smile from a few moments ago has now completely disappeared. She looks from Ben to me.

'What does he mean, Danni?'

'I found it, Mum – the place where they buried your baby. We wanted to bring you here so you could see where he is resting.'

I'm not sure how I thought Mum would react, but I didn't expect her to black out. It's only for a few seconds, but it scares me; for an awful moment I wonder if bringing her here has caused her to have a heart attack. Ben leaps out of the car, flings the rear door open and he still has his hand under her shawl checking for the pulse in her neck as she starts to come around.

'What are you doing?' she says, terrified.

'Don't panic, Diana,' he says, his voice calm and soothing. 'I was just checking your pulse. You gave us quite a scare.'

The explanation seems to satisfy her, probably because it has come from Ben rather than me.

'He really is dead then?' she says, adjusting her gaze to meet mine, her bottom lip quivering.

I nod. 'I'm so sorry, Mum. I know you've clung onto the hope that he made it and might eventually have come looking for you, but at least you know for sure now and you'll be able to picture this place when you think of him. Do you feel up to seeing his actual grave? We could always bring you back another time if it's too much for you.'

'I want to see it. I want to talk to him,' she says, starting to get out of the car.

Ben supports her by the elbow while I climb out of the other side and walk around to join them. I link my arm through hers, keeping her close on the narrow path with Ben following behind us.

'It's so peaceful here,' I say. 'I think the spot was chosen by the groundsman when he and his wife lost their own child.'

We're at the break in the picket fence and I can feel Mum trembling as her eyes scan the dozens of crosses before us. It's an overwhelming sight even though Ben and I have seen it before.

'Where is he?' Mum says, her voice shaking with emotion. 'Where's my boy?'

'Here he is, Mum; here's Jason.'

Not long after, the snow that has been threatening all morning starts to fall in large flakes which immediately settle. The path, already precarious underfoot, is fast disappearing under a layer of snow and I'm worried that if any of us inadvertently step off the path into the undergrowth it could be disastrous.

Once I've led Mum to Jason's grave, I move back to stand with Ben, giving her some space and privacy to reunite with her son. I can't hear what she's saying, but she talks constantly for the fifteen or so minutes she is stood over his burial spot, the snow falling around her. I'm pretty sure Mum isn't religious – she's never attended church since we've been back in her life – but it's almost as though she's praying.

As more and more flakes settle on the grey woollen hat she is wearing, I take a few steps towards her.

'Mum, I think we're going to have to go now. The snow is getting quite heavy.' She turns to face me, and I'm surprised to see that she is dry-eyed and smiling. 'Are you okay?' I ask.

'Thank you for finding him for me, Danni. You're a good girl.'

I have a huge lump in my throat as I reach for her arm to help guide her back along the path towards the car. In all my thirty-five years, that's the nicest thing she has ever said to me.

CHAPTER TWENTY-SEVEN
Sunday, 13 January

It's past four o'clock by the time we've dropped mum off, collected the girls and finally pulled into our driveway, which in itself is no mean feat as the snow has drifted in the wind and in places is over a foot deep. Jade has gone upstairs to have a bath and Amber is in the kitchen with Ben making a start on the dinner. I ring Mum to let her know we've arrived home safely.

'Danni, at last,' she says. 'I was starting to get really worried. Do you think he'll be alright?'

In light of where we've been earlier in the day, I presume she means Jason. 'He'll be fine, Mum. Think of the snow as a thick blanket to keep him warm.'

'A blanket? He didn't have a blanket with him. He was wearing his navy-blue duffle coat.'

Now I'm totally confused. I have no idea who she is talking about, unless she means Martin. Maybe she sent him out to run an errand and he hasn't returned. 'Who do you mean, Mum?'

'Adam. He went to the corner shop to get some sweets and he's not back yet. I wish I hadn't let him go; I don't like him going out on his own. Do you think I should go and look for him?'

Mum's having one of her confused episodes. I'm pretty sure she can't get out of the front of the house because I remember locking everything from the outside when we left, but the last thing I want is for her to go outside at all in the driving snow. If she slips and falls, she could freeze to death.

'It's probably best if you stay at home while I go and look for him,' I say. 'You wouldn't want the house to be empty if he finds his way back on his own.'

There's a short pause before she says, 'But he's not going to, is he?' I could hear confusion in her voice. 'I've waited for him to come and find me for all these years, but he's dead; you showed me his grave yourself.'

Mum has clearly got muddled up between Adam and Jason. I glance out of the window. The snow is still falling heavily and there's very little chance of Ben and I being able to get over to Mum's house. I need to speak to Martin and get him to go around to Mum's as quickly as possible, but I can't while she's still on the line. I'm about to speak when she starts shouting down the phone line at me.

'Unless you were lying, of course. I'll bet that wasn't his grave at all; you probably just stuck a cross with his name on it in the ground to make me believe he's dead. What is wrong with you, Danielle? Why have you always been so jealous of your brother?' she screams at me.

I put my hand over the mouthpiece of the phone and call out to Ben who hurries into the room. 'You need to ring Martin and get him round to Mum's now,' I say, throwing him my mobile phone. 'She's having a memory lapse and I'm worried she might try and get out of the house.' Ben retreats to the kitchen to make the call while I try to calm my mum.

'I wasn't lying to you about Jason, Mum. That was his grave we took you to this morning, I promise.'

There's another pause, quite a lengthy one this time, and when she speaks, she sounds a lot calmer.

'I want to believe you, but how can I be sure? I want to see the little blue box you claim he was buried in. I want to feel close to my baby son and say goodbye to him. That's all I've ever wanted. Can you do that for me, Danni and then I can die happy?'

As she finishes speaking, I can hear Martin's voice in the background. 'I thought I'd pop around and see if you need anything, Diana.'

'I've got to go now, that man's here again,' Mum says, before abruptly hanging up.

I sink down onto the sofa, relief flooding through me to know that Martin is with Mum. I'm just thinking that he deserves a medal when Amber's voice breaks into my thoughts.

'Who is Jason, and why were you showing Nana his grave?'

I turn to see Amber in the kitchen doorway with Ben standing behind her. There's a difference in not telling someone the whole truth and outright lying to them.

'When Jade comes down from her bath, I'll tell you both all about it,' I say.

Although it's only half past ten, I'm absolutely shattered when I climb into bed and snuggle into Ben's back. He's as warm as a piece of toast.

'Hey,' he says, 'keep your freezing cold feet to yourself. Same goes for your hands,' he adds, as I reach my arm around him.

'You never used to tell me to keep my hands to myself,' I say.

'I'm pretty sure I did if they were cold,' he says, turning to face me. 'Are you alright? It's been a pretty challenging day.'

I rest my cheek against his chest and close my eyes. He's not wrong.

'You were right to tell the girls about Jason after Amber overheard you on the phone and I think you told them just enough.'

'Really? I'm wondering if I should have told them about Aunt Susie's boyfriend being the father.'

'I don't see the point. They don't know her and she's unlikely to be a part of their lives, so do they really need to know all the sordid details? I think it was enough that you said that baby Jason wasn't planned and also how you reassured them both that if anything like that should ever happen to them, they shouldn't be afraid to tell us. You really are an amazing mother,' he says, planting a kiss on my mouth.

'But a pretty rubbish wife at the moment,' I say once my lips are free.

'Sex isn't everything, Danni, and besides, I'm looking forward to you making it up to me once things are a bit more normal.' He tickles my waist until I'm crying with laughter.

When I can speak, I say, 'Have I told you lately that I love you?'

'Are you just quoting a song lyric, or do you mean it?'

'What do you think?' I say hugging him tightly, and this time he doesn't complain about how cold my hands are.

'I think we are very lucky to have each other. It just goes to show that not all lies are bad. If you hadn't pretended to be your friend on that blind date, we may never have got together.'

'I know, but I still shouldn't have lied to you. Speaking of which…' I bring the conversation back to my mum. 'Mum thinks I was lying to her about that being Jason's grave.'

'When did she say that?'

'On the phone, after she'd calmed down from the state she got herself into. She says she wants to see his little blue coffin.'

'You can't seriously be thinking about digging it up?' Ben says.

'Mum sounded so sad. She said she would die happy if she could be close to her baby for a few moments to say her goodbyes. I just want to make her happy.'

'Listen to yourself, Danni. You're talking about digging up a grave. I'm not sure that's even legal. Just leave it, you've done enough.'

'Couldn't we at least try?'

'Absolutely not,' Ben says, with a finality to his voice. 'You found your half-brother's grave and you took your mum there so that she could see where he was laid to rest and grieve for him. That's what you set out to do and it's the end of it. I'm not digging up his grave and to be honest I'm amazed that you'd contemplate it. Leave Jason alone now. He's part of your history and that's where he should stay,' Ben says turning away from me and switching off the bedside lamp.

I know he's probably right, but as I lie in bed trying to get to sleep, the germ of an idea starts to form in my mind. Would it be possible to exhume Jason's remains and move them to our family plot in the cemetery? We could even hold a small funeral service for him. The image of my mum lying in her casket cradling a tiny blue box is the last thing I remember before finally drifting off to sleep. Mum and Jason couldn't be together in life, but maybe they can lie together in death.

CHAPTER TWENTY-EIGHT
Sunday, 20 January

We haven't seen much of Mum for the past week because of the dreadful weather conditions. The snow eventually stopped falling late on Tuesday afternoon, but the temperature is still below freezing and there's no sign of a thaw. School has been cancelled all week while the snow ploughs and gritting lorries tackle the small side roads, having cleared the main roads first. A lot of my time has been taken up with home schooling the girls, but that's okay because the library has also been closed.

We've managed to get out to the shops a couple of times on foot to get the basics, but mostly we've been living on store-cupboard and freezer stuff. I've enjoyed spending more time with Ben and the girls. Building a snowman in our back garden and the snowball fight we had afterwards was great fun, but now I'm keen for things to get back to normal.

Ben and I haven't talked about Jason again. There doesn't seem much point. He's adamant that we've done everything we should, and I don't share his opinion.

The most amazing thing about this week is that Mum actually asked Martin if he would stay over at hers and offered him one of the spare bedrooms rather than the couch. He's rung a couple of times a day with updates, and the girls have chatted to their nana for hours, but I've only actually spoken to her a couple of times. Maybe she's regretting shouting at me and calling me a liar, or maybe she can't even recall it. I hope she's remembered visiting the little graveyard; she looked so happy when she turned to face me after her lengthy conversation with my brother. It's funny how I think of Jason as that now even though I never had the opportunity to know him.

I'm just unloading the washing machine when my mobile rings. I experience the flutter of mild panic that I always do when I think it might be Martin calling with a problem. It's a relief when I see that it's Maxine.

'Hi Danni,' she says, 'I'm just ringing to see if you'll be okay to come into work tomorrow? I was listening to the local news on the radio and the schools are re-opening so I'm going to open the library. I can ask Ella if she can do a couple of hours if it's too tricky for you.'

'It should be fine, Max. To be honest, I was just thinking how much I'm looking forward to getting back to normal. We're going to drive over to Mum's this afternoon so I can get an idea of what the roads are like then, but I'm sure it won't be a problem.'

'How is Diana? Has she had any delayed reaction to seeing your brother's grave?'

Without intending to I'm sure, Maxine has made me feel guilty. She lives alone, so it's pretty selfish of me not to have rung to check she was okay at some point this week considering all the stuff she does for me.

'I'm sorry,' I say, 'I should have called.'

'Don't be silly, you've had your hands full with Amber and Jade off school, and I don't expect Ben's been able to get to work either.'

She has such a generous spirit.

'Mum did have a bit of a moment when I spoke to her after picking the girls up from yours. She questioned whether it was really Jason's grave.'

Now that Maxine has raised the subject, I'm wondering whether to tell her about my idea, despite originally thinking it would be better to talk it over in person. Ben is out at the supermarket and the girls are up in their bedrooms doing their homework, so there is no one around to overhear our conversation.

'I did wonder if she might,' Maxine says, before I can speak. 'Look Danni, this might not be the right thing for Diana, but I've been doing a bit of research on how best to help mothers of stillborn babies who were never given the opportunity to grieve. There's this woman, Rowena Nash, who started a charity to offer support to these mothers after she'd helped trace where her best friend's daughter had been buried. She witnessed first-hand how locating the graves helped in terms of achieving closure.'

'But we've already found Jason,' I say, wondering where she is going with this.

'I know, but I was reading how in some cases parents had requested that the remains be moved to be with the rest of the family graves. I was wondering if that might be something you think would help Diana?'

I can hardly believe what I'm hearing. Ben, my usually sup-portive husband, made me feel as though even suggesting that we should move Jason's remains was somehow ghoulish and yet here is Maxine telling me that other families have already done exactly that.

'Are you still there, Danni?' Maxine asks, a hint of anxiety in her voice. 'Obviously, if it's not something you think would be right for your family, you can forget I ever suggested it. I just thought you should know it's an option.'

'Max, you have no idea how much this means to me,' I eventu-ally manage. 'I've been thinking along similar lines, but Ben is vehemently against it.'

'Try not to blame him for that,' Maxine says. 'It must be difficult for men to imagine the bond that develops between a mother and her unborn baby, even someone as intuitive as Ben. Let's face it, before the 1980s, when the rules surrounding stillborns changed, nobody, not even the health professionals, realised how cruel it was to simply remove a dead infant, without allowing the mother to hold it and say their goodbyes. They didn't think they needed to tell the parents what had happened to their son or daughter and seemed to have no concept of the guilt the mother experienced. Thankfully, attitudes have changed now, but I think some men still find it hard to understand what it does to their partner emotionally.'

I don't know if I'm imagining it, but Maxine's voice is tinged with a sadness which feels personal. I really know very little about my boss's past; maybe she's speaking from experience.

'I know it's a big ask, Max, but if I tell Ben about this and he's still reluctant, would you help me find out how I can go about reuniting Jason with the rest of my family at the cemetery?'

'You know you don't even need to ask,' she replies.

'You see, I've got this image in my head of my mum being laid to rest cradling Jason's little blue burial box. I know it might not be possible, but I'd like to give it a try.'

'I agree. Look, why don't I email Rowena Nash and ask her to help us. Our problem is time. If permission needs to be obtained from the authorities it could take months and we may not have that long. But we might only need permission from the hospital because they own the unconsecrated ground where Jason's buried and I can't really see why they would refuse.'

I love the fact that Maxine is saying 'we' and 'us'. I've never really been one for making friends, always believing that Ben and our girls are enough for me, but I have to admit that since Maxine came into my life, her friendship has given my world a whole new dimension, one that I would hate to be without now. I hear the jangle of keys and realise Ben is back from the supermarket.

'I'll have to go, Max. Ben's home and now is not the moment to talk this through with him. But yes, please send the email. And Max,' I say before ending the call, 'thank you for being such a wonderful friend.'

CHAPTER TWENTY-NINE
Tuesday, 22 January

It's a big day for Mum today and she seems to have made a special effort with her appearance as though to acknowledge it. She's wearing an olive-green wool dress, but that's probably out of necessity as all her skirt and trouser waistbands are far too big for her now. She's also wearing a small amount of make-up – a light dusting of powder, a bit of blusher and lipstick – and her hair is freshly washed. Not only has she got an appointment at the breast clinic for a scan to find out if the cocktail of drugs she's been taking has slowed down the spread of her cancer, she's also aware that the estate agent is returning for the re-arranged viewing with his clients while we're out. Perhaps she wanted to look presentable in case they are still viewing her house when we get back, after the not so favourable first impression she'd given.

It's not only Mum who looks smart, I've never seen the house looking so clean and tidy. I can only assume that Martin has been helping her while they've been prisoners of the snow. The bathroom taps are positively gleaming when I pop upstairs to use the loo before we head off to the hospital, and everywhere smells so fresh, which I put down to the little glass jars with wooden reeds in them that have appeared as though by magic in various places around the house. Mum's newspapers and magazines, which are usually scattered haphazardly over the sofa, have been neatly stacked in a pile on the coffee table and everywhere has been dusted and vacuumed. Even the kitchen is immaculate with all the dishes washed, dried and hidden away in the cupboards. The redecoration after Mum's kitchen fire has been a blessing as everywhere is painted in ivory rather than covered with the loud geometric design wallpaper that had graced the walls since I was a child. All in all, the place looks very presentable and ready to move into, which will hopefully mean a quick sale.

Mum has asked Martin to stay for the viewing as she doesn't like the idea of people touching her personal things. Standing in the doorway waving to us as we walk down the driveway, he looks resigned to the fact that he is going to lose his neighbour one way or the other. I've unlocked and opened the big wooden gates to show the amount of off-road parking the house has and although the garage doors could do with a coat of paint and a few of the trees need pruning, the overall impression is a good one.

'I still might not sell,' Mum says, as I help her into the passenger seat and hand her the end of the seatbelt so that she doesn't have to twist around in her seat for it. 'If the drugs haven't worked, I might only have a few more weeks to live, so it would be pointless putting everybody through all the upheaval. It's worth them having a look today though; if they like it, you'll have buyers lined up when I'm gone.'

I turn away so that Mum can't see my face and the impact her words have had. She has days like this where she's resolved to the fact that her days are numbered. Other times she rails against the injustice of the old age she is being denied. And then there are the days when she can't even remember her name, let alone the faces of the people who are trying to care for her. Martin copes fine with being referred to as 'that man', but Jade still gets upset when Mum calls her Danni, although it's preferable to the days when she doesn't recognise her at all.

As I'm getting into the driving seat, she says, 'Have you had any more thoughts about Jason?'

It takes me by surprise. She didn't mention it when we visited her on Sunday, and she's said nothing so far this morning, but maybe that's because she doesn't want to talk about it in front of Martin. The funny thing is, I do have news but I'm not sure I'm ready to share it with her now because I'm yet to decide what to do.

Maxine emailed Rowena Nash straight after our telephone conversation on Sunday morning and heard back within the hour. Rowena said she was going to check with her contact at her local council, but she was pretty sure that we'd only need the hospital's permission to move my brother's remains because they owned the ground where he had been interred. By coffee-break time on Monday morning, Maxine had received a second email, which she showed me straightaway:

Dear Maxine,

As I thought, the only permission your friend would need to move her brother's remains is that of the hospital, although it would be advisable to check with your local cemetery that they are happy to receive them in the family plot. Are you considering some kind of funeral service? If so, I can assist you in finding someone to perform it if your local vicar is unwilling.

Please let me know if you'd like me to approach the hospital on your behalf and if there is anything else I can do to help. I hope this brings closure for both your friend and her mother.

Rowena

'So, there you have it,' Maxine said. 'Now it's up to you to decide what will be best for your mum.'

'What do you think I should do, Max? I did try to talk to Ben about it again last night after the girls had gone to bed, but he said he wasn't prepared to discuss it, even though I explained that other families have done it before.'

'Did he give you a reason?'

'Only the same one he'd already given. He thinks Jason has lain in that place for forty-four years and shouldn't be disturbed. He just doesn't seem to get the emotional side of this situation at all.'

'How do you think he would react if you went ahead and did this anyway?'

'I honestly don't know. We've never disagreed about anything this major.'

'It's a tricky one,' she said. 'Clearly this is important to you and you believe it would be the right thing for your mum…'

'But?'

'Is it worth letting this come between the two of you?'

Yesterday, while we were sitting discussing it in the kitchen at the library, I could see that Maxine had a point about not allowing my attempt to please my mum come between Ben and me, but things have moved on yet again. Although I didn't ask Rowena to approach the hospital on my behalf, she did it anyway, thinking she was being helpful. They've given their blessing for us to remove Jason's remains and bury them in the cemetery with the rest of our family.

And now Mum has asked me a direct question, I feel backed into a corner. I could make any numbers of excuses to Mum, including telling her the hospital wouldn't give us permission, but that would be an outright lie and it feels wrong to deceive a dying woman. I'm going to stall her until after we get the results of the scan, which will give me a bit more time to reach my decision.

'I'm going to ask the hospital if there's a correct procedure for lifting Jason's coffin,' I say, being very careful to give her a truthful response. 'But first, I need to approach the cemetery to get permission to have him reburied.'

'Really?' she says, placing her hand on my forearm, her eyes filling with tears. 'You're willing to do that for me?'

The expression of hope on Mum's face brings about my decision earlier than I'd anticipated. Unlikely as it may seem, the very tragedy that had stopped Mum from being able to show me love is now bringing us closer than at any point in our lives.

'If that's what you want and it will make you happy, then yes,' I reply, turning on the ignition and pulling into the flow of traffic.

According to Martin the viewing went well, and this is backed up when Ballard and Ross call me while I'm waiting for the girls to come out of school. The Watsons have made an asking-price offer and are keen to exchange contracts within six weeks with a completion date to follow soon afterwards. I tell the estate agents I'll put it to Mum and that we should have an answer for them the next day. After hanging up, I ring Ben.

'Hi,' I say, 'good news on Mum's house, we've got an offer at the asking price.'

'Wow, that was quick. You don't think Ballard and Ross undervalued it because they knew we needed to sell, do you?'

I can hear the worry in his voice. Ben is so honest, he might have let slip that we had to sell quickly because of Mum's worsening health.

'No. I just think the Watsons really want to live on that road,' I say to reassure him. 'The thing is, they need a quick decision otherwise they'll be tied into another six months renting, so I'm going to take the girls over to Mum's after all. Depending on how she is, I'll get her on her own and tell her the situation.'

'She's not likely to have changed her mind about selling, is she?' Ben asks.

'I don't know, Ben. This morning she hinted that she wanted to know the results of today's scan before she made her final decision, but unlike you, she changes her mind like the wind these days,' I say, regretting the words the moment they are out of my mouth.

He sounds quite aggressive when he says, 'What's that supposed to mean?'

'Nothing. I'm just tired I guess.'

'Bullshit. Are you still going on about digging up your brother's grave?' he demands. 'Do it if you want to, just don't expect me to be part of it.'

'I may just do that,' I reply, matching his aggression. 'The hospital has given us their blessing to move him to consecrated ground. It seems you're the only one that has a problem with it. I've got to go, the girls are at the car,' I say, hanging up.

It's almost true; they're actually saying goodbye to their friends at the school gates, but I need a couple of moments to compose myself. I hate arguing with Ben, even over petty little things like the girls watching too much television or one of us overspending on the weekly shop. In fact, we've never really had a major disagreement about anything because we're usually able to see both sides of every situation. But he is resolutely refusing to even try to understand why I feel I need to do this one last thing for my mum. Maxine's words are turning over and over in my mind. Ben and I will hopefully have many years together when Mum has passed on, and in truth I'm going to need his support to get through what will undoubtedly be a very difficult time. Is it worth risking our future to try and mend Mum and my broken past?

CHAPTER THIRTY
Thursday, 24 January

Amber and Jade have gone through to the lounge to watch a bit of television with Ben, leaving me to put away the dinner plates they have just washed and dried without me asking them to. As Mum's health has declined over recent months and I've had to spend more time looking after her and less at home, the girls have been increasingly helpful around the house. A smile plays at the corner of my mouth as I recall the conversation Ben and I had during the Easter holidays last year, when we'd discussed whether we could afford to get a dog. He hadn't thought our girls would be capable of sticking to a programme of household chores. I'm pretty sure he now realises he underestimated what they were capable of if they put their minds to it, not dissimilar to the way he underestimated my determination to have Jason reunited with his family.

The exhumation is taking place on Sunday and the reburial service on Tuesday. With Ben still refusing to be part of it, Maxine has offered to drive me to Beechmede as she doesn't think I should be on my own for what is definitely going to be a very emotional moment. I'm desperate for the tiny coffin to still be intact as I want to give my mum her wish to sit with her baby son for a short time in the privacy of the Chapel of Rest before he is reburied. She knows nothing of my plan and I'm keeping it that way until Tuesday morning. Although Ben has refused to be present at the exhumation, he is coming to the small service at the cemetery, but we both agreed that our girls should not.

We are having to make a lot of major decisions surrounding Amber and Jade's wellbeing, when a few short months ago our biggest decision was whether or not they could have a dog. The funny thing is, we've now concluded that getting a puppy might be the best thing to help the girls come to terms with the grief when they lose their nana. We haven't given any serious thought to what kind of puppy we should get, but it will most likely be a crossbreed from the animal shelter. Nevertheless, I've taken to scrolling through cute images of dachshunds and cavapoos on my phone when I get a spare minute. That's exactly what I'm doing after putting the dinner dishes away, when my phone starts to ring in my hand.

'Hi Danielle, it's Adam.'

I can hear the excitement in his voice.

'Guess what? I've just booked my flight.'

'That's fantastic,' I say. 'When?'

'I leave here on the 7th of February and arrive around midday on the 8th. I've got a bit of a stopover in Paris but that was the cheapest flight and I wanted to get back as soon as I could. How's Mum holding up?'

'Pretty good most of the time. Obviously, she has her ups and downs. We're waiting for a letter with the results of a scan that she had on Tuesday to see if the drugs she's taking are halting the spread of the cancer.'

'Email me when you get them,' he says.

'Of course. How long will you be able to stay?'

There's a slight pause before Adam says, 'As long as it takes. I've only been doing temporary jobs and I don't have my own place, so I thought I'd come back and be with Mum for as long as she has.'

I'm so glad Adam's reached this decision. I know he thought I exaggerated how quickly she was deteriorating in terms of her mental health, but since the diagnosis of terminal breast cancer he's done all he can to raise money to fly home to England and spend some time with her.

'I presume you're intending to stay at Mum's?' I say.

Adam knows nothing about her house being sold with a view to moving Mum into a care home, but there's no point in going into that with him now. She accepted the Watsons' offer and they're not part of a chain, but even so, the conveyancing will take six to eight weeks. Now I know Adam is booked on a flight home in two weeks' time, I'm pretty sure Martin and I will be able to continue to care for her until my brother arrives if he's planning on staying at the house with her. And when the house sale does complete and she moves into a care home, Adam can come and stay at our house for a while.

'That's the plan,' he replies. 'I thought you could probably do with a break from going over to look after her every day. I'm sorry it's all fallen on your shoulders; you must think I'm really bloody selfish.'

That's exactly what I'd thought in the days and weeks following Mum's dementia diagnosis, when Adam had stuck his head in the sand over what was happening and wouldn't accept how desperate she was to see him. He'd also been too proud to admit that he wasn't working and couldn't afford the plane fare home. Things are much better between us now that we're being more honest with each other. That said, I haven't told him about Jason yet. I'm intending to show Adam where our brother has lain for all the years that none of us knew of his existence, before taking him to our family plot. I hope he'll approve of my decision to move him there.

'Maybe I used to before I understood how much you needed your freedom, but everything is so much clearer now. We've got a lot to talk about when you get home,' I say, 'and a lot of catching up to do.'

'I can't wait to see you all even though I wish it could have been in happier circumstances.'

'I know; but if all this stuff hadn't happened with Mum, we might not be having this conversation now.'

'True. It's brought us closer, so in some ways we should be grateful. You're all the family I've got when she passes, sis.'

I'm feeling a bit choked up. We haven't been close, but life is offering us a second chance.

'Email me all your flight details and I'll come and meet you at the airport,' I say.

'You don't have to do that.'

'I know, but I want to. Mum is going to be so excited when I tell her we've got an actual date to look forward to.'

'Give her my love, and to Amber and Jade too,' he says before ending the call.

'I thought I heard voices,' Ben says walking into the kitchen. 'For a minute I thought you were talking to yourself.'

'It was Adam,' I say, wafting my mobile phone at him unable to suppress the happiness in my voice and with a broad grin on my face. 'He's booked his flight; he's coming home.'

CHAPTER THIRTY-ONE
Sunday, 27 January

Ben hasn't been completely unsupportive today. Although he wouldn't come to Beechmede with me, he did volunteer to take Amber and Jade around to Mum's and cook Sunday lunch for them all to keep them out of the house for a few hours. I think he knew how emotional I would be feeling and thought I would need a bit of space. He's right.

Maxine was at my side when the tiny blue casket saw the light of day for the first time in forty-four years and was handed to the undertaker's to be taken to the Chapel of Rest until the burial service on Tuesday.

She hasn't tried to engage in conversation on the journey back from Beechmede, much to my relief. I've sat silently next to her clutching the wooden cross that for so many years had marked Jason's grave.

When she pulls the car onto our driveway, she asks, 'Would you like me to come in with you?'

I'm about to say no and then realise that I really could do with her support. 'Do you mind?'

'I wouldn't have offered if I did,' she replies. 'Come on, let's get you inside and get the kettle on.'

I nip upstairs to use the loo and when I come down Maxine has her back to me and is throwing a tissue in the bin as I push open the kitchen door.

Without turning to face me and in a voice that's a fraction too bright, she says, 'Shall we have that cup of tea now?'

I can't be certain, but she appears to have been crying, which surprises me. Maxine is not usually given to emotional outpourings; that's more my thing.

'Tea would be good,' I say. 'Are you alright, Max?'

She turns and in that instant I recognise the look in her eyes. I've seen it before when my mother first told me about Jason being stillborn.

My hand goes up to my chest as I gasp, 'Oh my God, Max, did this happen to you?'

She shakes her head. 'Not me; my younger sister, Beverley.'

I cross the kitchen and throw my arms around her. 'I'm so sorry for involving you in all this. It must have dredged up some devastating memories for you.'

She holds me very close for a few seconds and then removes herself from my embrace and walks over to flick the switch on the kettle before turning back to me, with a much calmer expression on her face.

'I wanted to help you and your mum because I know what Bev went through after being denied the chance to say goodbye to her daughter,' she says, momentarily closing her eyes. 'She was completely unable to cope with her grief and ended up pushing her husband away. After he'd left her, Bev couldn't see a reason to live. She took an overdose of the tranquilisers and sleeping tablets that the doctor had prescribed to help her "get over her loss",' she says.

I don't know how Maxine is remaining so calm. I can already feel tears welling in my eyes just thinking of the desperate action of a young woman whose whole world had collapsed around her.

'It took me years to come to terms with what she'd felt compelled to do. I blamed myself, you see.'

'Why, Max? You didn't take her newborn baby away from her,' I say, leaping to her defence.

'I know, but she tried to tell me how desperately unhappy she was and how worthless she felt. I didn't listen. I was too busy planning my wedding to have time for my sister.'

The click of the kettle switching itself off interrupts her and she turns to the mugs she has already got out of the cupboard to pour boiling water onto the tea bags. I don't know what to say to comfort her, or even if she needs comforting. She seems so calm, detached almost. She's relating the story as though it happened to someone else. I've sometimes wondered if Maxine had ever been married and now it seems she was. The things we don't know about the people we spend so much time with. The regret she feels for not making time for her sister when she needed her has clearly had a profound and lasting effect on her.

The spoon chinks against the side of the mugs as she retrieves the teabags and places them on the draining board to cool before throwing them in the bin. She adds milk, gives another stir and then turns to hand me one of the mugs.

'Thanks,' I murmur.

'I didn't go through with the wedding,' she says, a brief flash of sadness crossing her face. 'In fact, I broke the engagement off and finished things with Barry. It didn't feel right for me to be happy.'

'Oh, Max, I'm so sorry,' I say, but it's almost as though she hasn't heard me.

'Before long, I'd spiralled down into a similar type of depression to Bev. I was luckier than her though. Instead of giving me drugs, the doctor sent me to see a counsellor. Those sessions went on for years before I could eventually forgive myself.'

I blow gently on my tea before taking a sip. I don't want to interrupt her. This is the first time she's ever opened up to me in all the years I've known her and although she always appears so self-assured, maybe she finally feels the need to confide in someone.

'Even after I'd forgiven myself, I still felt as though I wanted to do something to make amends. That's where Rowena Nash came in.'

My hands are gripping the mug of tea I'm holding.

'So, you were already aware of her?' I say.

'I knew her from school,' Maxine says. 'She was my sister's best friend. Rowena and I used to meet up each year on Bev's birthday and she knew how the suicide completely devastated me. I used to say that I wished there was something we could do to reunite Bev with her baby. Remember I told you Rowena set up her charity after helping her best friend to locate her daughter's burial place?'

I nod.

'The first baby she set about looking for was Bev's daughter, Rebecca. She helped her best friend posthumously. After she discovered where Rebecca had been buried, we obtained permission to rebury her alongside my sister. I can't begin to describe the closure that gave me, knowing that they would be together for eternity. It was seeing the effect it had on me that made Rowena decide to set up the charity. That was over fourteen years ago, and since then she's helped hundreds of people to locate their stillborn children.'

'She sounds like an amazing woman.'

'She is, which is why I asked her if she could do anything to help you. I could sense you were wavering, so I asked her to approach Beechmede on your behalf. Yes, it will help Diana in her final days, but it will also help you, Danni. I think you would have forever regretted not reuniting her with Jason while you had the opportunity. It could have driven a wedge between you and Ben, and I didn't want that to happen. I hope he'll come to understand that this is the right thing for you as much as for your mother.'

Thinking of his consideration in taking the girls to Mum's this morning to give me some time for myself, I say, 'He's getting there in his own way. I'm so sorry that you felt too guilty to marry your fiancé. It doesn't seem fair that you missed out on a happy family life.'

'I don't view it like that,' she replies. 'But for the counselling sessions, I might have followed my sister's lead and taken my own life, so I see every day as a bonus. And as for missing out on a happy family life, it might not have been. Not everyone is lucky enough to have a Ben in their life, but don't tell him I said that,' she adds smiling. 'We don't want him getting big-headed.'

'I'm glad you felt you could talk to me, Max,' I say.

'You're the only person, apart from Rowena and my counsellor, that I've ever discussed this with,' she says, 'and I must admit it felt good to open up to you. What's the saying: a problem shared is a problem halved?'

Once we've finished our hot drinks, Maxine says she needs to make a move. After another hug, I wave her off and go upstairs to my bedroom to fetch the pretty notepad she bought me for Christmas. Ben has said he will be back with the girls at around 5 p.m., which gives me plenty of time to write to Ray Pullinger and thank him for all his kindness.

After writing my address in the top right-hand corner, I sit for a few minutes at our kitchen table trying to decide whether I should address Ray as Ray or Mr Pullinger, but once I've decided the words of gratitude pour from me.

Dear Ray,

You don't know me, but I felt compelled to write and thank you for the kindness you showed in giving my brother such a beautiful resting place in the grounds of Beechmede Hospital. I've only seen it in the winter, but I understand the whole area is covered in bluebells in the spring. It made me smile to think of that beautiful carpet of blue.

I knew nothing of my brother's existence until very recently. My mother, Diana Willetts as she was then, has kept it secret throughout her life, but sadly, she is now suffering from dementia and she mentioned her stillborn baby in one of her confused episodes. After contacting the hospital, I was able to speak to a nurse who attended my mother during her labour, under the supervision of your wife.

She confirmed that my brother, Jason, was stillborn, and she also told me about the blue and pink boxes you made for the babies so that they could be buried with dignity. I must admit I'd imagined something far less extravagant than the beautiful blue coffin we exhumed this morning in order to reunite Jason with his relatives in our plot at the local cemetery. At first, I was reluctant to move him because the resting place you chose for the babies was so peaceful but, after a lot of soul-searching, I decided that my brother should be with his family.

Believe me when I say I have no wish to pry, but while we were searching for Jason's grave, we noticed two crosses bearing the last name Pullinger who I'm assuming were your sons. I'm so sorry for yours and your wife's loss, but immensely grateful that you took the decision to allow other babies to share such a beautiful peaceful place to sleep.

I hope you don't mind me reaching out to you in this letter. I just wanted to communicate my heartfelt thanks to you for keeping my brother safe this past forty-four years,

Yours truly
Danielle Harper

I've left a space on the envelope for the address which I'll get from Linda at Jason's burial service on Tuesday. Across the bottom, I've written, 'Please return to sender if not known at this address'.

I've only just sealed the letter when I hear Ben's keys in the lock. Hurriedly, I drop it into my handbag and head through to the lounge.

'If you've got any homework to finish, go and do it now,' Ben says. 'I'll do pizza for half past six,' he adds over the thunder of footsteps on the stairs.

'How was Mum?' I ask.

'On good form, actually. Obviously, she asked where you were, but when I said you were spending the day with Maxine, she accepted it without question. She didn't really bother with me much as she was too busy with the girls. I didn't see Maxine's car when I pulled in, so I presume she's gone?'

'Yes. She stayed for a cup of tea and then headed off home,' I say, turning away from him so that my face doesn't give me away. Maxine confiding in me was a big step for her and I wouldn't want to betray her confidence. 'Do you want one? The kettle has just boiled,' I add over my shoulder as I head back into the kitchen.

He follows me and slips his arms around my waist, pulling me into his chest. 'More importantly, how are you? Did everything go okay?'

Although he still disagrees about moving Jason from his resting place, I think he's finally realising how much it means to me and how much it will mean to Mum. I allow myself to relax back against him, dropping my head forward slightly so that he can kiss my neck. Whatever else happens in my life, Ben is my rock, the person I rely on and I never want to be without him.

'Gross! Get a room you two,' Amber says from the kitchen doorway.

Ben jumps away from me as though he's been caught doing something he shouldn't; we were only cuddling, for goodness' sake.

'I thought you were upstairs,' Ben says.

'Clearly,' Amber replies reaching for the orange squash and the jug of filtered water in the fridge. 'I'm getting me and Jade a drink,' she adds, waggling the squash bottle. 'I think your gravy was a touch on the salty side, Dad.'

'Nothing wrong with my gravy,' he says, getting two mugs down from the cupboard for our teas.

The moment of intimacy has gone, but that's what family life is all about and to be honest, I wouldn't change it for the world.

CHAPTER THIRTY-TWO
Tuesday, 29 January

'Where are we going?' Mum asks when I unlock her front door just after nine o'clock on Tuesday morning. 'You were very secretive on the phone.'

I'm pleased she's remembered that we're going out. I didn't tell her too much during our phone conversation yesterday evening apart from that we were going somewhere special today and suggested she might want to wear something smart. She's chosen her navy-blue wool dress and as usual has her multi-coloured shawl around her shoulders. I think I can detect a hint of blusher on her cheeks. I was worried that if I mentioned Jason and the burial service I've arranged, she might have become over-excited and been unable to sleep. When she's tired, she tends to have her forgetful episodes and I want her to be fully aware of what we are doing today.

'Come and sit down, Mum,' I say, taking her hand and leading her through to the lounge. 'We don't have to go just yet.'

As I sit down on the sofa opposite the fireplace, I notice an official-looking white envelope propped up on the mantelpiece. My heart starts thumping against my ribs. It will be the results of the MRI scan she had last week.

I can see Mum follow my gaze. 'It arrived this morning,' she says.

'And?' I say trying to keep my voice upbeat.

'I haven't opened it; I thought maybe you would want to.'

'Right, yes, it's probably a good idea if we do it together. Do you want to open it now or after our day out?' I ask, hoping that she will be happy to wait until later. If it is bad news, I don't want anything to spoil her precious time with Jason.

'Shall we leave it here and do it when you bring me home. It's nothing that can't wait a few more hours whether it's good news or bad,' she says. 'Now, are you going to tell me where we're going?'

'We're going to the cemetery, Mum. We're going to lay Jason to rest in our family plot.'

She gasps, her hands flying up to her mouth. 'Really?'

'Yes, really. I've asked the undertaker if you'll be allowed to sit with him before they carry him out to the grave and they've agreed. You said you wanted to be close to him, Mum.'

'Yes,' she says, tears spilling down her cheeks and creating streaks in her blusher. 'That's all I ever wanted to do.'

In that moment I know I've made the right decision.

It's strange to think that some people can be so organised about death. The Willetts – my ancestors – had bought a family plot in the early twentieth century which has gradually been filled with my relatives. Jason will be temporarily laid to rest next to my grandparents, in the plot that has been reserved for my mother since the day she was born. There's still plenty of space for me, Ben and our girls, and future generations, although, unlike Aunt Susie and Mum, our plots have yet to be allocated.

The service itself is shorter than I imagined it would be, but nonetheless very touching. After we've all said a prayer, the chaplain ends his blessing with the words, 'May the little lad rest in peace with his family for all of eternity.'

The five of us stand watching in silence as the tiny blue coffin is lowered into the ground, until Mum cries out, 'Don't worry, Jason, I'll be with you soon.'

Even though I know she's right, it's heart-breaking to hear her say those words. Over the past few months, Mum and I have grown closer than at any time in my life. It's sad to think that we weren't able to enjoy a normal relationship because of what happened to her as a teenager. It's going to be difficult for me not to be over-protective with Amber and Jade like my mum was with Adam. I haven't told her he's booked his flight home yet. I thought she might need something to look forward to if the letter on her mantelpiece contains bad news.

As the box disappears from view, we each throw a white rose that Maxine has thoughtfully brought with her onto the top of the coffin. We've also brought along Ray Pullinger's original carved cross, which will mark Jason's grave until my mother joins her son and they have a joint headstone.

Ben squeezes my hand reassuringly. 'It was the right thing to do,' he whispers.

I return his squeeze, muttering, 'Thank you.'

We turn away from the grave and Mum seems happy, if that's an appropriate description. Ben takes her elbow to support her and Maxine falls into step on her other side, while I move ahead on the path to catch up with Linda.

'Thank you for coming,' I say.

'Thank you for inviting me. It was good to be reacquainted with Diana after all these years.'

I'd wondered how Mum would react to meeting Linda, even fearing that it might trigger one of her episodes, but I needn't have worried. She was fine, remarking that she would have recognised Linda anywhere because of her startling blue eyes. The two of them spoke for several minutes before the short service, ending their conversation with my mum taking Linda's hands in hers and Linda releasing them to give Mum a full-on hug.

'When she first told me about Jason's birth, she spoke very highly of you and all you did for her,' I say. 'Remembering your

kindness probably helped her get through the dark months following Jason's birth.'

'I wish I could have done more, but at least I was able to
reassure you that she had a friendly face with her at that terrible
time. Oh, and before I forget, here's the Pullingers' address,' she
says, pulling a slip of paper from her pocket and handing it over.
'Not that you need it now really.'

'I've already written Ray a letter to thank him for the respect
he showed my brother,' I say. 'I was intending to post it, but now
I'm wondering whether to deliver it in person to show how truly
grateful I am.'

'I'm sure he'd appreciate that, if he's still at that address, of
course. I don't suppose many of the bereaved families he helped
have gone to the lengths you have to locate their stillborn babies,
so he's probably unaware of how important what he did for them
all those years ago was. You must love Diana very much.'

I turn back to glance at my mum who is walking along the
path towards us. For years we barely spoke and when we did it
usually ended in an argument, and yet Linda is right. For all her
faults, she's my mum and I do love her.

A movement in the trees behind them catches my eye. The
sun is quite low in the sky making me squint, but unless I'm very
much mistaken, my Aunt Susie has been standing watching the
proceedings half-hidden behind an oak tree. I rang her yesterday
to tell her about Jason's burial as I thought she had a right to know.
After accusing me of meddling in things I didn't understand, she
hung up on me.

As though aware that she's been spotted, she turns and walks
away in the opposite direction. What a shame she can't put aside
her prejudice and support her sister by allowing Jason to be
recognised as a member of our family. A gesture like that would
have meant the world to Mum.

When we reach the car park, Ben, Linda and Maxine all head off back to work. After watching them go, Mum turns to me and gently runs her gloved hand down my cheek.

'You really are a kind and thoughtful girl. I wish I'd been able to love you in the way you deserved.'

I wish she had too, but today is not about me.

'You did your best, Mum,' is all I can say in response. 'Come on, let's get you home.'

CHAPTER THIRTY-THREE
Tuesday, 29 January

By the time we got back to Mum's house and I'd made us a bit of lunch, it was almost time to go and collect the girls from school. I didn't want to open the letter from the hospital and then have to rush straight off, particularly if it was bad news, so I suggested that Martin went around to hers for a while, telling her that I'd come back later for dinner and stay over with her.

I arrive back around seven o'clock and am reaching into the back seat for my overnight bag when I notice Martin coming out of his house and heading in my direction.

'Is everything alright?' I say locking my car door and immediately feeling anxious when I see the look of concern on his face.

'Not really; your mum had a funny turn just after you left.'

'You should have called me.'

'There didn't seem much point in worrying you when I knew you'd be at the school waiting for your girls. I managed to get her upstairs to her bedroom for a lie-down. She had that blank expression in her eyes, the one where she doesn't know who I am or where she is.'

I'd worried that she might experience some kind of delayed reaction and it would seem that my concerns were justified. It's obvious the day has had an unsettling effect on her, which is not surprising really, although she'd seemed to be coping really well when I'd left.

'How long was she like that?' I ask, unlocking the front gate, waiting for Martin to come in behind me, then locking it after us.

'Probably about fifteen minutes, but then she started asking me what I'd done with the baby. When I said I didn't know what baby she was talking about she began shouting at me, telling me to stop lying to her and that she was going to call the police and report me for breaking into her house and stealing her baby. I didn't know what to do, Danni. She was as bad as the day the estate agent turned up unexpectedly. No matter what I said, I couldn't calm her down.'

This latest episode of Mum's has clearly upset Martin. He's been so supportive over the past year, but I think even he realises that she is becoming more and more unpredictable when she's having one of her funny turns, as he put it. I'd originally worried that he might feel a little as though his nose is being pushed out of joint when Adam gets home from New Zealand but actually, I'm now thinking my younger brother's return can't come a moment too soon for all of us.

'Did she calm down eventually?'

'To be honest, she was getting so hysterical that I thought it was best to leave her on her own in her room. I waited downstairs in the lounge and when it all seemed quiet, I went back to check on her and she'd fallen asleep.'

'How long ago was that?' I ask.

'That was about five o'clock and I've popped back a couple of times since. The last time was half past six and she was still out for the count. She must have had a pretty exhausting day,' he says.

I'm guessing that he wants me to elaborate but, on this occasion, I'm not going to. If Mum wanted Martin to know about baby Jason, she would have told him.

'Yes,' is all I say. 'It's getting tougher for all of us. I hope you know just how much we appreciate all you do for her.'

Martin colours up slightly before letting himself out of the kitchen door.

*

I'm whisking the eggs to make me and Mum an omelette for our dinner, before going to wake her, when she appears at the kitchen door.

'I don't know what happened there,' she says. 'I only went for a lie-down; I must have fallen asleep.'

'You've had a busy and emotional day, Mum, I'm not surprised.'

She frowns. 'Have you been here long? I thought it was Martin banging around down here.'

'He was here looking after you. You really should try and show him a bit more gratitude.'

'Oh, he enjoys fussing around me,' she says. 'Let's face it, he hasn't got much else to do. Goodness knows how he's going to fill his days when I'm dead.'

A shiver runs through me. I hate that word. It sounds so final. She's right about Martin though; his world has revolved around my mum since her dementia diagnosis. I hope he'll be able to get back to some semblance of normality once she's gone.

'Well, you can fill this part of your day by getting the knives and forks out,' I say while tipping the beaten eggs into the sizzling butter in the frying pan.

Five minutes later, we're sat opposite each other at the kitchen table tucking into cheese omelette and peas. It's good to see Mum still has her appetite. She looks so frail, as though a puff of wind would blow her over, and yet today she has shown a tremendous amount of inner strength. On the table in front of me, propped up between the salt and pepper pots, is the letter from the hospital which she must have fetched from the mantelpiece in the lounge while I was busy cooking. Mum requested to receive her scan results by mail as she couldn't see the point in wasting the consultant's valuable time, as she had put it. Mr Goldsmith had reluctantly agreed, making it clear that she could call to speak to him if she was unsure about anything he'd written. It's the elephant in the room, which we both know has to be addressed.

The moment I put my knife and fork down on my empty plate, she says, 'Go on then, we might as well get it over with.'

The awful thing is, I think we both know what the letter is going to say. Mum is much thinner than when she stayed with us over Christmas and gets tired far more easily. My hands are shaking as I tear open the envelope and scan the few lines that have effectively signed Mum's death warrant.

'Well?' she says impatiently.

I bite my bottom lip hard to stop myself from crying. Mum needs me to be strong and that's what I have to be. I lower the letter so that I can make eye contact with her.

'The drugs haven't worked,' I say in as steady a voice as I can muster. 'The cancer has spread.'

'That's no great surprise,' she says, holding my gaze. 'How long have I got?'

She sounds so matter-of-fact.

'They don't say exactly but suggest you should consider moving into a hospice for your final weeks because they will be able to control your pain.'

I detect a flicker of fear in her eyes. I'm not sure if it's the thought of moving to a place where people go to die, the idea that she might have to endure a lot of pain or the final realisation that her life is almost at an end.

'I'd rather stay here, Danni,' she says quietly. 'Can't you come and stay with me until my time comes? We could have a nurse visit to give me any extra pain relief I might need if they won't allow you to administer it. I don't want to leave here, even though I know Jason won't be looking for me. It's my home. Please, Danni,' she begs, finally allowing herself to cry over the news she has just received.

I reach for her hands across the table and squeeze them tightly. 'You can stay here Mum, but you won't need me to be here for long; Adam's coming home.'

I experience a pang of jealousy at the pure unadulterated joy in her eyes. I thought I was past those feelings towards my younger brother, but after a lifetime of being second best, I guess it's not that easy.

'It won't change things between us, Danni,' she says, seeming to understand the impact her reaction to Adam coming home has had on me. 'It will be the three of us together for the time I have left.'

How desperately sad that it couldn't always have been that way, but I suppose I should feel grateful that finally we will be a proper family.

CHAPTER THIRTY-FOUR
Thursday, 31 January

The news of Adam's imminent arrival has lifted Mum's spirits to such an extent that I've felt confident enough to leave her in Martin's care today while I make the journey to Yorkshire. I'm hoping to find the Pullingers at the same address that they moved to when they left Woldington, which I realise is a bit of a long shot. I'd probably have settled on just sending the letter if they'd moved further away, but as it's only a couple of hours' drive, I'm prepared to risk the disappointment of them no longer being there, weighing it up against the enormous satisfaction it will give me to be able to say thank you to Ray Pullinger in person.

If I'm honest, I'm enjoying the drive. It's given me a sense of freedom to escape from the intensity of the situation with my mum. Ben offered to come with me, but I said no. This is something I want to do on my own, although if I didn't have a satnav, I would definitely have needed his map-reading skills as the Pullingers' house is in the middle of nowhere.

Even with electronic guidance I make a couple of wrong turns up single-track country lanes, so it's a relief when I finally pull up outside a stone cottage, having not seen another house for a mile or more. It has a small wooden sign attached to the gate saying 'Overdale Cottage'. I can see a wisp of smoke escaping from the chimney into the almost white skies overhead. I reach for my handbag from the passenger seat and climb out of my car just as an elderly man appears at the front door of the house.

'Are you lost, dear?' he asks. 'Your best bet is to reverse into my driveway and then head back the way you've just come until you get to the T-junction at the bottom of the hill. This road turns into a dirt track in a couple of hundred yards.'

Without asking, I know this is Ray Pullinger, even though we've never met.

'Actually,' I say, walking around the back of my car, 'I was looking for Overdale Cottage.'

'Really? In that case, well done; you've found it. How can I help?'

'Are you Ray Pullinger, by any chance?'

The friendly smile from moments earlier is replaced with a warier expression.

'Who's asking?'

'My name's Danni Harper, but you don't know me,' I add, responding to his puzzled expression. 'I wanted to come and thank you in person for something you did for my brother many years ago.'

The tension in his face relaxes slightly. 'You'd better come in then,' he says, stepping back into his hallway and holding the door open to allow me to pass. 'Let's go through to the sitting room. Can I get you a cup of tea?'

It's plain to see that this man's generosity of spirit hasn't waned over the years.

'I don't want to put you to any trouble.'

'No trouble at all. I don't get many visitors out here. How do you take it?'

'Milk but no sugar, thanks.'

'Won't be a jiffy,' he says. 'The kettle's always warm on the Rayburn.'

True to his word, he's back a couple of minutes later with my hot drink in a china cup and saucer, carrying a plate of digestive biscuits which he offers to me, but I decline. He takes two and puts the plate with the rest of the biscuits on a small wooden table at his side before settling into what I'm assuming is his favourite chair next to the wood-burning stove, as it has a well-worn look about it.

'So, Miss Harper, have you come far?' he asks, taking a bite of his biscuit and sending crumbs scattering down the front of his knitted pullover.

'Please, call me Danni,' I say taking a sip of the strongest tea I've ever tasted. I'm wishing I'd accepted a biscuit now to take away the taste. 'I live in Woldington, where you used to live.'

He nods acknowledgement but doesn't say anything, so I carry on talking.

'My brother was stillborn. We've only recently learned where he was laid to rest, and I wanted to thank you personally for choosing such a beautiful spot, although I also wrote you a letter of thanks.' I reach into my handbag with my free hand, withdrawing the envelope.

A flicker of pain momentarily distorts his amiable features. My intention isn't to dredge up unhappy memories, so I press on quickly.

'My mother has never really come to terms with her baby's stillbirth, partly because she was never allowed to hold him and say her goodbyes, and partly because no one ever told her what had happened to his body. It was a huge relief to learn that you treated the babies with such respect.'

'Poor little mites,' he says, 'denied a chance at life.'

The pain of losing his two boys is obviously still very raw, even after all these years.

Careful to avoid mentioning Linda's name, for fear of any repercussions after she passed on Ray's address unofficially, I say, 'A nurse who worked alongside your wife told me about the blue and pink boxes and the burials in the grounds. I had no idea how beautiful the tiny casket would be.'

'You've seen your brother's coffin?' Ray asks.

'Yes. Once we'd found him, I wanted to grant my mother's lifelong wish to hold her boy close and say goodbye to him properly. We obtained permission to move him to our family plot in the cemetery. My mother's terminally ill, so she wasn't strong enough to actually hold the coffin, but she sat with him for a while, and that was enough for her. When her time comes his little box will lie on her left-hand side close to her heart.'

'Reunited in death,' Ray says. 'What a beautiful idea. I wish I'd thought of that for my poor dear wife.'

'I'm so sorry, I had no idea,' I mumble.

'Of course not. Why would you? She's been gone almost five years now, although in a way we lost her when she had her stroke. Luke always said it must have been a blessed release for her when she was finally taken. She loved to talk, did Sarah, but after the stroke she could only make sounds instead of words, poor love.'

'Luke?'

'Yes, our lad. He was devastated. He and his mum had a very special relationship.'

My heart leaps. I'm so pleased the Pullingers finally had a living child, although I'm not sure I would have been able to call him by the same name as a baby I'd lost.

'I hope he's coming to terms with it now,' I say, painfully aware that I will soon be facing something similar.

'He's getting there,' Ray says. 'Luke was an only child. I think the bond is always stronger with an only child. You must have a pretty special relationship with your mother too, going to the trouble of finding your brother to bring her closure. Are you an only child by any chance?'

I smile and take a sip of tea so that I can take a moment. One of the things I've realised since Jason's reburial is that this hasn't only been about making Mum happy, it's also been about me striving to win her approval. When Adam left for New Zealand, there was a glimmer of hope that I could replace him in my mum's affections, but she soon made it clear that wouldn't be the case. Whatever she may think, Mum will always love my brother more than me. Ben was right when he said I don't need her approval or her love, but I think I've finally gained a degree of both and that will be enough.

'No,' I say, replacing my cup on its saucer and placing the whole thing on the dark oak table at my side. 'I have a younger brother, Adam, although you'd never know we're related to look at us. He has jet-black hair and light green eyes, exactly like our mum. He's been in New Zealand for the past two and a half years, so he doesn't know about Jason yet.'

Ray suddenly starts coughing violently as though he's breathed in sharply and a biscuit crumb has gone down the wrong passage. I spring to my feet and rush over to his chair prepared to help if he's really in difficulty. On the small table at his side, I notice a family photograph of Ray, his wife and their son. I only get a fleeting glimpse before Ray reaches out and places the photograph face down, but it's enough. The young man standing proudly between his two fair-haired parents is the image of my brother Adam. The blood in my veins turn to ice. Ray has stopped choking and looks up at me with fear in his eyes.

'What are you going to do?' he whispers.

'I don't know,' I reply, stumbling across the room in a daze to retrieve my handbag. 'I have to be going now. Thank you for the tea.'

It's only when I'm halfway down the hill, driving far too fast for a single-track road with passing places, that I realise I must have dropped the letter I wrote to Ray Pullinger in my haste to rush to his aid. He's already afraid of what he thinks I may have seen, but once he's read my letter, he'll know I'm aware of his two sons buried beneath the oak tree at Beechmede Hospital. In my mind I'm picturing Baby Luke's wooden cross with September 1974 carved into it. He was laid to rest around the time that Jason was born. Is it possible that my mother was right all along, and her baby wasn't born dead? Is it possible that the young man in that photograph is actually Jason?

CHAPTER THIRTY-FIVE
Saturday, 2 February

The last two days have passed in a blur of confusion and indecision. I don't suppose I'll ever know for certain what took place in the birthing room of Beechmede Hospital all those years ago, but I now feel sure of one thing: Luke Pullinger and my half-brother Jason are the same person.

Throughout the drive home from Ray Pullinger's house, it was difficult to concentrate on the road ahead, partly because of the shock of my discovery but mainly because my mind was filled with thoughts of what my next steps should be. I hadn't voiced my suspicions to Ray, but there was no need to, the look in his eyes had given him away. After forty-four years, he knew his carefully kept secret had been discovered.

I wasn't ready to have a conversation with Ben about it. We usually talk everything through, but I felt like I needed to give the idea of Jason being alive some careful consideration first. When I arrived home, I left a note on the kitchen table saying I had a migraine and that I'd gone to bed to try and sleep it off. I heard the door open and close a couple of times throughout the evening when Ben had obviously come up to check whether I needed anything, but I pretended to be asleep. I didn't like deceiving him, but I needed space to think.

The following morning, I feigned sleep again and he thoughtfully left me in bed. As soon as I heard him leave with the girls, I got up and packed my overnight bag – and since then I've been staying here with Mum. I've been tempted to call Maxine and ask for her advice, but for once I've kept it to myself while I weigh up what the consequences of any actions I take might be.

It's been difficult being around Mum, knowing what I do, but she's been very calm after laying the little blue coffin to rest, and I've got no intention of ruining that memory for now. Mum's focus has switched to living long enough to see Adam. She's literally marking off the days on the calendar; his arrival home can't come quickly enough for her – or for all of us if truth be told. Even with the increased pain relief medication she's taking, I've caught her wincing a few times and her appetite, which had been quite good up until receiving the letter from Mr Goldsmith, seems to have deserted her.

When Ben and I talked briefly on the phone last night after Mum had gone to bed, we decided that the time had come to have the difficult conversation with Amber and Jade about their nana only having weeks to live. Ben is due here with them this morning; it's a conversation I'm not looking forward to.

Understandably, both girls dissolve into floods of tears when they hear that their nana is very poorly indeed. She reaches her skeletal arms around them and pulls them into a hug.

The three of them sit huddled together for ten minutes or so before I finally say, 'Come on girls, let Nana come up for air.'

'Can we stay over tonight?' Jade pleads.

I start to say that I think it might be too much for Mum, when she interrupts me.

'I think that's a wonderful idea. I want to spend as much time as possible with all my girls. What shall we do? Watch a film or listen to music?'

In the end, we decide to have a 'girls' night in'. Hairstyling, make-up and nail painting might sound like odd things to do in

MY MOTHER'S SECRET 213

the circumstances, but I want us to have a fun time together and not dwell on what lies ahead. Amber and Jade write out a list of the things that will be needed for Ben to fetch from our house after lunch while we 'girls' sit around for an afternoon of looking through old photographs.

Mum doesn't have that many considering all the years she's lived, but she discovered some more in an old shoe box at the back of her wardrobe yesterday, after asking me to help her sort through her possessions. 'I don't want to burden you with having to do all this when I'm gone,' she said, handing over a tatty old box containing memories of a life that could have been so much happier if circumstances hadn't conspired against her. While I'm in the kitchen making us a cup of tea, I quickly ring Ben and ask him to pop into town and buy some photo albums. Mum's face is a picture when Ben gets back loaded down with overnight bags and hands the albums to her.

Organising the photos into the four albums Ben bought takes up most of Sunday. When all of them have been sorted out, it becomes glaringly obvious that there are very few pictures of me compared to those of Adam and each one of him makes me think of the photograph I'd seen at Ray Pullinger's house and what I'm going to do about it.

With the innocence of youth, Jade remarks about the lack of photos of me and there's an uncomfortable moment while she waits for an explanation. I'm about to jump in and say that I didn't like having my photo taken when I was younger, but Mum starts to speak before me.

'I wasn't always as nice to your mum as I could have been,' she says, 'something I deeply regret.' Her honesty touches me, and I only just manage to hold it together in front of the girls.

There are a few photos of my grandparents which the girls have seen before, especially the ones of me with them in their garden in Mablethorpe, but also one or two of my father which I'm surprised Mum has kept.

'So that's where we get our red hair from,' Jade says.

'And our freckles,' I add.

'Amber's more like Uncle Adam and Nana,' she says.

In my head, I add, *and Luke Pullinger*.

There are also a few photographs of Mum as a teenager that are ripped on one side suggesting the original had been of two people. I know who's missing, but I'm not sure if Mum will mention her sister to the girls. She must have noticed Amber fingering the torn edge before sticking one of the pictures into an album.

'I was about the same age as you are now when that was taken,' Mum says. 'I'll bet you're wondering who is missing aren't you?'

Amber nods.

'I had a sister,' Mum begins before correcting herself, 'or more accurately I should say I have a sister. Her name is Susan, but we fell out a long time ago because of something I did.'

Mum pauses, struggling to find her next words, and both girls turn to look at me, as though to question whether I know about her. I nod, trying to keep the frustration from my face. Despite me repeatedly telling Mum that Kevin was to blame for what happened, not her, she refuses to accept it.

'We were always very close, just like you two,' Mum says, 'but we haven't seen or spoken to each other in a very long time. You must never let anything come between you like we did.' She has a pained expression on her face. 'I've missed her terribly.'

Although I know the circumstances are completely different, it makes me think of the difficult relationship I've had up to this point with Adam. I'm determined that things will be better between us in the future. And now, I also have the problem of Luke Pullinger. I'm wondering if I should write to him and tell him my suspicions. If he is my and Adam's half-brother, surely he has a right to know.

CHAPTER THIRTY-SIX

Sunday, 3 February

Martin is staying with Mum for the next couple of nights. It will be good for him to spend time with her before Adam arrives, so we've decided to do two nights on, two nights off until he's here. I'm feeling guilty about neglecting the girls and Ben even though the situation has demanded it, so the arrangement suits me too and I'll still see her every day.

As soon as we are all in the car heading home, Amber says, 'What did Nana do that came between her and her sister?'

Ben casts a sidelong glance in my direction. I think he's wondering how I'm going to answer, but I've been expecting the question, so I'm prepared.

'It's less what your nana did and more something that happened that she feels she could have prevented,' I say carefully. 'If my grandma and granddad had been more supportive and tried to talk things through as a family, like Dad and I try to with you girls, it could maybe have been resolved.'

'Was it about the baby?' she asks.

'Yes, it was,' I say. I don't offer any more information and I'm hoping that Amber will pick up on the hint that I don't really want to talk about it.

It's Jade who speaks next.

'I feel sorry for Nana. She's missed her big sister. I can't imagine how sad I'd feel if Amber and I weren't friends.'

In the rear-view mirror, I see Amber reach for Jade's hand and squeeze it. A lump of emotion forms in my throat and not just because our girls are so close. They've got something that neither Ben nor I have ever had. Ben, because he was an only child and me because I never had a proper relationship with Adam. I close my eyes. I need to talk to Ben about what I may have discovered when I visited Ray Pullinger, but I'm worried about his reaction. He's had his concerns throughout the whole Jason episode, and there's no doubt it's put a strain on our relationship, but we've always been honest with each other and now is not the time to change that. I'll talk to him about it tonight, I decide, once the girls are in bed.

Jade is already asleep when I pop my head around her door to say goodnight, her coppery curls spread across her pillow like a fiery halo. I pad quietly across her room to turn off the bedside lamp and drop a gentle kiss onto her forehead before heading back towards the door, which I pull closed behind me. It's been an emotional but rewarding weekend and Jade had been particularly pleased with the job she'd done on her nana's nails. I smile. I'm not sure Mum would have chosen the blue-green metallic shade that Jade applied, but she'd allowed her to do it when Jade had insisted the colour would remind her of her granddaughter whenever she looked at it. I'm still smiling when I push open the door to Amber's room.

'That's a big grin,' Amber says. 'Did Jade say something funny?'

'She was already asleep. I was just thinking of the colour she painted on Nana's nails. You didn't mind, did you?'

'Of course not. I've already picked out the colour I'm going to do them in a couple of weeks' time: Amber Glow,' she says, winking at me.

'I'm sure Uncle Adam will be thrilled at having a "girls' night in",' I say.

'I don't mind painting his too,' she says. 'Anyway, it's not about Uncle Adam, it's about making Nana happy. We did make her happy, didn't we?'

I reach my arms around my beautiful girl and hug her tightly.

'Yes, we really did,' I mumble into her hair. 'You two girls make me so proud. I hope you know how much I love you.'

'We love you too. Like it says on your mug, you're the World's Best Mum.'

The mug had brought tears to my eyes when the girls had presented me with it on Mother's Day a couple of years ago.

'So long as I'm the best mum I can be to you and Jade, that's all that matters to me,' I say, flicking the switch on her lamp and dropping a kiss on her forehead too.

'Night, Mum,' she says as I head towards her bedroom door.

'Night, sweetheart. See you in the morning.'

I'm tempted to stay upstairs and get ready for bed, but we've just had hot chocolate drinks and I hate leaving the mugs overnight. I push the kitchen door open to find Ben already at the sink washing them up.

'I was just coming to do those,' I say.

'I thought I'd save you the trouble. By the way, a letter came for you yesterday. I put it on the shelf in the hall to bring over to your mum's and then forgot it. Don't worry, it doesn't look like a bill,' he says over his shoulder.

I retrieve the letter from the hall and head into the lounge to read it, which is where Ben finds me a few minutes later.

'Bloody hell, Danni, what's up? You look like you've seen a ghost.'

Little does Ben know how close to the truth those words are. The letter, although it could barely be called that, is from Luke Pullinger, and if it's possible to shout in the written word he has. It contains just a few lines of pure vitriol:

*Who the hell do you think you are upsetting my dad like you
did? He could have had a bloody heart attack!! Whatever may
or may not have happened in the past is exactly that – THE
PAST! None of it matters. My DAD is RAY. My MUM was
SARAH and I loved her. Don't you dare try to ruin her memory.
Never contact either of us again. Do you hear me? NEVER!*

My hands are shaking as I pass the letter to Ben. He scans the
page briefly, and then looks up with a horrified expression on his face.

'What is this, Danni?' he says. 'Who is it from?' He turns the
letter over to check the back for a signature, before fixing his gaze
back on me.

'Oh, God,' I say, dropping my head into my hands. 'What
have I done?'

'I don't know, Danni. I'm hoping you're going to tell me. Who's
written these vile words?'

'Luke Pullinger,' I say, lifting my eyes to his.

Ben frowns. 'But Luke Pullinger's dead. We found his cross
when we were searching for Jason.'

'All I wanted to do was thank Ray Pullinger in person for his
kindness. I had no idea that this was going to happen,' I say, tears
pricking the back of my eyes.

'Wasn't Luke buried in the little graveyard shortly before your
brother?' Ben asks.

'Yes, he was.'

'Then who is this other Luke Pullinger? Did they have another
baby and call him by the same name? That seems a bit morbid
to me.'

Ben is missing what became glaringly obvious to me the
moment I saw the Pullinger family photograph.

'You need to start talking, Danni. I want to know why this
bloke thinks he can write to you in this way. And another thing,
where did he get our address?'

'I wrote Ray Pullinger a letter before I decided to go and thank him in person and I put it on the envelope as a "return to sender" in case the Pullingers no longer lived at Overdale Cottage,' I explain. 'I must have dropped the letter without realising when Ray started choking and I went to help him. That's when I saw the photograph.'

'What photograph?' Ben demands.

'There was a family photograph of the Pullingers with their son, Luke.'

'What of it?'

'He doesn't look anything like either of them.'

'So? You take after your dad and don't bear any resemblance to your mum. You said so yourself just this afternoon. I can't see where you're going with this.'

'Adam does. He looks exactly like Mum… and so does Jason.'

'Jason? I'm sorry, Danni you've lost me. What are you getting at?' he says impatiently.

'The boy standing between the Pullingers in the photograph. It was like looking at a picture of Adam in his late teens,' I say, watching as Ben's expression changes from confused to incredulous. 'I think the Pullingers may have taken my mum's baby after they had their second stillborn child.'

'That's a very serious allegation, Danni. No wonder Luke Pullinger wrote this letter,' he says, shaking the piece of paper in my direction. 'You can't go around accusing people of stealing other people's children based on one child bearing a resemblance to another in a photograph! God, Danni. I've had a bad feeling about all of this from the start, but I've gone along with what you wanted because I knew how desperate you were to win your mum's approval. But this… this is madness. You've completely overstepped the mark here.'

Tears are trying to leak from the corners of my eyes, but I won't let them. Ben has always had my back. He's the person I normally depend on in a crisis and yet here he is assuming I'm in the wrong.

'I didn't accuse Ray of anything,' I sniff defiantly. 'I saw the photograph before he was able to hide it. His expression told me that he feared his secret was out. I'm not the one that's done anything wrong and it would be nice if my husband believed me rather than a complete stranger.'

We're facing each other, eyes blazing. I'm angry with Ben and he obviously feels the same way towards me. I don't want to argue with him. I want him to consider the possibility that I might be right.

As though he's reading my mind, he says in a calmer voice, 'Let's think about this logically. How could Sister Pullinger have smuggled a living baby from the delivery room? Surely it would have cried.'

'Not all babies do,' I say, relief flooding through me that at least Ben is prepared to give it some consideration. 'Adam was born with the cord around his neck and had to be resuscitated. If Sister Pullinger whisked away a limp, lifeless-looking baby, my mum and grandmother could easily have been misled into thinking he was stillborn. Mum told me she heard Jason whimper; maybe he did.'

'But how could they have hidden a newborn baby? People must have been curious as to where he'd come from.'

'They moved away. Linda told me the Pullingers left Woldington a couple of weeks after Jason was born. If they arrived in Yorkshire with a newborn son, why would anyone ask any questions? Would we? If someone moved in next door with a baby, we'd just assume it was theirs.'

Ben is looking thoughtful.

'The thing is, Danni, Luke has made it very clear that he doesn't want to change his history. As far as he's concerned, the Pullingers are his parents. Are you able to accept that?'

For the past few days, I've been wrestling with my conscience wondering what I should do about the information I've unwittingly uncovered. Luke has taken the decision out of my hands. He's happy with who he is and isn't interested in who he might have been. Mum is comforted by the thought that she will soon be lying next to her son in our family plot. Although I now know that's a lie and it pains me to think of her being alone, she doesn't know and nothing would be gained by me telling her the truth.

'I guess I'll have to accept it. I can't force Luke to want to get to know his birth family and besides, if he suddenly appeared in our lives how would I even begin to explain things to Mum,' I say. 'She's just started to trust me. If she thought I'd lied to her about baby Jason she'd never forgive me and our relationship would be back to square one. I can't risk that, Ben, not now that I've finally experienced her love.'

Ben reaches his arms around me and pulls me close.

'That's agreed then,' he says. 'This is our secret, just between the two of us. The fewer people who know, the better.'

I assume he's referring to Maxine. He knows we talk most things through, but I'm not sure this is something I want to share even with her.

'What Adam doesn't know won't hurt him,' he adds.

Until Ben mentioned his name, I hadn't given any thought as to whether or not I was going to tell Adam about our half-brother. But now Ben has mentioned it, I'm thrown back into indecision. I intended to tell him about our baby brother when I thought he was dead, so surely, he still has that same right to know. Not for the first time, I question whether I should have left well alone and not gone in search of Jason's resting place, but then I think of the closure Mum finally gained when she said goodbye to her baby. I did the right thing, and if it means not telling Adam about our half-brother until after she has passed, then so be it – but I will tell him because there have already been too many secrets.

CHAPTER THIRTY-SEVEN
Tuesday, 5 February

I can hear Mum's voice as I let myself in through the front door of her house. Whatever she and Martin are talking about must be quite amusing as she starts to laugh. It's not a sound I've heard that often over the past few weeks and it warms my heart. I'm hanging my coat up when I hear a different female voice. I can't be certain because it's slightly muffled through the wooden door, but it sounds like Aunt Susie.

'Is that you, Danni?' Mum calls out. 'You'll never guess who's here.'

I arrange my features in a neutral expression so that I can feign surprise when I push open the door. I've no idea why my aunt is here, but Mum sounds happy and that's all that matters to me.

'Aunt Susie,' I exclaim. 'What a surprise.'

Mum is looking animated, and younger than she has in a while. Even so, she looks at least ten years older than her elder sister. She is wearing her olive-green dress with her shawl around her shoulders, which she wouldn't normally do if it was just the two of us at home. She must have been expecting her visitor.

'Hello Danielle,' Aunt Susie says. 'I hope you don't mind me calling around?'

'Of course not, why would I?'

'Well…' She pauses, a look of embarrassment enveloping her features. 'I was a little rude hanging up on you when you called to tell me about the memorial service.'

'In fairness, it must have come as quite a shock,' I reply.

'That's a bit of an understatement,' she counters. 'At first, I couldn't understand why on earth you would want to have Di's baby buried in our family plot, but when I stopped to think about it, why not? Di's child, stillborn or not and conceived in whatever circumstances, has the right to lie with his relatives for eternity. Who am I to judge?'

For a moment, I picture the tiny blue coffin that we'd lowered into the ground less than a week ago. Baby Jason is not inside it. He's not lying with his relatives for eternity, he's living in Yorkshire refusing to acknowledge that his parents stole him from my mother. Living with this lie is never going to get any easier for me, but I'm going to have to try.

'I'm so pleased to hear you say that, and even more pleased to see you here with Mum,' I say. It didn't escape my notice that she used the abbreviation of her sister's name suggesting that the two of them are getting along just fine.

'We've been reminiscing,' Mum says, her eyes glowing. 'I've spent so many years feeling aggrieved about the cards life dealt me that I'd forgotten all the fun stuff Sue and I used to get up to when we were children. It made me realise how much I denied you, Danni.'

'None of that matters, Mum,' I say crossing the room and throwing my arms around her in a hug, before extending my left arm to include Aunt Susie.

It's sad to think about all the wasted years when the sisters had no contact, despite living less than five miles from each other, but hopefully that's all water under the bridge. I'm so relieved to see Mum reunited with Aunt Susie for however short a time she has left, and once Adam is home too, I really will feel as though my efforts to make Mum happier in the final stages of her life have all been worth it.

'Look, seeing as it's almost midday and we have nothing decent to offer a guest for lunch, how about we all go to Poppy's?' I say, grasping the opportunity for the two of them to spend as much time together as possible. 'If you feel up to it of course, Mum?'

'I'd like that very much. I haven't been anywhere apart from hospitals and graveyards for ages,' Mum says. 'Is that alright with you, Sue? Unless of course you have somewhere else you need to be.'

'Even if I did, I'd cancel it,' she says, squeezing my mum's arm. 'They do the most delicious custard tarts in Poppy's. They were always our favourites, if you remember, Di, when we used to go to Carter's Bakery with our mum on a Saturday morning to buy cakes for lunch.'

'Yes, yes I do remember. Mum always had an iced fresh cream slice, Dad had a chocolate éclair and we had egg custard tarts.'

I'm beginning to feel a bit like a gooseberry, but in a nice way. I can't wait to sit down with the two of them to hear more about their lives before Jason. It will fill in some of the gaps in my family history.

'We'd better make a move before the lunchtime rush,' I say, ushering Mum out into the hallway and reaching her coat down off the row of pegs.

'I like what you've done with the place, Di,' Aunt Susie says. 'In my head I was remembering that hideous 1970s geometric wallpaper and the swirly carpets.'

Mum opens her mouth to speak, but I catch her eye and shake my head. I'd rather my aunt believe that Mum has decorated because she wanted to rather than because she almost burned the place down.

'It was pretty dreadful, wasn't it?' she says instead, giving me a knowing smile.

As I pull the door to and lock it, a thought occurs to me. How did Aunt Susie get into the house with the front door and gate locked and the keys in my possession?

'I know what you're thinking, Danni,' Mum says. 'How did Sue get in? I might have my moments of craziness, but when she rang and asked if she could visit and my jailer wasn't here to unlock Fort Knox, I told her to go next door to Martin's and come around the back.'

That's the thing with dementia; at times Mum is as sharp as a pin and at others she can't work out how to operate the tin opener. There is a tiny part of me that is relieved that the cancer will take her body before her mind deteriorates to the point where she would no longer recognise any of us.

I'm glad we get to Poppy's early as we manage to get a table at the back of the café. It's further away from the takeaway bakery counter, so we stand a better chance of having a decent conversation without constantly being interrupted by the bell over the door as customers come in and out.

I order a mozzarella, tomato and basil panini and Aunt Susie has quiche Lorraine, but Mum sticks to her guns about not having foreign food and orders an individual cottage pie. When it arrives, I have to admit it looks and smells very appetising.

'Do you want to try some?' Mum asks.

'If you're sure you don't mind,' I say, sticking my fork in the creamy mashed potato topping which has been liberally sprinkled with cheese and browned under the grill.

'I won't be able to finish it all anyway,' she says. 'You know I've got the appetite of a sparrow these days.'

To be fair, she starts off pretty well, but after a dozen mouthfuls she puts her fork down on her plate and sits back in her chair while Aunt Susie and I plough on with our respective lunches.

When we've finished, the waitress comes over to take our plates and ask if we'd like to see the dessert menu. I get the feeling that

Aunt Susie would have liked a custard tart for old times' sake, but Mum has obviously had enough to eat, so we settle on three coffees instead. Funnily enough, Mum agrees to having a cappuccino, so obviously her dislike of anything foreign doesn't extend to drinks.

While we're waiting for our coffees to arrive, Mum says she needs the loo.

The moment she's out of earshot, Aunt Susie says, 'Goodness, Danni, I had no idea she was this poorly. I'm so grateful that you came to see me, whatever your real motivation was. I would have hated to have read her obituary in the paper without us having made our peace.'

'And did you?' I ask.

'Yes,' she says, pressing her lips together as though she's not going to elaborate, but then she seems to change her mind. 'Di told me what happened with Kevin and I believe her. It's such a shame that the truth has taken this long to come out. I've missed my little sister dreadfully.'

'You know, it's funny that you should ring today. Over the weekend, me and my girls were looking at old photographs and there were a few that had been ripped in half with your side of the picture missing. Mum told them about you and how she'd missed you too. I think if you hadn't contacted her, she would have reached out to you.'

The bell over the front door of the café tinkles again and I glance over to see the back of someone wearing something brightly coloured disappear from view. I push my chair back with a scraping noise and hurry towards the toilet cubicle. It's empty.

Calling out to Aunt Susie as I head towards the exit, I say, 'I think Mum's wandered out onto the street. Can you get the bill and I'll settle with you back at home?'

My heart's thumping in my chest as I rush out of the café and look right and left down the street. At first, I can't see Mum, but then I notice a flash of vibrant fabric emerging from a shop doorway. I make a dash towards it, apologising to the people I'm bumping into as I run to try and catch up with my mum before she attempts to cross the road. Putting my hand on her shoulder, I spin her around to face me.

'Mum,' I say, breathing heavily after my exertion, 'where are you off to?'

'What are you doing?' she says. 'Don't touch my shawl please.'

'Mum, it's me, Danni.'

'I'm sorry, I don't know you and I'd thank you to keep your hands off my clothing.'

My heart sinks. I've come to know only too well the vacant look in Mum's eyes when she's having an episode.

'I'm sorry,' I say, taking my hand off her shoulder, 'I thought you were someone else. Can I help you across the road, maybe?'

'I'm not an invalid; I'm perfectly capable of crossing the road,' she says, about to step off the pavement into the oncoming traffic, making it necessary for me to reach for her arm again.

'Steady,' I say, 'you almost overbalanced. Are you sure I can't help you get somewhere? I can ask my aunt to fetch her car and we could maybe drop you off?'

'You must think I'm stupid. I'm not getting into a car with strangers. But you can help me out by giving me directions to the station. I seem to have lost my bearings and I don't want to miss the train, or I'll be late for the theatre.'

It must be years since Mum last went to the theatre – probably when she used to take Adam to see the pantomime in Oakbridge. Looking back along the street to Poppy's, I can see Aunt Susie coming out, arms laden with our coats and bags that I'd abandoned in my rush. She's heading this way towards her car.

'It's just along here,' I say, steering my mum in that direction. 'I'll walk with you if you like.'

Mum gives me a weird look but doesn't raise any objection. As we approach the back of Aunt Susie's car, the rear door opens and I'm able to bundle Mum onto the back seat much to the consternation of some passing pedestrians.

'It's alright,' I say. 'She's my mum and she's suffering from dementia. We need to get her home.'

I'm pretty sure one of the passers-by has just taken a photo with her mobile phone and will no doubt report it to the police, which is actually reassuring. If I witnessed what I thought was a kidnap, I'd do exactly the same thing.

'Is she okay?' Aunt Susie asks from the driving seat as she pulls hastily away from the kerb.

'Who are you talking about, Sue?' Mum asks.

Aunt Susie and I exchange a glance in the rear-view mirror.

'Are we going to Poppy's now?' she asks. 'I'm starving.'

When we get back, Mum says she's tired, so I take her upstairs to her room and settle her into bed. Aunt Susie is still in the hallway when I come back downstairs, despite me telling her to make herself at home.

'How is she?' she asks.

'She's fine now. She'll probably sleep for most of the afternoon and wake up remembering very little about her morning.' I notice Aunt Susie's expression. 'On the other hand, she may recall everything.'

'I do hope it's the latter. We had a really good chat earlier and, apart from the Kevin stuff, it was lovely remembering how close we were and how I looked out for my younger sister.'

The image of Amber and Jade walking across the playground happy and smiling on Jade's first day of senior school floods my mind. I can hardly believe that was only five months ago; how my life has changed since.

'You know,' she continues, 'I'd started to wonder if you were exaggerating how bad she is with the dementia. She seemed so... so normal this morning.'

'My brother Adam thought the same thing. It wasn't until she had the terminal breast cancer diagnosis that he started saving up for a flight home.'

'You should have told me. I could have helped him out with that; I've no one of my own to spend my money on,' Aunt Susie says, a hint of sadness in her voice.

'That's very kind, but he's bought his ticket now, in fact, he's due to arrive home on Friday. I'm so looking forward to seeing him. On the subject of money, how much do I owe you for lunch?'

'Nothing. My treat,' she says. 'It's the least I can do.'

There's no point protesting, I can see she won't take no for an answer, so I just say, 'Thank you.'

'I should be going really, Danni. Do you think Di would like me to call in again?'

'I think she would love it. She was having such a good time before the episode.'

'Well, I'll give it a few days for her to spend some time with your brother and then I'll give her a call.'

It's only after I've waved her off and gone through into the kitchen that I notice there is a cardboard box on the table next to my bag. I lift the lid. Inside are three custard tarts.

CHAPTER THIRTY-EIGHT
Friday, 8 February

I arrive at Manchester airport ridiculously early for two reasons. Firstly, I've never been here before and was afraid of getting lost even with instruction from my satnav, and secondly, I wasn't sure how bad the traffic would be. I didn't want to be late for Adam after he'd been travelling for almost thirty hours. His connecting flight from Paris is due in at 11.40 a.m. and I can see from the arrivals board that it's on time. As it's only just past ten, I head to the coffee shop for a caffeine hit and a bite of breakfast, but first I pop into WHSmith for a card.

On the drive here, I've had plenty of time to think about the note from Luke Pullinger. Although it had been really upsetting when I'd first read it on Sunday night, I can now understand what a state of shock he must have been in. I have no idea what Ray told him, but for Luke to react as he had, Ray must have revealed that he and Sarah were not Luke's natural parents. I can understand him not wanting to change his history, but I've reached the conclusion that for my own peace of mind, I have to let him know that I didn't visit his home with anything but the best of intentions.

There isn't a great selection of 'left blank inside for your own message' cards, but the one I choose with a picture of a bluebell wood on the front feels appropriate. I settle down at a table for two and stare down at the card. It was much easier to think about what I wanted to say than it's proving to actually write the words.

Eventually, after a fortifying pain au chocolat and a second cup of coffee I start writing:

Dear Luke,

I know you were quite insistent that I shouldn't contact you and I promise I won't bother you after this, but I think you deserve to know that the woman who gave you life, my mother, loved you with every fibre of her being. She was only fifteen when she fell pregnant with you and would never have given you up had she not been forced to by her parents.

She was told that you had died at birth, something she didn't really believe and so has always hoped that you would find out about your past and come looking for her.

Mum didn't tell me any of this willingly. She has dementia and the truth spilled out. Please believe me when I say that I had no idea that my mum was your birth mother. All I knew was that there were two Pullinger babies buried in the beautiful little graveyard that your father created. I merely wanted to thank him in person for treating my brother, and the other stillborns, with the same compassion as his own lost children.

There is no ulterior motive for telling you any of this, I just thought you had a right to know that you were always loved.

I hope you and your dad will forgive any upset caused and I wish you both well for the future.

Danielle

Without re-reading my words, in case I change my mind about sending the card, I seal the envelope, address it and stick a stamp on it, before dropping it into the airport post box. On my way to the arrivals gate, I can't help thinking how desperate Sarah Pullinger must have been to risk everything in order to have the baby she craved, and how much Ray must have loved her to go along with it. My heart goes out to both of them.

Standing among the other friends and relatives, and taxi drivers holding up placards with the name of their client on, feels like the end scene of the film *Love Actually*, which I always watch when it's on the television over Christmas. My excitement grows with each joyous reunion that is marked with hugs and kisses. Soon it will be my turn and I'm barely able to contain myself. Not only for the first time in my life am I genuinely looking forward to spending time with my younger brother, it's also a massive relief that Adam has made it home in time to see Mum.

Her deterioration is really accelerating now. I truly believe that the only thing keeping her going is her determination to see Adam. She sleeps the majority of the time and as Tuesday at Poppy's had emphasised, her appetite is woeful. She seemed to enjoy the custard tart that Aunt Susie had bought for her though, which I gave her with a cup of tea when she'd surfaced around half past four. And she remembered seeing her sister without me having to give her any clues. She was in such a good mood when I left her in Martin's care for the evening that she gave him the third custard tart. I don't know who was more surprised, me or Martin.

Another flurry of people wheeling cases or carrying overstuffed rucksacks are surging towards those of us standing behind the barrier. I scan the crowd looking for my brother. Unsurprisingly, there are lots of men with beards, but there's no sign of Adam yet. That's the thing when you're waiting for someone in the arrivals hall. Although you know their plane has landed on time, there's no way of knowing how long they will have to wait by the carousel for their luggage to appear.

*

Forty-five minutes has passed and I'm starting to feel a little anxious. Surely Adam should have come through by now? All sorts of possibilities start to run through my head.

Maybe the flight from New Zealand was delayed and he missed his connection? If that was the case, I'm pretty sure he would have let me know. I reach into my bag to check that there are no text messages or missed calls from him. Nothing. Perhaps he's been stopped by customs for carrying something illegal. I don't know my brother that well. For all I know he may have a recreational drug habit and has been hauled into an office to be searched after being caught out by sniffer dogs. I try his mobile number, but it goes straight to voicemail. He's probably forgotten to turn it back on after clearing passport control. I have a quick look around me for an information desk. If he hasn't come through in the next fifteen minutes, I'll have to see if they can find out if he was on the plane that arrived from Paris.

Thirty minutes later I'm standing at the Air France desk while the man behind the counter checks to see whether or not Adam was on the flight that arrived from Paris almost two hours ago. I've been directed here after the woman at the information desk spoke to her colleagues in customs to see if my brother was being held by them for some reason. Once she'd ascertained that he wasn't, I tried his number again, but it still went straight to voicemail. I left him a short message.

'Hi Adam, it's Danni. Did you have a problem with your flight? If so, can you let me know as soon as you get this and then I can plan whether to hang around here at the airport a bit longer or head home.'

I'm tapping my index finger on the counter in impatience. I can't believe it's taking this long to find out whether a particular passenger was on board a flight or not. Surely everything is computerised these days? Anyway, I thought most airlines had a policy of selling seats to stand-by passengers if travellers didn't check in on time. Finally, the man gets off the phone.

'I'm sorry to have kept you,' he says. 'I wanted to check something with our baggage handling team in France. You told me the Air France part of your brother's journey was a connecting flight following his arrival from New Zealand with Qatar Airways?'

'Yes, that's right.'

'Well, I've checked, and his luggage was booked all the way through to Manchester, so our ground crew staff in Paris would have put it on the connecting flight had it arrived.'

I stop tapping.

'Are you saying it didn't?' I ask.

'It would appear so, but it would be as well to check with Qatar Airways. They'd also be able to confirm whether or not your brother boarded the plane in Auckland. Do you know where their desk is?'

At that moment, my phone starts to ring. I reach into my bag for it, assuming it's Adam returning my call from a few moments ago, feeling a mix of irritation that he may have missed his flight and relief that he's okay. It isn't Adam, it's Ben.

'Hi Danni, where are you?' he asks. His voice sounds a little strange.

'I'm at the airport waiting for Adam. It's looking like he may have missed his flight. I wish he'd let me know and then I wouldn't have had a wasted journey.'

'I meant where in the airport are you?'

'That's a weird question,' I say. 'I'm at the Air France information desk. It was them that told me Adam wasn't on the flight from Paris.'

'Okay,' he says, 'just hang on there a minute…'

He's stopped speaking, but he hasn't terminated the call. I'm trying to work out what I can hear in the background; it doesn't sound like his office. An announcement asking people not to leave bags unattended is in progress and I realise I'm not only hearing it in real life but also via Ben's phone. Then my eyes pick out a familiar figure hurrying towards me through the crowds. Even from this distance I can see the expression on his face. In that instant, I know something is terribly wrong. Things start to move in slow motion and the edge of my vision is peppered with sparkling lights. I'm clinging onto the counter, but my legs start to give way beneath me as Ben makes a lunge for me and catches me before I hit the ground.

For a moment I'm disorientated. I'm lying on something very hard and the overhead lights are harsh and bright. I can hear low voices and one of them is my husband.

'Ben?' I say.

'I'm here, I'm here,' he says, instantly at my side and holding my hand.

I look up into his eyes. They are full of compassion.

'What happened?' I ask.

'You fainted. You're in the Air France office; they've just sent for the airport doctor.'

'I mean, what happened with Adam?' I say, struggling to form the words.

In his eyes I can see pain. I know my husband so well. He wants to protect me from something but knows he can't.

'Ben. Tell me.'

'There was an accident, Danni. The taxi Adam was travelling to the airport in was involved in a head-on crash with a lorry.'

My world starts spinning again. My breath is coming in shallow gasps.

'He had to be cut from the wreckage and was in surgery for hours, but…' He pauses, gently stroking my forehead. 'I'm so sorry, Danni. They couldn't save him.'

'No,' I manage. 'No, there must be a mistake. It's not him. He wouldn't have been in a taxi. He didn't have any money. There's a mistake... there must be. It can't be him.'

'Sh... sh...' Ben urges trying to keep me calm. 'There's no mistake, Danni. The New Zealand police rang Diana's number as she was named in his passport as his next of kin.'

'Oh, God. They spoke to Mum?' I say, panic rising in my chest.

'No. Fortunately, Martin answered the phone and explained that Diana is unwell. He gave them my mobile as he didn't think you should be alone when you received the news.'

'What am I going to do, Ben? How am I going to tell Mum?' I say through the tears streaming down my cheeks. 'If I hadn't pressured him to come home, he wouldn't have been in that taxi... he'd still be alive. It's all my fault...'

'Come on, Danni you know that's not true,' Ben says, gathering me up in his arms and rocking me. 'You had to tell him his mother was dying. He made the decision to come home, so how can it be your fault. Do you hear me, Danni? It's not your fault.'

I hear him, but I don't believe him. Adam is dead because of me.

CHAPTER THIRTY-NINE
Friday, 8 February

I don't remember much about the first part of the drive home except that Ben and I were very quiet. The mild sedative injection the airport doctor gave me to help me cope with the trauma of Adam's death no doubt contributed in my case, but Ben seems stunned into silence.

At the start of the journey, he asked me several times in the space of a few minutes if I was okay. I know he was only trying to be kind, but it wasn't helping. At first, I simply hadn't answered, but eventually something inside me snapped and I rounded on him.

'No, Ben, I'm not okay. My mother is dying, my brother is dead, and my half-brother doesn't want anything to do with me. I'm not bloody okay, so please stop asking.'

I immediately felt dreadful for shouting at him, but I couldn't bring myself to apologise. He hasn't spoken since. I don't know if he's respecting my wishes or if he's sulking, but I'm beyond caring. All I want to do is curl up in a ball and go to sleep and wake up to find this has all been a horrible dream. Even that has been denied me despite having my seat reclined and my eyes closed. I keep hearing the excitement in Adam's voice at the prospect of finally being able to get home to see our mum even though it was tearing him away from his new life in a country he loved. The waves of guilt keep washing over me. I didn't have to tell him Mum was so ill; I didn't need to pressure him to come home.

It's a relief to eventually feel the car slowing down, signalling that we are about to get off the motorway so are only twenty minutes or so away from home. I'm craving the comfort of a hot bath, sinking into the foamy water to soothe my aching heart. It will only be postponing the inevitability of having to tell my mum that her son is dead, but I can't face her right now. I need time to think about how I'm going to break it to her. Involuntary tears trickle down my cheeks.

'Can I speak without you shouting at me?' Ben asks gently.

I sniff and brush the tears away.

'I'm sorry I shouted,' I say. 'It's not your fault. You were only trying to be nice.'

'I should have chosen my words more carefully,' he replies. 'Of course you're not okay. It was a stupid thing to say.'

I open my eyes for the first time since we got in the car and am surprised to see it's snowing quite heavily.

'Apology accepted,' I say, looking up at him and giving him a watery smile. 'How long has it been snowing?'

'About an hour. It was more like sleet to start with, but in the last few minutes it's got heavier, and it looks like it's settling.'

'For once, the weather forecasters were right when they prom-ised us an arctic winter,' I say, realising that the slowing down of the car was probably due to the worsening weather conditions rather than us nearing our turn off. I put my seat in the upright position. 'Where are we?'

'Near Pontefract,' he says. 'In these conditions we'll be lucky to be back much before five.'

'Oh my God, the girls!' I say, panicking. 'You were supposed to be picking them up from school today.'

'It's all under control,' Ben says. 'I asked Maxine if she'd be able to collect them when I realised I was going to need to come and fetch you. She's taking them back to the library with her to do their homework and dropping them back at ours when she's finished work.'

'Did you tell her about Adam?'

'No. I told her something urgent had come up at work and I wasn't able to get away.'

'Why didn't you tell her? She's going to find out soon enough and she'll be upset that you lied to her.'

'We need to think carefully about how we're going to handle things, Danni. Obviously, telling Diana is going to be horrendous. I'm wondering if we should maybe put that off for a few days.'

'Why? Mum's expecting me to walk in with Adam. She'll already be stressed out that we're so late.'

Ben is concentrating studiously on the road ahead.

'We can say he missed the flight, or that it was cancelled, or even overbooked. It'll give us a few days to think about how to break it to her gently.'

He's never been a good liar. I think I know why he's suggesting that we delay telling Mum about Adam. She hasn't got long to live, possibly only days, and he's thinking if we make excuses for Adam's non-appearance for long enough, we could avoid putting her through the agony of knowing the truth. She could go to her grave unaware of the tragedy.

'It's a kind thought, Ben but it won't work.'

'What?' he asks, feigning innocence.

'Mum will cling on to life with every fibre of her being. I'm pretty sure it's only the thought of being reunited with Adam that has kept her going these past few weeks. We'll have to tell her the truth at some point even though they may well be the final words she hears,' I say battling to keep hold of my emotions. 'But you're right, we won't tell her straightaway. She made a wish on that wretched Christmas bauble and I'm going to make it come true if it's the last thing I do for her. It won't be the happy reunion we'd all envisaged, but we'll bring Adam home and she will see him one last time before she dies.'

It's heart-breaking to think that it's only been a little over a week since Mum sat in the Chapel of Rest and said goodbye to her first child and now she has to do it all over again. The difference is, this time one of her sons will be in the coffin.

Ben momentarily releases his left hand from gripping the steering wheel and gently squeezes my hand.

'I think that's the right decision,' he says, 'but we do have a problem. What are we going to tell Amber and Jade? The moment they see you, they'll know something is terribly wrong. I think we're going to have to tell them the truth.'

'How can we? Once they know, we'd have to keep them away from their nana for fear of them letting the truth slip out. That wouldn't be fair on Mum or the girls in the little time she has left.'

'Well then, we'll have to tell them the same as we tell Diana. Adam missed the flight; we're not lying, just not being completely truthful. Do you think you can cope with that?'

'For Mum's sake, I have to.'

Because of the snow, it's another hour before we finally reach home, but thankfully, Maxine's Mini is not yet parked outside our house, meaning I won't have to face her or our girls. Ben's going to tell them that I've gone to bed with a migraine because I'm upset that Adam missed the flight which, although only a half-truth, isn't lying to them.

I'm sitting on the edge of the bed staring into space when he comes upstairs with a hot water bottle and a cup of tea a few minutes later.

'I've just spoken to Martin and asked him not to say anything to your mum about Adam,' he says, undoing my trainers and pulling the covers back for me to get into bed. 'I told him I'll ring and speak to her once I've got you settled into bed and that I'll call him back later to explain things.'

I nod as he hands me my tea and two white pills that the airport doctor gave us. I swallow them and lie back on my pillow. 'Thank you' is all I can manage to say to Ben before the sleep that eluded me on the journey home from Manchester finally engulfs me.

CHAPTER FORTY
Monday, 11 February

Without Ben's support, I would never have got through the past weekend. He came with me and the girls to visit Mum on Saturday morning rather than letting me go on my own with them as I usually did.

Although desperately disappointed, Mum accepted the explanation Ben gave her on the phone on Friday evening about Adam missing his flight because of traffic in Auckland. He'd told her that Adam would be on another flight as soon as it could be arranged, which was true as Ben had also been on the phone to the British Embassy to find out the procedure for bringing Adam's body home.

We both made every effort to be as normal as possible around Mum and the girls, listening to music and watching television, although I had to absent myself when they started looking through her newly organised photo albums yesterday morning while Ben was out doing our weekly shop. The very last thing I wanted was to see Adam smiling up from the pages at me, so I went into the kitchen to make some hot drinks. I was waiting for the kettle to boil when Martin had popped around to ask if I needed him to stay over with Mum last night. The sympathetic look in his eyes almost pushed me over the edge.

I managed to hold it together until we were back at home yesterday evening and Amber and Jade had gone to bed. I cuddled into Ben on the sofa and started to cry: tears for Adam that his

life had been cut so tragically short; tears for Mum in anticipa-
tion of the heart-breaking news I was yet to impart; and tears for
myself too. Ben just let me cry without asking me any questions,
but when my tears finally dried up, he said, 'I'm not sure you
should be going in to work tomorrow.' I insisted that I needed
the normality of routine, but now that I'm here, I'm wishing I'd
taken his advice.

Maxine knows something is wrong. I've felt her eyes on me at
various points in the morning when I've been putting the returned
books back in their places on the shelves. I know she's going to
quiz me the moment we're alone together and I won't be able to
lie to her because she knows me too well.

It's been a pretty quiet morning, probably because there is still
some lying snow after the fall on Friday and there is no one at
all in the library when I head to the kitchen for my lunchbreak.
Minutes later, Maxine joins me.

'Who's manning the desk?' I ask.

'Nobody. I've put a note on the front door saying we'll be open
again in fifteen minutes due to staff shortages. What's going on,
Danni? Did Adam change his mind about coming home at the
last minute?'

The bite of sandwich I'd been struggling to swallow before
Maxine had come into the room now feels as though it's the
size of a brick and seems firmly wedged in my throat making it
impossible for me to speak, so Maxine continues.

'He's not coming, is he? You shouldn't cover for him, it's not
fair on you.'

The sound of chair legs scraping against the floor tiles seems
deafening in the quiet of the empty library as I push my chair
away from the table and rush to the toilet where I'm promptly
sick. Maxine is by my side seconds later with kitchen roll and a
cool damp tea-towel which she holds against my forehead just as
I always do with Amber and Jade when they're ill. I thought I was

all cried out after the episode on the sofa with Ben last night, but clearly my body has other ideas.

'There, there, let it all out,' Maxine says in a soothing tone. 'You're too kind and caring for your own good. People will always take advantage of that.'

'It's not what you think,' I say, sniffing to try and bring my sobbing under control. 'Adam didn't deliberately miss his flight. He was in a road traffic accident on his way to the airport. He's dead, Maxine, and it's all my fault.'

I hear her gasp and then feel her arms around me as she gently lifts me to my feet and ushers me through the kitchen and towards one of the comfy sofas in the main body of the library.

'I shouldn't have been so quick to judge,' she says, sitting down next to me and rubbing my hands gently.

'You weren't to know,' I say, feeling guilty that we didn't tell her the truth when she brought the girls back to our house on Friday. 'Adam's been putting off coming home for so long. If only he'd told me about his money worries earlier, maybe Ben and I could have scraped together the airfare and then he wouldn't have been in the back of that taxi. He'd have been safely home with Mum weeks ago.'

'Does Diana know why Adam isn't home?' Maxine asks.

'No. We told her he missed the flight, but didn't tell her the real reason.'

'Are you going to?'

'Yes, but not until Adam's home. Ben's already spoken to the British Embassy and we should be able to get him on a flight at the weekend. The plan is to take her to the Chapel of Rest so that she will be with Adam when we tell her.'

'Make sure you've said your goodbyes,' Maxine says. 'She may not survive a shock like that.'

'I know, but I think it's the right thing to do. At least she'll know that Adam wanted to come home to her, before fate stepped in.'

Someone is knocking on the front door of the library.

'I need to open up, Danni. I can manage on my own this afternoon if you want to go home.'

'I'd rather stay, if you don't mind. I need to be busy to keep my mind off things.'

'Of course,' Maxine says heading towards the door where the knocking has increased in volume. 'I'll always be here for you, Danni; you're like the daughter I never had.'

Although I hate myself for thinking it, she's like the mother I might have had if things had been different.

CHAPTER FORTY-ONE
Sunday, 17 February

Adam is finally coming home today. The plane carrying his coffin arrived at Manchester airport at six o'clock this morning according to our local undertaker's, Farrell and Farrell, who were there to meet it. Once we've received confirmation from them that they are back in Woldington, we're taking Mum to the Chapel of Rest to be with her son when we break the tragic news.

Ben and I agree that it's better to tell her without Amber and Jade present, so he's taken them over to spend the morning with Mum, before dropping them at Maxine's for the afternoon and coming back to collect me. Poor Ben, I'm sure he could never have imagined a scenario like the one he is currently coping with when he made his wedding vows fifteen and a half years ago. Not only has he been there to comfort me throughout my frequent bouts of guilt and grief, he's also had to act as though everything is completely normal in front of the girls and my mum. The foundations of our relationship, which have felt a little shaky at times over the past couple of months, are now rock solid again. I couldn't have got through the past ten days without him and I never want anything to threaten to come between us again. This afternoon is going to be unbelievably difficult, but with Ben by my side to help support Mum when the bottom falls out of her world, we'll manage.

I've been trying to keep my mind off this afternoon by busying myself with household chores. The kitchen is spotless, the bathroom is gleaming, and I'm halfway down the stairs, my arms filled with the sheets off the girls' beds after deciding to change the bed linen a day early, when the doorbell rings.

'Hold on a minute,' I call out, taking the last few stairs at a pace and hurrying through to the kitchen where I bundle everything into the washing machine. 'Sorry about that,' I say, opening the front door, 'I was just…' I stop mid-sentence, the words freezing on my lips. In front of me is a man who for a millisecond I think is Adam before my brain registers that it can't be. Feeling light-headed, I reach my hand out to steady myself against the door frame.

'Danielle?' the man says. 'I know it would have been better if I'd called first, but I didn't have your number. I'm Luke Pullinger. Have I caught you at a bad moment?' he asks when I don't respond. 'I can come back another time if you're busy.'

My heart is thumping in my chest. The dark hair, the green eyes, the shape of the nose: the likeness is uncanny.

'Are you okay?' he says, concern evident in his voice. 'You look like you're about to pass out.'

I take a couple of deep breaths to calm myself. Quite apart from his resemblance to Adam, what on earth is Luke Pullinger doing on my doorstep?

'I'm fine,' I say. 'It was just a bit of a shock to open the door and see you there.'

Luke shifts uncomfortably.

'I got your letter,' he says. 'Thank you for writing to me even though I told you not to. Look, I understand if you'd rather I leave.'

'You'd better come in,' I say, taking a step backwards into the hallway to allow him to pass before following him through to the lounge and sinking onto the sofa.

'You're probably surprised to see me,' he says.

That's an understatement. After what happened with Adam, I'd more or less forgotten about the card I posted to Luke at the airport.

'Yes.'

'Why did you bother writing to me after the awful note I sent?' he asks, a flush of embarrassment creeping up his cheeks.

'I wanted you and Ray to know that I wasn't going to cause any trouble. I didn't want to destroy the lifetime of memories you made with the Pullingers, but I thought you should know that our mum really loved you.'

'I showed your card to Dad. That's when he told me the rest of the story.'

'The rest of the story?' I say.

'Yes. Originally, all he told me was that he'd had a visit from my half-sister and explained that I'd been given up for adoption. Obviously, I was upset to learn that my parents weren't my natural parents, but more than that, I was angry to think I hadn't been wanted by my birth mother. That's when I wrote the note saying those terrible things. I regret them now.'

I don't say anything. His words really upset me and there's no point pretending otherwise.

'When I showed Dad your card he started to cry. I asked him why neither he nor Mum had ever told me that I'd had two brothers who had died. That's when the truth came pouring out. Graham was stillborn, but Luke survived his birth. My parents were ecstatic to finally have the baby they craved after trying for five years following Graham's death. He lived for several weeks until the morning my mother found him dead in his cot.'

I gasp. My heart contracts for Sarah Pullinger. I can't even begin to imagine her despair on finding her baby's lifeless body.

'The baby's birth had been registered but my mother was so utterly crushed by losing a second son that she couldn't bear to register his death because she wasn't ready to say goodbye to him.'

For a moment I allow my thoughts to wander to Mum and how desolate she is going to be when she learns she has lost a second son. I reach for the tissue I have up my sleeve and pretend to blow my nose. Luke has no way of knowing that my mum is about to endure a similar devastation.

'Dad told me that he tried to prevent Mum from going to work the day Luke died because she was in such an emotional state, but she insisted. I guess we'll never know for sure whether she had it in her mind to take Diana's baby, but when I was born with the cord around my neck, looking limp and lifeless, she saw an opportunity and seized it.'

I'm trying to put myself in Sarah Pullinger's shoes; to feel what she must have been feeling. She had just lost a second child and yet hours later was instrumental in bringing a healthy baby into the world. She had so much motherly love to give and no one to give it to. It was little wonder it pushed her over the edge.

'Dad said he was frantic when Mum arrived home with a stolen baby, even though Mum explained that I was being given up for adoption, so my mother wasn't going to keep her baby. He knew if he'd made her take me back, she would have lost not only her job but her whole career. But more than that, he was afraid she might take her own life and he couldn't let that happen because he loved her,' Luke says, his voice cracking. 'They really were the most devoted couple and were wonderful parents.'

'What a dreadful position for your dad to find himself in,' I say, wondering what Ben would do in similar circumstances. He has shown his love for me time and again, but I'm doubtful whether he would have broken the law to protect me. I suppose none of us know what we are capable of until we are faced with the situation.

Luke seems to have recovered his composure.

'In the end, Dad came up with a solution to cover up what Mum had done. He made two blue coffins: one to secretly lay Luke to rest because he wanted him to have his own little cross, and the other, Jason's coffin, to be buried empty, in case anyone ever came looking for his resting place. They had a birth certificate for Luke, so they were able to pretend that the baby they arrived in Yorkshire with was him. I would have lived my life none the wiser if you hadn't searched out my dad to thank him for the way he looked after me forty-four years ago. You weren't to know he'd actually been looking after me for all of that time.'

'I'm sorry. I had no idea what the search for Jason's grave would unearth. I couldn't believe my eyes when I saw the photograph.'

'There's no need for you to apologise. I think Dad was relieved to finally be telling me the truth. If anything, I should be apologising for my parents' actions. However desperate Mum was to have a child she shouldn't have lied to your mother.'

'She's your mother too,' I remind him.

'The only mum I've ever known is the one who raised me,' he says.

I understand why he feels that way, but I really want him to understand that it wasn't her choice.

'Like I said in my letter, Mum never truly believed you were stillborn; she was certain she would have known if you'd died because she already loved you so much before your birth. She was adamant you made a sound before you were whisked away from her. All her adult life, she's lived in her childhood home because of her refusal to accept you were dead and her hope that one day you would come looking for her. It's no exaggeration when I say that the whole pregnancy and what followed totally ruined Mum's life.'

Luke has been listening intently, holding my gaze while I've been talking, but when I finish his head drops forward for a moment. His eyes when he raises them again are filled with confusion.

'I don't know what you want me to say, Danielle. I was never destined to be Diana's child because she wouldn't have been able to care for me. I would still have grown up with an adoptive family, not knowing her as my mother.'

'All I ask is that you don't judge her too harshly,' I say.

'I'm not judging her at all. How can I when I don't know her? Diana may be the person who gave me life, but she's not my mother, she's not the person who shaped who I am.'

I know he's right, but it's upsetting to hear Luke say those words.

'She never had the opportunity to "shape you", as you put it, and yet she still held so much love for you in her heart. Seeing her joy when we thought we'd found your grave is one of the most heart-rending things I've ever witnessed. She's never been able to love me the way she loved you.'

We're both silent. I hope I've made Luke realise how much Diana loved her first child, even though she never knew him, but that presents me with a dilemma. I'd reached the conclusion that there'd be no point in telling Mum that Jason had survived his birth, a hope she'd clung on to for so long, but that was when I thought he was going to refuse to have any part of our lives. Now he's here in person in my home, I'm wondering whether I should tell her the truth. Her words, 'a mother would know if her baby had died', fill my mind. She's been proved right, but would she benefit from knowing?

'Why did you come here today, Luke?' I ask, hoping his answer will help me reach a decision.

'I came here to apologise for my rudeness, but also to meet you. You'd made a great impression on my dad before the incident with the photograph.'

I smile, remembering Ray's generosity at inviting me into his home and offering me tea and biscuits.

'He was right about you,' Luke continues. 'I think your willingness to see things from my mum's point of view only adds to the kindness you've already shown in wanting to thank my dad in person for what you thought he had done for your brother.'

The words 'your brother' immediately conjure up a picture of Adam in my mind. Fairly soon, I should be getting a call from the undertakers to say they've arrived back in Woldington with him. A tiny part of me wonders whether finding out that Jason is alive might help lessen the blow for Mum of learning that Adam is not.

'I had another brother,' I say, my voice barely above a whisper.

'Had?' Luke says.

'Yes,' I say, looking directly into those green eyes which are so like Adam's. 'H… he was on his way home from New Zealand last week to see Mum before she dies. She has terminal breast cancer,' I say in response to the questioning look on Luke's face. He shakes his head from side to side as though struggling to comprehend that the birth mother he has only recently learned about is gravely ill. 'Adam was involved in a road accident,' I say, a tear squeezing out of the corner of my eye before I can stop it. 'He never even made it to Auckland airport.'

Luke gets to his feet and rushes over to me. I think he might have been about to put his arms around me, but he seems to think better of it, instead standing awkwardly in front of me.

'Oh my God, Danielle,' he says. 'I'm so sorry, I had no idea you were in mourning. Look, I should probably be going. Maybe we can talk again when you've had a chance to come to terms with your loss.'

I reach my hand out to his saying, 'Please don't go.'

He drops down onto his haunches at my side.

'Of course, if that's what you want. Is there anything I can do to help?'

I swallow.

'The thing is, I haven't told Mum about Adam yet.'

'Why on earth not?'

'I just don't know how to. She was expecting me to arrive at her house with him having collected him from the airport. She was so excited at the thought of seeing him.'

'So your mother knew he was coming home? How on earth did you explain his non-appearance?'

'I didn't. My husband, Ben, rang her to say he'd missed the flight. I couldn't face Mum straightaway and it's been torture seeing her over the past week knowing that eventually I'm going to have to tell her what happened and worrying that the shock will kill her.'

'Poor woman. As though she hasn't been through enough in her life,' he mutters, squeezing my hand.

It warms my heart to see this side of Luke. After his horrible letter, I'd initially been quite glad that someone so hateful hadn't wanted to be part of my life, until I realised it was a knee-jerk reaction to a complicated situation that threatened to undermine all he'd ever known.

'I'm just wondering if the knowledge that you didn't die at birth would help to lessen Mum's grief at losing Adam. It might give us a little bit of extra time for my girls to spend with their nana.'

Luke is staring at me as though I'm crazy.

'I'm not sure about that, Danielle. If the dementia already makes her confused, it might be difficult to explain to her that I'm still alive.'

'But is it fair for her not to know that she was right all along? I just don't know what to do for the best.'

It's true; I'm torn. Mum said her goodbyes to baby Jason. Meeting a grown-up Jason, who is now called Luke might be too much for her to comprehend – and could destroy the trust she now has in me if she thought I'd deliberately deceived her. And yet, it could give her closure in the fullest sense of the word, getting confirmation of what she had always believed was true. In a few short hours, I'm going to have to break the crushing news to her about Adam, maybe the only thing that will prevent her heart from breaking is knowing that her other son is alive.

'How long does she have?' Luke asks.

'Weeks… at best,' I reply, battling to hold back the tears which want to flow each time I think about losing Mum.

He seems to be having an internal battle with himself. Eventually he says, 'I think maybe you are right. Knowing that her first son is alive might help her cope with her second son's death. If we go and see her now, it might help you to find the words to tell her about Adam.'

'You'd be prepared to do that for Mum?' I ask.

'For her, but also for you, Danielle. You were kind and forgiving when you wrote to me, the very least I can do is repay some of that kindness.'

CHAPTER FORTY-TWO
Sunday, 17 February

Luke and I arrive outside Mum's house fifteen minutes later and I unlock the front gate while he finishes parking his car. I'm hoping she'll be in reasonable spirits after spending the morning with Amber and Jade. I let us in through the front door and call out to her.

'It's only me, Mum.'

There's no reply. I stick my head around the lounge door and then have a quick glance in the kitchen; she's not there, but I'm not worried. Having spent the morning with the girls, she's probably gone upstairs for a lie-down.

'Like I was telling you before we left my house, Luke, she gets easily tired. She must be resting, so it looks like we'll have to do this another time, after all.'

'Danni? Is that you?' Mum's voice is coming from upstairs. 'Ben said you were coming over later this afternoon.'

'You wait in the lounge,' I say to Luke in a hushed voice, 'and I'll call you to come up when I've had chance to explain things to her.'

He nods his understanding and I make my way up the stairs. The curtains are drawn across, so Mum's bedroom is in semi-darkness when I push the door open.

'Sorry, Mum, I didn't mean to disturb you. Were you sleeping?'

'No, I only just came up,' she says, inching her way up the bed to prop herself up on her pillows.

'Did you have a good morning with the girls?' I ask, crossing the room to sit on the edge of her bed.

She holds up her hands to show me her nails, which I can barely make out in the dim light.

'It's called Amber Glow,' she says, smiling. 'Don't tell Jade I said so, but I think it's a better colour on me than the metallic blue.'

'Our secret,' I say conspiratorially, 'although we're not supposed to be keeping secrets anymore.' Instantly, I feel guilty, knowing that I've been keeping a monumental one for the past ten days. Although the consequences of telling Mum about Adam's accident terrify me, I'm relieved that the ordeal of keeping it from her is almost over.

'But this one is to protect Jade's feelings. We're being kind,' she says. 'I wish I'd always appreciated how good it felt to be kind.'

I swallow the lump in my throat. We both know she's referring to the way she treated me, but I don't want to talk about that now, so put a different slant on it.

'I'm sure Martin will be delighted to hear that. Has he been in today?'

'He was here last night and brought me my breakfast, but he disappeared as soon as Ben showed up with the girls. Actually, I'm a bit worried about him. He's been a bit weird this week. I can't quite put my finger on it, but not his usual self. I hope he's going to be alright when I'm gone.'

I can feel the colour rising in my cheeks and I'm glad of the lack of light in the room. Poor Martin – he's had to face Mum's daily excitement at the prospect of Adam coming home, all the while knowing that he's dead. I'm not sure how I'll ever be able to repay him for what he has done over the past year. Like Mum says, I hope he'll be alright when she's gone.

'Any news from Adam yet?' she adds.

It's usually her first question for me, but showing off her newly painted nails must have distracted her. I take a deep breath.

'Actually, Mum there is. I didn't want to tell you until I was sure he'd made the flight.'

A floorboard creaks on the landing and I turn just as Luke appears in the doorway, despite me asking him to wait downstairs.

'Adam?' Mum says, her voice high-pitched with excitement. 'My God, Adam, is it really you?'

Luke doesn't move. He has the look of a deer caught in the glare of headlights. Framed in the doorway, I can understand why Mum has mistaken him for Adam. They are the same height and build, they have the same dark hair and beard, and even I'd momentarily been fooled by the similarity of their appearance earlier, despite knowing that it couldn't be Adam because my younger brother is dead. I can feel the blood pulsing through my veins. I need to put Mum straight before she gets too excited, but I don't know how to break it to her. I turn back to face her, but before I can speak, she rushes on.

'I can't believe it's you,' she says, her face the most animated I've seen it in a long time, her eyes positively sparkling. 'I'd almost given up hope that I'd see you in real life again after you missed your flight. Danni, why didn't you tell me he'd arrived?' she scolds. 'I'd have put on one of my nice wool dresses with my shawl. Ah, wait a minute,' she says as though something has just occurred to her. 'You wanted it to be a surprise. I'll bet that's why you didn't come over with Ben and the girls this morning. Had you gone to fetch him from the airport? Come here, Adam,' she says, reaching out her hand towards him, 'let me get a proper look at you.'

It's like a machine-gun; Mum's firing questions and comments non-stop. How am I going to tell her she's made a mistake? I turn back to look at Luke, silently appealing for his help, but it doesn't look as though it's going to be forthcoming; he's still firmly rooted to the spot. I have no idea what I'm going to say, but I have to say something.

'Mum,' I start to say, 'it's not…'

Luke interrupts. 'She was about to say it's not her fault, which it isn't really. I didn't tell her I was coming today,' he says, moving towards the bed and taking her outstretched hand in his.

The situation seems to be slipping from my control. I've no idea what Luke's intending to do. Is he going to try and explain that he's Jason, her long-lost baby, or is he going to try and pass himself off as my younger brother? I'm not sure I should allow him to do the latter. When she realises it's not him she'll be distraught.

'Oh my God, I can hardly believe my eyes. I'm still not keen on that beard though. It makes you look older, don't you think, Danni?' she says, raising her hand to touch Luke's facial hair and then recoiling from the feel of it. 'It changes your face a bit too, but I'd know my boy anywhere.'

This is my opportunity. I need to tell Mum it's not Adam, but I just can't find the words.

'I've missed you terribly, Adam,' she adds, finally seeming to run out of steam and sinking back on to her pillows.

The silence that follows her outpouring of emotion seems to last forever but it's really only a couple of seconds before Luke speaks.

'I've missed you too, Mum,' he says, leaning in to kiss her on the cheek. 'It's been far too long.'

Tears are pricking the back of my eyes. Although I know Luke is pretending to be Adam, by calling her Mum, it feels as though he has just acknowledged her as his mother.

'It's been such a struggle holding on to see you and now here you are, home at last,' Mum says with something approaching content-ment in her voice. 'I always knew you'd come back to me in the end.'

I think my heart might actually break. Mum is saying those words without realising that she is talking to Jason, the son she has prayed would come and find her all her life. And now he's finally here, she doesn't know it's him.

'I want to hear all about New Zealand,' she says, but even as the words come out of her mouth her eyelids are starting to droop.

'Of course, Mum, all in good time, but right now I think you need to rest. All this excitement has worn you out,' he says, pulling her covers up to her chin as though it's the most natural thing in the world.

'Thank you for coming home to me and thank you for bringing him, Danni. I feel so blessed to have you as my children.'

'Why did you let her believe you were Adam?' I ask, once we're safely downstairs and I'm sure we're out of earshot.

'I don't know,' Luke says. 'Until I saw her, I don't think I'd realised just how sick she was. She looked so frail and ill, but then her face lit up when she saw me and thought I was her son home from New Zealand. I couldn't spoil that moment for her.'

'But what am I going to tell her when she wakes up and you're not here?'

'She has dementia, Danielle. There must be times when she doesn't know whether something really happened, or she imagined it. You could say that she must have dreamt she'd seen Adam because she wanted it so badly.'

'It seems a bit cruel to deceive her like that.'

'Sometimes we have to be cruel to be kind. She won't know you're deceiving her and it just felt right to let her have her reconciliation with her son.'

There's something about the way Luke said 'reconciliation with her son' that makes me realise the moment was as special for him as it was for Mum. There was also a finality to it. Having agreed to come with me today and be reintroduced into Mum's life, it now feels as though he may have changed his mind.

'Where does that leave things with you?' I ask. 'She thinks you're Adam; you can't suddenly claim to be Jason.'

'I know,' he says, his voice tinged with sadness. 'It's too late for us to form a relationship. She's reconciled to the fact that her baby died, and in a way he did. She believes she'll soon be lying next to her son for eternity; I'm not going to interfere with that.'

The tragedy is, Mum will soon be reunited in death with her son, just not the one she thought it would be.

'I'm sorry she mistook you for Adam,' I say.

'I'm not. It gave her pleasure,' Luke replies.

He's right. Even though I'm going to tell her that Adam wasn't in her bedroom, and explain to her why he couldn't come home, she had those precious moments of total elation and at least I know her feelings were real.

'So, what's next for us?' I ask, hoping that Luke will want to stay in touch.

'I've never had a sister before, let alone nieces. It would be good to meet them one day.'

'I'd like that too,' I say.

Once Luke has gone, I ring Ben and tell him what's happened. We agree that it would be best to put off telling Mum about Adam's death until tomorrow. He's going to take the day off work so that the three of us can go to the Chapel of Rest to see Adam together.

I check on Mum several times throughout the afternoon. She's sleeping peacefully with a smile on her face. At around six I go up to wake her for dinner.

'Mum,' I say, switching on the bedside lamp as the room is now in total darkness. 'It's dinner time. Are you going to come down or shall I bring you something up?'

She doesn't stir. I check to make sure she is still breathing. She is, but it's very shallow, and in that moment I know that she's going. With dogged determination, she forced herself to hang on to life just long enough to see Adam, but in truth, she's been ready to go for a couple of weeks. I sit down on the edge of her bed and reach for her hand. Her nails, freshly painted with Amber

Glow, start my tears flowing as I realise my girls have laid eyes on their nana for the last time. I can take comfort that throughout her final day she has been surrounded by love.

My tears have dried, but I'm still holding her hand an hour or so later when she takes her last breath. I expect the tears to return in floods, but they don't; I just feel numb. I sit with her in the warm glow of the bedside lamp trying to feel thankful that she was spared the latter stages of dementia but nonetheless sad that she was struck down with it at all. Then I remind myself that if it hadn't been for the dementia, I may never have found out about Jason and she and I might not have become as close as we did in her final months. Some of the things she said to me after I found what I believed was my baby brother's grave, I've written down and placed in a keepsake jar, along with a piece of the original shawl that she had cut to shreds. And the photograph I took of her with my girls after they'd decorated their first Christmas cake together will always have pride of place on my mantelpiece. Mum might not always have loved me, or at the very least been able to show her love for me, but those precious things will act as a reminder that she did in the end.

I finally release her hand a couple of hours later and tuck it under her brightly coloured shawl which I've laid over her bed covers so that its softness is touching her skin, before going downstairs to call Ben. He picks up on the second ring.

'She's gone,' I say, my voice devoid of emotion.

'I'm sorry, Danni,' he says.

'What do I have to do?' I ask.

'We'll have to report Diana's death to the authorities and they'll send someone to confirm it.'

'If we report it now, will they take her away from her house tonight?'

'Probably,' Ben replies.

'Can we leave it until tomorrow then? I want her to have one last night in her home.'

'I don't suppose leaving it for a few hours will make any difference,' he says gently. 'Are you going to stay with her? Do you want me to call Maxine to sit with the girls so that I can come over and be with you?'

'No, I'm coming home.'

CHAPTER FORTY-THREE
Easter Monday, 22 April 2019

The easterly wind is biting as it whips in across the beach from the North Sea, but at least there's no sign of the predicted rain yet, despite the storm clouds gathering on the horizon. It's too cold for a picnic lunch and lazing around reading, but we decided to visit Mablethorpe anyway exactly as we had done last Easter Monday. None of us could possibly have predicted the changes to our lives that the next twelve months would bring as we'd splashed around that day in the shallow waters on the shoreline.

It's not just the four of us today though. One of the most important things I've learned over the past year is that although I love and cherish Ben and our girls, it's important to allow people outside of our tightknit family unit to enrich our lives and for us to contribute positively to theirs.

Maxine has always been a wonderful boss and work colleague, but she's now so much more than that. We've started inviting her to have Sunday lunch with us whenever she chooses, which I'm delighted to say is most weeks. Martin is also a regular at our table and the two of them have become good friends, frequently going to the cinema and theatre together. They're even talking about going on a cruise, something Maxine has always fancied doing. She assures me that their relationship is purely platonic, but time will tell. It would be wonderful for two such kind and caring souls to have partners to share their lives with.

They've come out to the coast with Aunt Susie and Uncle Colin. It was decided that they travel in the luxury of Aunt Susie's BMW rather than them all trying to cram into Maxine's Mini. Picturing my generously proportioned aunt and uncle squashed onto the back seat brings a smile to my face.

'What's so funny?' Ben asks.

'I'll tell you later,' I say, not wanting to risk my words being carried away on the buffeting wind and offending my relatives.

Considering that Amber and Jade knew nothing about Mum's sister until the day we were sorting through the photographs and sticking them in albums, it's amazing how they've accepted my aunt into their lives. A big hole was left when their nana passed away and Aunt Susie has willingly stepped up to fill it. Much as she wants to shower them with generous gifts, I've made it clear that we want the girls to appreciate the value of money, so I've asked her to only indulge them on birthdays and at Christmas and then nothing wildly expensive. I did however back down when it came to the puppy.

The moment Ben and I told Amber and Jade we were thinking of getting a dog, they could talk of nothing else and must have mentioned it in front of my aunt. She'd set them a secret mission to find out which was my favourite breed and had turned up at our house the following week with an eight-week old bundle of fluff. I wanted to say no to her extravagant gesture, but one look into the little cavapoo's trusting brown eyes won me over.

Teddy is enjoying his first experience of chasing a ball on a beach despite the restriction of wearing a harness and being on a leash. We were right to get a dog and even though money isn't quite as tight now that the sale of Mum's house has gone through, we're still paying the girls to do chores, with the money going into the dogfood collection box. I'm just wondering who'll tire of the game more quickly, the girls or the puppy, when my phone starts to ring. Glancing down at the screen, I can see it's Luke. He wasn't able to join us today as it's the fifth anniversary of his mother's death and understandably he wants to spend it with Ray. I unlink my arm from Ben's and hurry towards a brightly coloured beach hut for some shelter from the wind so that I will be able to hear him better.

'Hi Luke, how are you doing?'

'Hi Danni,' he replies.

I'm so pleased he's started calling me Danni. It makes me feel as though our relationship is moving towards that of brother and sister rather than just acquaintances. The girls think it's cool to have a long-lost uncle and are already badgering us to take them to Yorkshire for a visit during the summer holidays.

'I can't hear you too well,' I say, pressing the phone closer to my ear and turning my back against the wind which is somehow managing to creep its way around the side of the hut. 'It's blowing a gale here.'

'I'm sorry I couldn't come today, but Dad wanted to visit Mum to lay some flowers. He's sitting on the bench opposite her grave having a chat with her now.'

The image of a different cemetery fills my mind. It's only a few weeks since we laid my mum to rest in our family plot. There's a space left for Aunt Susie and her family between Mum and her parents. It comforts me to think that she will be lying between people who love her when Aunt Susie eventually passes, after the two of them reconciled their differences and ended up as close as they had been when they were children. Aunt Susie gave the eulogy as she knew more about Mum's life than anyone, and it was good to hear some of the antics the pair of them had got up to as teenagers; it lightened what would otherwise have been unbearably sad.

Having the joint service for Mum and Adam was a good decision as the two of them had been so close in life, but it doubled the sadness of the occasion. His grave was dug alongside Mum, because although she grew to love me in the last few months of her life, it wasn't the special connection she'd always had with my brother. As the two coffins were lowered simultaneously into the ground, I needed to control my emotions in order to comfort Amber and Jade who were both inconsolable. Before the earth was filled back in, the little blue casket that Ray Pullinger had crafted was lowered into Mum's grave. Although it had always been empty, she'd believed that it held the body of her stillborn baby and so it felt right to have it lying close to her just as I'd promised her it would. The thought of being buried next to her son gave Mum comfort in her final few weeks and thanks to a cruel twist of fate, she had her dying wish.

'I'm sorry,' I hear Luke say, 'it's probably really insensitive of me to be talking about graves so soon after your loss, but I just wanted to let you know that I told Mum that you forgive her for what she did all those years ago. I wish you could have met her, Danni, you'd understand why I was reluctant at first to acknowledge that I had a different mother.'

The vision of Luke holding Mum's hands and calling her Mum, before tucking the covers under her chin as she drifted off to sleep, will live in my heart forever.

'I'm glad you were able to meet our mother, Luke.'

'Me too,' he replies.

I can see Ben walking towards me holding a sand-covered Teddy in his arms. It would seem the puppy tired of running on the beach before Amber and Jade did.

'I'm going to have to go,' I say. 'Remember to ask Ray if he'd like to come to lunch next Sunday.'

'I already did and he said yes please.'

'Great. See you then,' I say, ending the call.

'Are you okay?' Ben asks, when he's near enough for me to hear him above the howling wind.

The last time he asked me that, just after I'd heard about Adam's accident, I nearly bit his head off.

'Fine,' I reply stretching my hand out to tickle Teddy's ears. The grief of losing Mum and Adam is still very raw, but thanks to Ben and my friends and family, I'm taking each day as it comes and have accepted that some will be better than others. 'Did those naughty girls wear you out, Teddy?' I say.

'It's the other way around,' Ben laughs. 'Amber and Jade dumped him on me while they went ahead with the others to get a hot chocolate from the beach café. I told you the novelty of having a dog would wear off.'

I smile. I'm pretty sure he knows that's not true, but he probably hates to think he might have been wrong in not allowing the girls to have a dog before. They absolutely adore Teddy and there's no doubt that having him to cuddle and play with when they're feeling down has helped them to cope emotionally.

It hasn't been an easy year, but I'm glad I discovered why Mum always found it so difficult to love me. I'm comforted by the thought that she did in the end.

I reach for Teddy and tuck him inside my quilted coat before ducking under Ben's arm as we face into the wind and head back along the promenade to re-join the others. It might be my imagination, but it looks as though the storm clouds are receding.

A LETTER FROM JULIA

Thank you so much for choosing to read *My Mother's Secret*. If you enjoyed it and want to keep up to date with all my latest releases, just sign up at the following link. Your email address will never be shared and you can unsubscribe at any time.

www.bookouture.com/julia-roberts

The germ of the idea for *My Mother's Secret* came to me when I was recovering from ankle surgery and a subsequent broken wrist after falling off my crutches, so found myself watching more television than I normally would. I watched a news report about a woman who had set up a charity to help the families of stillborn children locate where their babies were buried prior to the change in the law in the early 1980s.

As a mother myself, I couldn't comprehend why mothers of stillborns were not permitted to hold their babies before saying their final goodbyes. Worse still, most had no idea where the tiny bodies were buried or even if they were buried, so they had nowhere to visit to allow the grieving and subsequent healing processes to take place. Once the graves had been located, the mothers interviewed said that they had finally achieved a form of closure after years of suffering, which had in most cases adversely affected the remainder of their lives.

This news story gave me a reason for Diana's awful behaviour towards her daughter, but there needed to be a way for Danni to find out about the stillborn baby in her mother's past that had so badly affected Diana's ability to love her daughter. My son was working in the mental health sector at the time and would sometimes come home quite affected by the dementia patients he had come into contact with. I've also been able to draw on my own personal experience of knowing people with Alzheimer's or other forms of dementia and the tragedy of seeing them struggle to remember things or even recognise their nearest and dearest. As a result of Diana's dementia, Danni finds out about her half-brother and in order to try and build a better relationship with her mum, sets about trying to find out where his body was buried. I like to think that there may have been a few Ray Pullingers in the world, who treated the stillborn babies with such respect, whatever their motive. I don't know about you, but I had a vivid image of the graveyard awash with bluebells in the spring.

Ray, of course, was protecting his wife and there is quite a focus on the loving relationship Danni has with her husband, Ben, which at times gets stretched to breaking point. Thank goodness Danni has a surrogate mother figure in Maxine – as I say in the book, 'everyone needs a Maxine in their life'.

I needed to accelerate Diana's decline by having her diagnosed with inoperable, stage four breast cancer which allowed me to bring in the urgency of getting Adam home from New Zealand in order for my final 'twist' to work. I will hold my hand up and say that I felt a little bit wicked killing Adam – I've never been able to read through the scene at the airport without a tear in my eye, and in my editor Ruth's notes there were several mentions of 'poor Danni'; I really put her through the mill, didn't I?

I've left you to decide how the relationship between Danni and her half-brother, Luke, develops and also whether kindly neighbour Martin will have a happy ending with Maxine.

This is a departure from my DCI Rachel Hart series, and I must confess it took me a while to get back into the emotional groove of my earlier self-published books, but now I'm back I'm looking forward to writing the next one.

I hope you loved *My Mother's Secret*. If you did, I'd be most grateful if you would take a few minutes to write a review. Not only is your feedback important to me, it can make a real difference in helping new readers to discover one of my books for the first time.

I love hearing from my readers – you can get in touch on my Facebook page, through Twitter, Goodreads, Instagram or my website.

Thanks,
Julia Roberts

 JuliaRobertsTV

 @JuliaRobertsTV

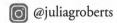 @juliagroberts

www.juliarobertsauthor.com

ACKNOWLEDGEMENTS

Once again, I would like to say a huge thank you to every member of Team Julia for their work on *My Mother's Secret*.

As with my previous Bookouture books, my editor is Ruth Tross and I have to thank her first of all for having faith in my change of direction. *My Mother's Secret* is very different from the Rachel Hart series, more akin to my early self-published books. She believed in this book from the initial idea and thanks to her patience and professionalism we have arrived at the story I wanted to tell. She is a pleasure to work with, providing feedback at every stage and an assured guiding hand if I went off piste, which I must confess I did in the first draft. She is also tremendously supportive, enthusiastic and honest, all vital attributes for an editor in my opinion. I feel very fortunate to be working closely with Ruth.

For *My Mother's Secret*, I've worked with a new copy editor, Dushi Horti. Relationships can take time to gel, but I must be honest and say that I felt comfortable with her immediately. As well as pointing out discrepancies in the timeline and making sure certain words weren't overused, she also posed questions if things were less than clear. Because Dushi is seeing the book with fresh eyes, she picks up on little things that are obvious to me because I know the story intimately but might not be to other people.

I absolutely love the title of this latest book. It's quite close to my original working title but better in my opinion and I hope you agree that the cover is a stunner – thank you, Alice Moore. I had lots of positive feedback when the cover was revealed by the

Bookouture publicity team, headed up by Kim Nash, and my thanks must go to Sarah Hardy in particular for the work she has put in to help spread the word.

I always thank my family for the part they play in each new book. They are the ones who see the hours spent at the computer throughout each stage of the process and have to put up with me vaguely nodding my head during conversations at the dinner table when my mind is clearly elsewhere. Because of the emotional nature of this book, I have often come downstairs from my writing loft with red-rimmed eyes or felt them watering when I tried to tell my husband, Chris, about the latest heart-breaking twist I've just created. He doesn't say much, instead handing me a box of tissues… he truly is the wind beneath my wings.

Thanks must also go to two of my fellow presenters at QVC; Katy, whose surname sounded perfect for Ray Pullinger and his family, and Chloe who has the most adorable cavapoo called… Teddy!

Finally, I want to thank you for reading *My Mother's Secret*. I love this book and I hope you did too.

Lightning Source UK Ltd.
Milton Keynes UK
UKHW010113200221
379053UK00001B/91